As far as the outlaws knew, Tilly and Nolan were husband and wife.

She'd been too stunned by the outlaws' unexpected attack to refute his words, but Nolan had latched on to the falsehood. He'd saved their lives, and her virtue, in the process. Though she wasn't adept at dealing with fugitives, she admired Nolan's ploy. He'd cleverly bargained his assistance for her safety and the safety of the girls.

Nolan led her to the meticulously ordered kitchen. He lit the stove and adjusted the flame. "The outlaws will expect the woman to prepare the food," he said. "Follow my lead and try to pretend you know where everything is located."

She and Nolan were treading through a minefield with this charade. Who knew what pitfalls they were bound to stumble over in the next few days? Her nieces had no idea of the danger, and she was determined to keep it that way.

Nolan was the best hope for the girls. He was the only one who could truly protect them. He was the one the outlaws needed for their plan to succeed.

If she wanted to live her life as a brave woman with purpose, then she'd better start acting like one.

D0037237

Sherri Shackelford is an award-winning author of inspirational books featuring ordinary people discovering extraordinary love. A reformed pessimist, Sherri has a passion for storytelling. Her books are fast-paced and heartfelt with a generous dose of humor. She loves to hear from readers at sherri@sherrishackelford.com. Visit her website at sherrishackelford.com.

Books by Sherri Shackelford

Love Inspired Historical

Prairie Courtships

The Engagement Bargain
The Rancher's Christmas Proposal
A Family for the Holidays
A Temporary Family

Cowboy Creek

Special Delivery Baby

Visit the Author Profile page at Harlequin.com for more titles.

SHERRI SHACKELFORD

A Temporary Family

HARLEQUIN LOVE INSPIRED HISTORICAL

Recycling programs
for this product may
not exist in your area.

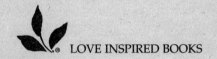

LOVE INSPIRED BOOKS

ISBN-13: 978-0-373-42515-0

A Temporary Family

www.Harlequin.com

Printed in U.S.A.

For thou, Lord, art good, and ready to forgive;
and plenteous in mercy unto all them
that call upon thee.
—*Psalms* 86:5

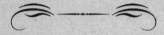

To Roy E. Shackelford, my greatest fan

Chapter One

Stagecoach relay station
Pyrite, Nebraska, 1869

Nolan West couldn't shake the feeling he was being watched.

He flipped open the cover of his timepiece and checked the hour. Twenty minutes before the next stagecoach arrived.

For the past year, he'd been manning the Pioneer Stagecoach relay station out of the abandoned town of Pyrite. Three years before his arrival, an overly optimistic prospector had discovered gold in the nearby Niobrara River. A town had sprung up practically overnight. Within a year, the claim had dried up, and the town was abandoned. Only the relay station remained occupied.

Prairie grass nudged through the slats in the derelict boardwalk, and a wet spring had fed the wild brush reclaiming the spaces between the empty buildings. A cacophony of crickets, frogs and birds called from the shelter of the lush buttress.

Nolan's sense of unease lingered, raising the fine hairs on the nape of his neck. He searched the shadows, catching only the rustle of the cottonwood leaves. He was alone. Yet the sensation lingered.

A bugle call sounded, startling him from his reverie, and Nolan replied in kind. He replaced his instrument on the peg just inside the livery door, ensuring the bell tube was directly vertical and the mouthpiece rigidly horizontal.

He slapped the reins against the rumps of the hitched horses. There was no time to waste. Because he worked the station alone, when he finished here, he'd have to hightail it back to the kitchen and serve the passengers dinner.

The rumble of hoofbeats sounded, and the distinctive orange Concord, with its gold trim, rumbled down Main Street. Harnesses jingled, echoing off the block-long stretch of deserted and dilapidated buildings. The driver swayed in time beside an outrider who cradled a shotgun in his arms. Reflections of the passing stagecoach appeared in the few windows that hadn't yet been broken or boarded over.

As the driver slowed the Concord parallel to where Nolan's hitched team waited before the town livery, the wheels kicked up dust. His horses surged forward.

The outrider stowed his gun and leaped from his seat. Bill Golden was a perpetually rumpled, stocky man in his midforties with a grizzled face and a mop of graying hair beneath his tattered hat. Considering he was usually drunk by this point in the journey, he appeared remarkably steady on his feet.

Bill lifted his hand in greeting. "Top of the day to you, West."

"You're early."

"We're traveling light."

The stocky outrider pulled down the collapsible stairs and swung open the door.

A little girl, no more than three years old, appeared in the opening. A passenger inside the traveling carriage held the child suspended with her legs dangling. Bill grasped the child around the waist and set her on the ground. Two more girls appeared—chestnut-haired, brown-eyed, identical replicas of each other, probably around five or six years of age respectively.

Nolan tilted his head. This route served Virginia City, Montana, and catered almost exclusively to prospectors seeking their fortune.

Bill extended his hand, and a woman grasped his fingers. Her bonnet concealed her face and hair, and Nolan allowed himself only one brief, admiring glimpse of her figure, which was encased in a lively green calico dress. Though he'd come to appreciate his solitude, he couldn't help but notice her. The last woman he'd seen had been the sixty-year-old wife of the traveling doctor.

"Thank you, Mr. Golden," she said, her voice at once crisp and soothing. "How are you feeling?"

Bill doffed his hat. "I feel all right, I guess, ma'am. I mean, Miss Hargreaves. Thank you for asking."

She fixed her gaze on the outrider as though she was peering into his very heart. The intensity of the moment raised Nolan's guard, but there was nowhere to hide while he held the horses. Shifting on his feet, he glanced away and back again.

"I know the change hasn't been easy." Her attention didn't flicker toward her new surroundings. She kept her interest directed solely on the outrider. "But you're doing well. I'm proud of you. Whenever you find yourself straying from the path, remember what we talked about."

"Yes, ma'am." A flush spread across the outrider's

face. "I will, ma'am. I surely do appreciate your kind words and all. I'll try and do my best."

She patted his arm. "That's all any of us can do."

Her words were gentle and sincere, and a pulse throbbed in Nolan's throat. He made a mental note to avoid the woman at all costs. Since returning from the war, he kept to himself. He didn't want anyone looking at him the way she was studying Bill. He didn't want anyone peering close enough to see the troubling battles he fought each day.

"I'd best see to the horses, Miss Hargreaves." The mottled blush on Bill's face deepened. "This here is the dinner stop. You can stretch your legs and enjoy some solid ground. If you need anything, let me know."

"You're too kind," she said. "Solid ground sounds marvelous. When I agreed to assist my sister, this was not at all what I imagined."

While Nolan pondered the odd change in the normally taciturn outrider, the second-oldest girl clutched her stomach and pitched forward.

"I don't feel so good, Aunt Tilly." The girl groaned.

"Are you certain, Caroline?" Miss Hargreaves was by the child's side in an instant. "Do you not feel good a little or a lot?"

"I'm certain," the girl replied with a gulp. "I don't feel good a lot."

"Oh, dear."

The woman glanced around and Nolan caught his first glimpse of her face. His curiosity deepened. She was younger than he'd expected. On first impression, her looks hovered somewhere between plain and pretty. On second glance he placed her nearer to pretty. She had eyes the color of a Virginia bluebell, a complexion bronzed by the sun and a pert nose. Though none of those features was particularly remarkable on its own, taken together they were uniquely pleasing.

She caught his interested gaze. "What should I do?"

Nolan placed a hand against his chest. "Are you asking me?"

Miss Hargreaves nodded.

Passengers rarely paid him any mind. Nolan frowned. He preferred it that way.

"Well, uh," he stuttered. "There's a privy out back."

"Excellent suggestion, thank you." She draped an arm around the girl's shoulders. "Mr. Golden, will you kindly look after Victoria and Elizabeth for a few minutes?"

"Absolutely," Bill said. "Take as much time as you need."

Nolan's frown deepened. The outrider rarely showed even the barest consideration to any of the passengers. Bill also loathed delays of any kind; he was scrupulous about the schedule.

Once she'd rounded the corner and disappeared, the driver leaped from his seat and set about unhitching the horses. With Bill's help, the three men had the horses switched out in record time. Throughout the well-honed operation, the two remaining girls assembled daisy chains with dandelions they'd plucked from the overgrowth between the unused buildings.

Nolan backtracked to the relay station and set the table for supper. When the passengers failed to appear, he returned to the corral and propped one foot on the lowest slat.

Bill sidled nearer. "Maybe you oughta go out back and see what's taking Miss Hargreaves so long."

"She's your passenger." Nolan hoisted an eyebrow. "What's gotten in to you today, anyway?"

"She has a way of talking to a fellow." The outrider

slid his hand beneath his coat, as though reaching for the flask he usually kept in his breast pocket, then stilled. "I told her things I ain't never told anybody. I even quit drinking."

"You were sober when you told her those things?" Nolan's curiosity swelled. "Why would you do that?"

"She asked."

"You've killed six highwaymen in the past ten years. You've fought Indians. You once outran a prairie wildfire. And you're telling me you're intimidated by that slip of a woman?"

"It's not like that." Bill swallowed, and his Adam's apple worked. "She never asked me to quit. Instead, she asked me why I drank as much as I did."

"What did you say?"

"I said I didn't know. Then she started asking me about my family, and about my experiences. The next thing I know, I was blabbering my whole life story."

Nolan's stomach dipped. He'd rather be sitting behind enemy lines again than prattling to a stranger about his life. After spending two years as a Confederate prisoner of war at Rock Island, he'd become intolerant toward people. While living in the prisoner camp, he'd acquired certain quirks that set him apart from regular folks. He'd become obsessively neat and austere about his possessions. Each evening he spent an hour checking the placement of each item and ensuring the buildings he occupied had been secured. If he didn't, he had nightmares that sometimes turned violent.

He'd survived the War for Southern Independence only to return home and discover his family farm had been confiscated. He'd gone adrift after that, moving from job to job and state to state. Over time his eccentricities had become increasingly difficult to disguise.

He'd gradually accepted that the war had changed him in ways that ran too deep to fathom. In order to camouflage his dilemma, he'd settled in this remote, abandoned town. He fully expected that after a few years away from the company of other folks, he'd be healed. Having strangers underfoot exacerbated his troubles. The sooner this bunch ate dinner and moved on, the better.

The woman finally appeared, her arm still resting protectively around the girl's shoulders. Nolan heaved a sigh of relief. They'd be gone soon.

Except Caroline looked worse than when she'd left. Her face was pale with an almost greenish tinge, her forehead was screwed up and both hands protectively covered her stomach.

Bill cleared his throat and elbowed him in the side.

Nolan flashed the outrider a questioning gaze.

"Tell her about dinner," Bill mumbled beneath his breath.

"There's dinner at the relay station," Nolan declared. "Boiled beans, bacon and bread."

The woman's nose wrinkled ever-so-slightly. "That sounds edifying. Let's have some bread, shall we, Caroline? Bread is good for an upset stomach, isn't it, Mr.—?" She raised her voice in question.

"Mr. West."

He hesitated in revealing something as simple as his name. He needed some distance between them. He'd considered Bill as tough as hardtack, and she'd somehow wheedled her way into the man's confidence.

Bill hitched his pants. "Me and Digger ate at the last stop. We're gonna catch some winks in the livery."

"You're going to sleep?" Nolan couldn't mask his incredulity. "Now?"

"I think that's a fine idea," the woman said with a smile. "Rest is often the best medicine."

"But…" Nolan's voice trailed off.

"But what?" The outrider bared his teeth in defiance. "I never argue with a lady."

There wasn't much Nolan could say to that, which left him alone with the woman and the three girls. With no other choice, he pivoted on his heel and trudged toward the sprawling relay station. The building had originally housed overnight guests, but since he'd taken over the post, there hadn't been any need. Another reason he kept this job. Except for twice a week when the stagecoach came through town, he was alone.

Ten minutes later they were all seated around the rectangular table. Despite his carful maneuvering, he'd gotten sandwiched between the woman and the youngest girl.

He held out the bowl of beans. "Mrs. Hargreaves."

"Not Missus," she amended. "It's just Miss. I'm not married. These delightful pixies are my nieces."

Keeping her head bent, Caroline broke off a small crust of bread and nibbled on the edge.

"After Aunt Tilly takes us to Omaha," Victoria said, reaching for the blackberries, "she's traveling to New York City."

Miss Hargreaves absently poured her niece a cup of water. "My father's cousin serves on the board of The New York Widows and Orphans Society. Since the war, they've been positively overwhelmed. I can't imagine a greater good than helping those displaced by the Southern rebellion, can you?"

Nolan flinched at the reference. "I guess not."

The war went by different names depending on which side of the Mason-Dixon Line a fellow called home.

Victoria nodded eagerly. "Aunt Tilly promised to post

us a letter every week and tell us all about her experiences."

Caroline's cheeks puffed out and she pressed two fingers over her mouth. Nolan's breath hitched, and he frantically searched for the slop bucket. The girl appeared worse with each passing minute.

"I should have plenty of fascinating things to write about," Miss Hargreaves said. "There are so many different people to meet. According to my father's cousin, the sidewalks are packed day and night in some places. You can't walk down the street without brushing into someone."

"You don't say." Nolan's gaze darted toward the sick child once more, but she appeared to be holding steady. "Aren't there any interesting people where you live now?"

"I've exhausted the supply in Omaha."

Following the war, he hadn't been able to tolerate anyone touching him. Pushing through crowded streets sounded like a nightmare.

"I'm dreadfully bored these days." Miss Hargreaves ladled a generous heaping of beans over her bread. "During the war, I helped my father with his law practice after his law clerk was conscripted. Since the war, there's been few opportunities for me. My sister, Eleanor, thinks I'll quit within the week, and I'm determined to prove her wrong. She thinks I'm flighty and lack direction. Have you ever felt as though people only see the worst in you?"

"Not particularly."

He'd felt exactly that, but he sure wasn't confiding in Miss Hargreaves. At least he had some sympathy for Bill. Her willingness to share her vulnerabilities naturally invited others to do the same.

"What about excitement?" She clasped her hands.

"Don't you get dreadfully bored out here all by your lonesome?"

"The quiet suits me."

"The solitude would drive me mad. There are more opportunities for women in larger cities. I'm not exactly certain what I want in life, but I know what I don't want. I don't want to feel useless. Women were perfectly useful during the war, I don't know why men believe we've suddenly become inept simply because peace was declar—" She glanced at her niece. "Oh, dear, Caroline. Do you need another trip to the privy?"

"Water."

Miss Hargreaves shoved a full glass across the table. The girl downed the liquid and sighed. "Better."

"See there?" Miss Hargreaves's smile brightened. "You'll be right as rain in no time."

Keeping a close watch on the girl, Nolan pushed back his plate. He'd been raised the only child of a dirt-scrabble farmer along the border of Virginia and Pennsylvania. As a child, he'd planned on farming like his father before him. Except his father had lost everything: his home, his land and his livelihood. Many of the farms on the losing side of the border had been confiscated during the war, and the land had never been returned. Following the war, his father had moved to Cimarron Springs, Kansas, to live near his sister, Nolan's aunt Edith.

Nolan had lived with his father for a time, but if he didn't follow certain patterns during the day, his sleep was marked by night terrors that sometimes turned violent. After nearly assaulting his own father during an episode, he'd retreated to the remotest location he could find. If he didn't show some improvement by the time the railroads shut down the stagecoaches, he'd travel farther west. Maybe California or the Wyoming Territory.

Miss Hargreaves rested her elbow on the table and planted her chin in her hand. "It's such a little thing, isn't it? Wanting to be useful? Getting married and having a family is all well and good, but I'd go mad if all I had was the washing up to keep my mind occupied each day. Do you know how many documents must be filed with the county before the railroad claims a plot of land?"

"Nope."

"One. But it's quite complicated. The Douglas County clerk said I had a talent for land negotiations. A lot of good that does me. No one will hire a female for land management. I told my father I'd do all the paperwork for the cases, and he could take the credit. I don't know what all the fuss is about."

"Fuss?"

"My father. He doesn't think that I know what I want. He's right, I suppose. Except I know what I don't want." She grimaced. "He thinks we should all be more like my sister, Eleanor. Content with supporting her husband, even if that husband drags her all the way to Virginia City and then dies. Sounds dreadful to me. I have grander plans."

Nolan had forgotten what it was like to view the future with hope rather than dread. Miss Hargreaves's unflinching optimism was as flawless and blue as a spring sky. She was like a flash of light illuminating the darkness.

Poisonous grief threaded through his veins. Some things were better left in the shadows.

The youngest child held out her sticky fingers. "Booberry."

The toddler rested a hand on his bent knee, smearing blackberries across his canvas trousers.

Nolan closed his eyes with a groan.

Miss Hargreaves absently grasped the tiny fingers and

blotted them with her napkin. "Gracious, where are my manners? I haven't even introduced us. Victoria is the oldest, Caroline is the middle child and you're sitting next to Miss Elizabeth. You can call me Tilly. That's short for Matilda."

"I three," Elizabeth stated, holding up the proper number of sticky fingers in confirmation.

Nolan scooted nearer the edge of the bench. "Pleasure to meet you."

"I Isbeth," the toddler said.

Tilly rolled her eyes. "My mother named my sister and me after her two favorite queens of England. Eleanor followed suit." Tilly leaned over Elizabeth's head and whispered in his ear. "That's probably the only good thing that came of my brother-in-law Walter's passing. Who wants a niece named Eadgifu? I'm sure she was a fine queen, but what an atrocious name."

Her breath raised gooseflesh along the back of his neck. This close, he noted the delicate sunburn on the apples of her cheeks. Her hair was the same chestnut brown as the girls, but streaked lighter from the sun.

A suitable reply escaped him. Nolan finally settled on "I'm sorry for your loss."

"Are you talking about Papa?" Victoria asked.

"Yes." Tilly covered the girl's hand. "I shouldn't have said anything. I didn't mean to upset you."

Victoria, her eyes solemn, only shrugged. "I don't miss him as much as Mama. He was never home. When is Mama meeting us at Nanny and Poppy's in Omaha? Will we visit you at your house after Mama arrives?"

Tilly's lips whitened and made an exaggerated point of smoothing her napkin in her lap. "Your mother is only a week or so behind us. Of course you'll visit me before I leave for New York. Your mother would never miss the opportunity to critique my efforts and find me wanting."

"What does *critique* mean?"

Nolan glanced between the two.

Miss Hargreaves blanched. "Never mind."

A bugle call sounded.

Instantly alert, his stomach muscles knotted.

Miss Hargreaves reached for his arm. "What's that?"

"The cavalry," Nolan said, stepping out of her reach.

"Is that good or bad?"

The arrival of his unexpected guests had distracted Nolan from his earlier unease. Had the cavalry been scouting him earlier? Captain Ronald, the leader of the local fort, had some odd notions. Nolan forced the tension from his shoulders and turned away from the four pairs of eyes staring expectantly at him.

"Probably nothing," he said. "Everyone stay inside until I know whether there's trouble or not."

This had better be a routine check, because as long as Miss Hargreaves and her nieces remained at the relay station, the girls were his responsibility.

And if there was one thing the war hadn't stolen from him, he took his responsibilities seriously.

After ten minutes, Tilly stood and tossed her napkin on the table. If only her brother-in-law hadn't gone and died. Walter's timing had never been good. Eleanor had married her father's law clerk, a handsome fellow who might have made a good husband if it weren't for the gold rush. Though her sister had wanted to remain living near Tilly and their father, as soon as the war ended, Walter had dragged Eleanor to the wilds of Montana in search of instant riches. They'd been gone nearly two years when he was killed in a mining accident.

Last month, Eleanor had written to say she was returning home to Omaha to live with Walter's parents. Staying with Eleanor and Tilly's widowed father was out of the question. Their father had never been much for disruption even before their mother's death.

Eleanor had demanded Tilly's assistance with their travels. Though frustrated by the delay in her own plans, Tilly had dutifully made the trip. Except nothing had gone as Tilly had expected.

Claiming she couldn't finish tying up the loose ends of Walter's passing with the children underfoot, Eleanor had sent Tilly and the girls ahead of her. Alone.

A fierce quarrel, conducted in hushed tones in deference to the girls, had ensued. In her usual high-handed manner, Eleanor had instructed Tilly to care for the girls better than Tilly had cared for her clothing and belongings as a child. The argument was old and recycled, and Tilly invariably lost. Eleanor was five years older and had an excellent memory. She'd dredged up every item of hers that Tilly had lost or broken over the years. When they'd reached the inevitable point in the argument when Eleanor recalled a borrowed dress Tilly had ruined with spilled punch, Tilly had thrown up her hands and relented.

Though not without a few muttered annoyances.

After all, if Eleanor thought so little of Tilly's abilities, why entrust her with the girls? Eleanor had responded by pointing out that Tilly merely had to board the stagecoach in Virginia City, and disembark in Omaha.

The unspoken words had been cutting and obvious— even Tilly couldn't botch such a simple task.

"I'm going to check on Mr. West," Tilly said. "You three stay here."

Elizabeth grinned. "I three."

The child was inordinately pleased with her recent birthday.

"You should be very proud. It's a very advanced age."

Tilly stepped outside and glanced at the sky. A flotilla of angry clouds had formed along the horizon. Perfect. More rain. For the past week, there'd been nothing but rain, rain and more rain. The stagecoach had nearly gotten stuck more than once, and floating across the Niobrara River had been precarious against the swift tide.

Tilly paused midstride. A half a dozen cavalry officers on horseback had mustered in the clearing between the relay station and Main Street. Their uniforms might have been crisp and blue at one point, but the men were covered in a fine coat of trail dust. The gold braiding on their hats was frayed, and their brass buttons tarnished from wear.

"You didn't tell us you had guests," a voice drawled. "Be careful, West, or you'll lose your reputation as a recluse."

The man speaking was clearly the leader of the bunch. He leaned slightly forward, letting the reins of his horse droop. The officer was handsome, with a straight nose and a strong jaw highlighted by his bushy muttonchops.

"Didn't have a choice," Nolan said.

The officer smoothed one hand down the front of his coat. "Introduce me."

Her gaze slid toward Mr. West. He stood with his feet braced apart and his arms crossed over his chest. Of the two men, she much preferred the clean-shaven stagecoach employee. He was too rugged to be strictly handsome. His jaw was too strong, his nose too aquiline and his mouth too hard for what passed for true masculine beauty. His hair might have been blond as a child, but had darkened to a tawny brown with age. Yet there was something compelling about him, a mystery in the depths of those hazel eyes. If she had more time here, she'd relish the challenge of solving the puzzle of his clipped answers and taciturn silence.

Except she wasn't sticking around any longer than absolutely necessary, especially now that Eleanor was returning. Being under Eleanor's thumb these past few days had only reinforced Tilly's decision. She was heartily sick of always being judged and found lacking.

Following the end of the war, when her father's law clerks had returned, the work she'd done in their absence had been gradually removed from her oversight. She was bored and restless.

The cavalry officer grinned at her, and touched the brim of his hat. "Captain Ronald, miss. At your disposal."

Tilly plastered a cheerful look on her face. His attention was less flattering than perfunctory. If Eleanor was here, she knew from experience that he'd hardly spare her a glance.

"Pleasure to meet you, Captain. I'm Miss Hargreaves."

"Where's Perry?" Nolan demanded.

At the growl in his voice, Tilly took an unconscious step back. Clearly there was animosity simmering between the two men.

"Perry is patrolling another area," Captain Ronald said. "You'll have to deal with me, much as it pains you." He turned his attention toward Tilly. "Don't you worry about the danger, ma'am. We've got extra patrols between here and Omaha. You'll be as safe as a baby in a cradle."

"Danger?" Shock rippled through Tilly. "What danger?"

"As I said, don't you worry your pretty little head, ma'am." The captain touched the yellow handkerchief knotted around his neck. "The mining company is sending a shipment of gold from Virginia City on one of the stagecoaches, and we've gotten word that Dakota Red and his brother are in the area. They busted out of jail and need money. Nothing for you to fret about, though. We're sending out a decoy to trap them. When they hold up the wrong stagecoach, we'll nab them."

"That sounds rather dangerous."

"Nothing my boys can't handle."

Tilly thought she heard a low guffaw, but when she turned toward Nolan, his face was impassive.

"Why the stagecoach?" Nolan demanded. "Why aren't they shipping the gold on the riverboat?"

"The last riverboat sunk, and they haven't replaced it yet. Why do you think your stagecoach traffic has doubled? There's a lot happening in the world. You ought to get out of the wilderness once in a while, Nolan."

The stagecoach man made a sound of disgust. "The mining company ought to wait on shipping that gold. That haul is as good as stolen."

His conviction chilled Tilly. What if the outlaws robbed the stagecoach near Pyrite?

"I'm traveling with children." She made a feeble gesture toward the relay station. "Are you certain it's safe for us here?"

"Children?" The captain's interest seemed to slacken at the mention of her nieces. "Dakota Red and his brother were spotted on the other side of the river. There's only one place to cross, which means they can't travel south without one of my men spotting them. This relay station is the best place to be, given the circumstances. You're safe under my watch."

He added a self-satisfied grin that was probably meant to inspire her trust.

"Thank you, Captain Ronald." She offered an overly bright smile in return. Since there was little chance of them meeting again, she might as well humor the man. For reasons she couldn't explain, she trusted Nolan's assessment of the situation more than the cavalry officer's opinion. "I appreciate both your concern and the protection of your men."

"My pleasure, ma'am." His sat up straighter, puffing out his chest. "If those boys so much as sneeze, we'll know."

"I'm sure your men are more than capable." Despite the captain's assurances, a nagging sense of unease lingered. "I appreciate your vigilance."

If something happened to the girls, she'd never forgive herself. Both her father and Eleanor had been frustrated by her irresponsibility in the past. Their criticism was exaggerated, though not entirely unfounded. She wasn't exactly irresponsible, she was simply distracted easily. While the two of them could focus on one task to the exclusion of all else, Tilly preferred flitting from activity to activity. Her lack of commitment drove them to distraction.

"Aunt Tilly!" Victoria hollered from the doorway of the relay station. "You'd best come quick. Caroline is sick again."

"Oh, dear. Duty calls, Captain Ronald."

"Don't let me keep you." The captain touched the brim of his hat, a slight hint of distaste marring his handsome face. "We'll scout the area. Those outlaws will be in custody in no time."

"Much obliged, Captain," Tilly said.

The captain signaled to his men, and the unit broke into a canter.

Tilly hastily returned inside. To her surprise, Mr. West was close on her heels.

Caroline had slumped over the table. Her arm was hooked over her head. "I feel worse, Aunt Tilly."

"I gathered as much," Tilly soothed.

Caroline was a replica of Eleanor at that age.

Because of their age difference, following the death of their mother, Eleanor had taken over the role of matriarch in the family. Eleanor had been a strict parent, stricter even than their father. Now the task of caring for Caroline fell to Tilly, though she was ill-suited for the role. She knew one thing for certain—she was going to be a far less severe guardian than Eleanor.

"I'll fetch you some water," Tilly said, uncertain how else to assist her niece.

She'd never been one to play house and care for dolls the way Eleanor had. She'd never been much for courting, either. Eleanor had always been the sister who attracted romantic attention, while Tilly had been the sister that men befriended. Usually in the hopes of getting closer to Eleanor.

Tilly had the uneasy feeling that her sister's marriage had not been entirely happy. Though Eleanor had always denied any discontent, with each subsequent visit home, she'd become a shell of her former self. If the life Eleanor had been dreaming about since she was a child had done that to her, Tilly wanted no part of marriage. She refused to suffer the same fate as her sister.

"There's a room in the back," Mr. West said. "Caroline can rest there."

Relief rushed through Tilly. "Thank you, Mr. West."

"Call me Nolan."

He scooped Caroline into his arms and carried her down the corridor. Grateful for his assistance, Tilly trailed after them. The room he'd chosen was sparsely furnished with only a bed and a small table, but the space was spotless. He rested Caroline on the counterpane.

Tilly touched his arm, and the muscles tensed beneath her fingers.

"Is she going to be all right?" she asked. "Do you think we should send for a doctor?"

"The nearest doctor is in the village of Yankton, and that's a two-day ride. There's a fellow who comes through town once in a while, but I never know when." Nolan pressed the backs of his knuckles against Caroline's forehead. "She's not running a fever. It's probably just something she ate."

Bill Golden appeared in the doorway, concern etched on his grizzled face. "Is there anything I can do to help?"

Tilly considered her options. Travel by stagecoach was uncomfortable in the best of circumstances. The air was stifling, the bumpy conditions grueling and the chance for rest all but impossible.

"I don't think she can travel." Tilly wrapped her arms around her midriff. "Can you wait until she's better?"

"I'm afraid not." Bill scratched his forehead. "This here is a mail coach. The mail has to go through. The passengers are secondary."

"When is the next stagecoach?"

"Thursday."

"We can't wait until Thursday."

"I'm afraid that's the best I can do."

Tilly's shoulders sagged.

Nolan scowled. "I can't have a bunch of greenhorns underfoot."

Her stomach knotted, and she pictured Eleanor's disapproving frown. The simple task of boarding the stagecoach in Virginia City, Montana, and exiting once they arrived in Omaha, had suddenly become a whole lot more complicated.

She clasped her hands before her. "Surely you can stay an hour or two. I'm certain Caroline will be much improved by then. This town doesn't appear fit for children."

"She's right." Nolan set his chin in a stubborn line. "This lady has no business being here."

Her spine stiffened. This lady? *This lady?*

The way he said the words made her sound singularly incompetent. She narrowed her gaze. At least Eleanor and her father had a basis for their criticism. She certainly hadn't traveled all this way to take orders from a man who knew nothing about her capabilities. The stagecoach man had no foundation for the contempt in his voice.

"You don't have a choice, Mr. West," Tilly challenged. "If Caroline is unable to travel, we're staying put, and that's that."

"I'm in charge." The stagecoach man propped his hands on his lean hips. "And I'll have the last say."

Chapter Two

So much for being in charge.

The day following the arrival of his unexpected guests, Nolan glanced up from placing a harness on the peg in the livery. A scrape sounded and Victoria appeared in the opening of the livery doors. Her two dark braids rested against her shoulders, and her blue calico dress was clean and neat with a starched apron tied around her waist, an improvement over her younger sister.

Nolan brushed at the phantom blueberry stain on his knee.

The girl jammed her hands in the pockets of her apron, stretching the material taut. "Whatcha doin?"

"Oiling the harnesses."

"How come?"

"Because dry leather cracks and breaks. Oiled leather is stronger."

"What happens if the leather breaks?"

"The horses get hurt."

"Can I help?"

"I'm finished," Nolan said.

Victoria grasped the oil can. "What's this?"

"Machine oil." Nolan reached for the tin and replaced

the base in the circle in he'd drawn on the workbench. "For machines."

He nudged the handle until the tin faced north.

"Oh." Victoria plucked a tool from the wall. "What's this?"

"Pincers." Nolan retrieved the tool and hooked the handle on the nail in the silhouette he'd drawn on the wall. "For shoeing horses."

"Are you a blacksmith?"

"No. But sometimes a horse will throw a shoe on the trail. I can do some basic repairs."

"It sure is quiet in this town."

"I like quiet."

"Hmph." Victoria tapped her chin. "Do you have any matches? I want to light a fire."

"Stay away from fire." Nolan slid his hand over the box on his workbench. He surreptitiously stowed the matches in his pocket. "Even with the rain, the buildings along Main Street are nothing but dry tinder."

"I just wondered." Victoria shrugged. "Aunt Tilly found some oil lamps."

"Where did she find them?"

"She and Elizabeth are exploring the town while Caroline sleeps."

"Your aunt sure keeps busy."

"Mama said that Aunt Tilly needs activity like some other folks need water or air."

"You don't say."

He'd managed to cover his outburst the previous afternoon with relatively little notice. He'd set up a cot in the livery, and let his guests take over the relay station. Mostly he'd spent his time avoiding Miss Hargreaves. She had a look in her eye that didn't bode well. She kept staring at him as though he was a knot she wanted to unravel. He wouldn't let her get to him like she'd gotten to Bill.

"I like Aunt Tilly," Victoria said, "but I miss my mama."

He was curious about the circumstances, but reluctant to pry. Pulling answers from a seven-year-old didn't sit well with him. "I'm sorry about that."

"Mama stayed behind to sell our furniture and stuff, but that's not what she told Aunt Tilly," the girl said matter-of-factly. "I don't think Mama wants Aunt Tilly to know that we're poor. Mama even sold our horse and our dollhouse. We're going to live with our nanny and poppy in Omaha because Papa spent all our money and left us with a worthless gold mine. Mama said that she wasn't surprised our pa died. She always said that gold fever was going to kill him. Can you catch gold fever?"

"No." Nolan cleared his throat. "Sorry about your pa, too."

He tugged on his collar. That was more information than he'd intended to learn. While he figured Eleanor ought to confide in her sister, pride was an emotion he understood all too well, and he certainly wasn't the man to pass judgment on someone else.

"I'm glad you can't catch gold fever," Victoria said. "I don't think Mama liked Pa very much. She complained that he worked all the time and made us live in Virginia City."

"I'm sure she liked your pa just fine. Sometimes folks say things they don't mean."

An ear-splitting scream sounded from the direction of the abandoned hotel. Nolan's chest tightened.

Victoria took off through the double doors in a dash but Nolan quickly outpaced the child. He crossed the street and vaulted over the boardwalk railing, then shoved open the door of the hotel. Frightened chatter reverberated from the recesses of the building.

He wove his way through the abandoned tables and chairs that littered the dining space and pushed into the kitchen. A small hand tugged on the hem of his shirt, leaving a purple print. A muscle throbbed in his temple.

The toddler seemed to have an endless supply of blackberries.

"Ti-wy," Elizabeth said.

The little girl appeared unhurt, and his heartbeat slowed a notch.

"It's all right." He patted her head. "I'll take care of this."

Tilly perched atop a single chair with a broom held protectively before her.

"What is it?" Nolan demanded. "What's happened?"

"In there." Tilly gestured with her broom handle. "There's something in the stove."

He motioned with his hand. "Hand me the broom."

While he'd known the hotel was equipped with a kitchen, he'd never explored the building. An enormous cast-iron stove took up most of the limited space. The chimney pipe exited through the ceiling, and light showed around the space.

Opposite the chimney, a bench and shelves lined the wall. The room smelled of neglect and dust coated every surface. The untidy mess triggered his unease, and he searched for something to ground him.

Disorder in the spaces surrounding him had a way of seeping into his mood. The previous owner had left behind only a few dented pots and pans, along with some chipped plates and cups. He snatched a bandana from his back pocket and pinched the edge of a plate between the unsoiled fabric. With his fingers protected from the dust, he stacked one dish atop another, then repeated the process.

"What are you doing?" Tilly wore a scarf wrapped around her hair, pulling the chestnut mass away from her face. "I wasn't shrieking my head off because the cupboards are in disarray!"

He nudged the handle of a cup toward the north, neatly folded his bandana and stuffed the square back in his pocket. "What's the matter?"

Even the simple task of straightening the plates had a calming effect.

She urged him forward. "Take a look."

The space between the workbench and the stove was narrow enough that she rested her hand on his shoulder and peered around him. The warmth of her touch seeped through his shirt and landed somewhere near his chest.

He grasped the broomstick once more and stuck the end through the oven handle. As the cast-iron door fell open, the rusted hinges squeaked. Tilly's fingers tightened on his shoulder.

Something growled.

An enormous raccoon bared its teeth.

Nolan surged backward.

Tilly shrieked. From her perch on the chair, she leaned around Nolan and kicked shut the door. "I told you something was in there."

"You can't just trap the animal." He splayed his hand to hold her back. "It'll suffocate."

Memories settled over him like a bleak dirge. He'd once spent an entire month in isolated confinement for a minor infraction of the rules. A month in complete and utter darkness with nothing but the scuttle of rats for company. His throat tightened painfully and he searched the open shelving behind Tilly's head. There were four plates, an even number, and the handles on the cups faced north. Restoring order forced calm. If he spun the last plate clockwise, he wouldn't even see the chip on the edge.

Tilly's face swam before him. "Thank you for coming to our rescue, Mr. West. That animal startled me. Not what I was expecting to find during our explorations."

"Explorations?" he said.

"Yes. Aren't you simply fascinated by this town? Think of all the stories people left behind. Haven't you ever wondered about who lived here and what they dreamed about?"

Frustrated by his inability to control the actions of others, he offered a curt "No."

"I do."

There was a gentleness and a guileless optimism about her that had been missing from his life for a very long time. An eternity. Part of him wanted to reach for the soothing comfort of her limitless hope in the world, but any thoughts in that direction were folly. He needed the distance. Nolan tore his gaze from the vulnerability in her clear eyes and stared at the dusty shelves.

Four plates. An even number. Even numbers symbolized order. With Tilly and the girls staring at him, he couldn't very well scrub the dusty surfaces. They'd think he'd gone mad for tidying an abandoned building. He'd wind up like his aunt Vicky, who lived near his aunt Edith in Cimarron Springs. Aunt Vicky kept fifteen goats and dressed them up on special occasions. He needed to be alone because hiding his affliction only increased his anxiety.

"I wouldn't waste time thinking about a bunch of strangers," he snapped. "I don't know why you'd want to meet a bunch of fool people who built a town without checking to see if there was actually gold in the river."

"I hadn't thought of it that way," she said, a thread of hurt weaving through her voice. "Still, they must have loved adventure to go to all this trouble for a chance at gold."

The adventure hadn't turned out well for her brother-in-law, but Nolan doubted she'd made the connection. That was the problem with optimists. They ignored the facts that didn't fit their rosy picture.

"Never mind," he said. Her wounded eyes had him feeling like a first-rate heel. "Let's see about this raccoon. I think there's a reason she's taken up residence in the kitchen stove."

"The raccoon is a girl?" Tilly laughed. "I didn't realize the two of you had met before."

She leaned over his shoulder, and her cheek brushed against his ear. His pulse thrummed. She must have rinsed her hair in lavender water that morning, and the delicate scent overwhelmed his senses. He'd forgotten how much he missed the simplest pleasures of female companionship: the soft laughter, the swish of skirts, the way they made even the starkest places feel like home.

Home. This wasn't his home, not permanently, and he didn't need a bunch of folks crowding up the place.

"Your raccoon is definitely female." Nolan focused his thoughts and eased the oven door open once more. "Look."

Four tiny pairs of black eyes shimmered in the ambient kitchen light.

"Babies." Tilly's lips parted in a gasp, and her warm exhale puffed against his neck. "Now what?"

The mother hissed and they both sprang back. Tilly teetered and he automatically caught her around the waist. His breath hitched. She was soft and yielding and undeniably feminine. Once she was steady, he swiftly released his hold.

"It's up to you," Nolan said. "If you really want, I can relocate them, but there's a good chance the mother will reject the babies if they're moved."

"No!" Caroline called from the doorway. "You can't kill them, Aunt Tilly. They're just babies."

"You're awake!" Tilly exclaimed. "Are you feeling better?"

"Much better."

"That's wonderful." The relief in Tilly's voice was obvious. "We'll be able to leave on Thursday."

Clearly she wanted out of Pyrite as much as he wanted them to go. The thought should have relieved him. Instead, her words left a deep, hollow ache in his chest. He'd lost his tolerance for people, though he hadn't entirely lost the need for human connection. Yet the longer they stayed, the more he risked revealing his eccentricities. He couldn't stomach watching their regard turn to disgust, or, worse yet, feel their ridicule.

Tilly took the broom from him. "If you don't want them harmed, Caroline, then we'll leave them be. It's almost suppertime—we should go anyway."

As they emerged into the dining room, a shadow passed before the front window. The five of them paused. The outline of a rider trotted down Main Street. The hollow thud of hoofbeats drifted through the partially open door.

An icy knot of fear settled in the pit of Nolan's stomach. A lone rider around these parts was unusual. Most folks traveled in pairs or groups through Indian country. There was safety in numbers.

Tilly squinted through the filthy glass. "I didn't think the cavalry would be on patrol again this soon."

"That isn't the cavalry," Nolan replied, his expression grim.

Chapter Three

Tilly scrubbed at the grubby pane. Two more riders trotted past. Beside her, Nolan's posture grew rigid and his expression was tense.

He urged her away from the window and held his index finger before his lips. "Stay inside," he said. "Don't come out unless I call for you."

"But Captain Ronald said the outlaws couldn't cross the river without being seen," she whispered. "That must be someone else, right?"

"The captain says a lot of things." Nolan yanked his gun from his holster, spun the chamber, then squinted along the barrel before replacing the weapon. "There's more than one rider. Stay out of sight. No matter what happens to me, stay hidden."

"You sound worried." Her heart beat a rapid tattoo against her chest. "Why are you worried?"

"It's probably nothing, but follow my orders, just in case."

Yesterday when the cavalry officer had warned her of danger, she'd been frightened. His assurances of safety had been confident, but he'd unleashed a nagging concern. When the stagecoach was moving, she felt safer, more secure. Stranded in this lonely town, they were vulnerable.

Nolan touched her sleeve and she stared at the spot where his fingers grazed the material. Though they'd only been in Pyrite for twenty-four hours, some things had become obvious immediately. More often than not, he kept his distance, moving out of her reach and avoiding her at every turn.

He kept a physical distance, but she sensed his protectiveness, his awareness of them. When she'd been startled by the raccoon, he'd been at her side in an instant. Yet she sensed his annoyance. As with Eleanor and her father, he seemed to find her inquisitiveness irritating. Despite the contradictions in his character, he inspired a curious reaction within her.

When he gazed at her with those intriguing hazel eyes, she was instantly tongue-tied.

"Don't come out of hiding until those men are gone," he said. "There's another gun in a box under the bed at the relay station. If anything happens to me, wait for them to leave, then lock yourselves up tight and wait for the next stagecoach. There are plenty of supplies."

Her knees turned watery. Surely he was exaggerating. There was no reason to assume the men outside meant them any harm. Captain Ronald's regiment was keeping a watch out for the outlaws. They'd know if something had happened. She glanced at the girls and quickly masked her expression. They had an alarming ability to read her moods.

"Let's keep an eye on the raccoon." Tilly urged the girls back toward the kitchen once more. "We should be extra-special quiet. We don't want to frighten her."

Victoria took Elizabeth's pudgy hand. "We'll be quiet. But what about the riders? What if they make noise?"

The girl's curious expression, so like Eleanor's, betrayed her skepticism. Victoria knew the distraction was about more than keeping an eye on the raccoon.

"Mr. West will take care of everything," Tilly said. "Don't worry."

His terse orders reminded her of her father, but she didn't doubt his ability. He had the bearing of a soldier and a hard edge to his eyes. She'd seen plenty of men with that same sharpness after the war. He was shielding them until he knew for certain the riders meant no harm, and for that she was thankful. He was the last bastion of safety in this untamed wilderness, and she clung to his unwavering self-assurance.

The girls scrounged chairs from the dining room and set up a horseshoe at the far end of the kitchen, safe from the riders and the mama raccoon, which, thankfully, had retreated deeper into the shadows.

"Keep your distance from the mama," Tilly ordered. "Don't touch her. Be as quiet as church mice. Stay here, and I'll be right back."

Unable to contain her curiosity, Tilly returned to the dining room. The warped door hadn't shut fully behind Nolan. Her pulse thumping, she pressed her ear near the opening. Nolan met the three riders in the center of the street. The strangers were dressed in rough canvas jackets with their hats pulled low over their eyes. Foam flecked the sides of their horses, indicating a grueling ride.

Tilly fisted a hand against the dread settling in her chest. She didn't like the look of the men. An air of menace hung thickly over them. There was something off-putting about the way they carried themselves—a desperation in the bedraggled cut of their clothing and the ribs showing on the sides of their horses.

Nolan propped one hand on his gun belt. "Where are you headed?"

One of the men tipped back his hat with his index finger. "We're on our way south."

"You're going in the right direction."

The second man chuckled. "Is this the route for the Pioneer Stagecoach line?"

"Yep."

The man crowded his roan horse nearer to Nolan. Unease skittered along Tilly's spine.

Nolan tensed, and he hooked his fingers around the barrel of the gun. He glanced over his shoulder with a piercing stare, and she scooted out of sight. He'd obviously sensed her scrutiny. Once again she marveled at his intuition. At home, her father rarely paid her any mind. He always had his nose in a law book. He rarely looked up except to scold her for interrupting him, or to admonish her for not being more like Eleanor. In contrast, Nolan was always aware of her movements. Not in a cloying, overbearing manner—but a watchful, comforting sort of a way.

The first man reined his horse around. "When is the next stagecoach due?"

"Week from Thursday," Nolan lied.

Tilly frowned at the falsehood.

"Why so little traffic?"

Nolan shrugged. "Why take the stagecoach when the riverboat is faster?"

"That's an odd thing to say. I heard the riverboat sank. You know something I don't know, stagecoach man?"

"This station is isolated. We don't hear the news except for when folks pass through."

"Then you won't mind if we stick around for a while."

Nolan drew himself taller. "There's nothing here. You might as well keep going south."

"You're all alone?"

"Just me."

The man rubbed one finger up and down the side of his bulbous nose. "No. I think this town will be perfect. Just perfect."

Nolan glanced over his shoulder once more. His lips were set in a hard line. Tilly shivered. Something brushed against her arm, and she stifled a shriek.

"Gracious, Caroline, you frightened me."

Caroline clasped her hands. "Elizabeth is gone."

"What do you mean?" Tilly demanded. "Where could she go?"

"Victoria and I only turned our back for an instant, and she was gone. There's a door leading to the next building. I didn't even notice because we were watching for the raccoon."

Tilly started back for the kitchen but Caroline pointed, her face pale. Tilly followed the direction of her niece's horrified gaze.

Elizabeth had exited the barbershop next door, and was clumsily navigating her way down the boardwalk steps and into the street directly before the strangers.

Tilly's heart jerked into her throat. "Stay here," she ordered the girls.

Her blood pounding, she pushed through the door and dashed after Elizabeth. Nolan spun around. She reached the errant toddler and caught Elizabeth beneath the arms.

"No-wan," the toddler declared, reaching for Mr. West.

"You lied to me," the outlaw declared. "I don't like liars."

In an instant the scene descended into a chaotic scuffle. The second man kicked Nolan square in the chest.

Nolan doubled over with a groan. The third men leaped from his horse and wrapped Nolan's hand behind his back. He struggled and the third man joined the effort to subdue him. The outlaw snatched the stagecoach man's gun and tossed the weapon to his companion.

The leader remained mounted. He edged his horse closer, then drew his sidearm and pressed the barrel against Nolan's head.

"You said you were alone here, mister. I don't like when folks lie to me."

The second man moved his horse between Tilly and Nolan. She clutched Elizabeth and scooted away. The third man blocked her exit. Frightened by the commotion, tears welled in Elizabeth's eyes.

"Mama," the toddler sobbed.

The mounted outlaw yanked on Tilly's hair, tipping back her head in a painful stretch. "You should have told me you had a wife, mister."

Chapter Four

A fierce haze clouded Nolan's vision. The pain in his chest sucked the breath from his lungs. With a burst of strength he broke free from the outlaw twisting his arm. At the same time, the third man released Tilly. She launched herself toward Nolan. With Elizabeth clutched between them, she threw one arm around his waist and buried her head against his shoulder.

He stiffened in surprise but didn't pull away. The toddler's eyes shimmered with unshed tears. He transferred Elizabeth into his arms and wrapped his free hand around Tilly.

"What do you want?" Nolan demanded, fearing he already knew the answer. "There's nothing for you here."

Tilly trembled and worked her hand between them, clutching her throat. Elizabeth hiccupped a sob.

"I'm Dakota Red." The red-haired leader grinned. "This fellow is my brother, Charlie, and Snyder here is a friend we busted out of jail."

Tilly gasped.

Though the brothers were similar in appearance, Charlie was at least a head shorter with small, sunken eyes and shaggy blond hair visible beneath his hat. Snyder was the largest of the bunch, a mountain of a man with a long, dark beard and heavy eyebrows. From the looks of the third man, Nolan guessed the brothers had busted Snyder out of jail for his brawn and not his brains.

Nolan slid his arm down Tilly's back and drew her closer. "I told you, there's nothing for you folks here."

"Not yet. But there will be." A scuffle sounded from the hotel and Dakota Red sighted his gun on the building. "Who's there?"

Tilly wrenched from Nolan's protective grasp.

Her eyes wide and frightened, she frantically splayed her arms. "They're children. Don't shoot."

Nolan moved before her, but there was no way for him to shield both her and Elizabeth from the outlaw.

"You heard her." Impotent fury settled in his chest. "Drop your weapon before you harm a child," Nolan said.

The outlaw's stance slackened, and the tip of his gun lowered.

His mocking laughter erupted in the strained silence. "How many young'uns you got, feller?"

"There's just my wife and our three nieces," Nolan answered quickly, his mind racing. They were outnumbered and outgunned. The safety of Tilly and her nieces mattered most. He grasped for any advantage he could exploit against the men.

"Where's their pa?" The outlaw narrowed his gaze. "And don't lie, or I'll know."

"Dead," Nolan replied shortly.

Dakota Red didn't ask about the mother. The outlaw must have assumed she was dead or he didn't care. Another piece of information Nolan tucked away for future reference. The man clearly didn't see women as a threat.

"Charlie." Dakota Red motioned for his brother. "This place will work just fine."

A muscle twitched in Charlie's cheek. "You sure?"

"I'm sure."

Tilly's hair had come loose from the coil at the nape of her neck, and the tangled mass tumbled around her shoulders. A break in the clouds sent a shaft of sunlight glinting off the silken strands. As though drawn by an invisible force, Charlie sidled nearer. He caught a handful in his gloved hand and brought the strands toward his face. Inhaling deeply, his eyes glittered dangerously.

Tilly shuddered and strained to get away.

"Let her go," Nolan growled.

"Charlie," Dakota Red barked out. "You heard the man."

The outlaw's brother remained defiant for a beat, then chuckled and shoved Tilly away.

The moment Charlie released his hold, Nolan twisted her free from the outlaw and tucked her against his side once more.

Dakota Red swung his leg over his horse's rump and dropped to the ground. He tossed the reins to Snyder, then paced the distance, his hands planted on the double gun belts strapped around his hips.

"You and I both know what has to happen here. There's a shipment of gold coming out of Virginia City. Without the usual steamship, that shipment has to travel over ground. The way I see things, trying to steal the gold outright will only get us shot. Which is why you and your wife are going to help us out. When the stages come through town, you're going to steal the gold for us. By the time them cavalry boys figure out it's missing, we'll be long gone."

Tilly stiffened. "What happens if we don't help you?"

"I guess I'll just have to kill you, won't I?"

"No!"

"We'll cooperate." Nolan rapidly worked through his options. "On one condition. Neither you nor your men lay a finger on my wife or the children. If anything happens to one of them…" With a fixed stare in Charlie's direction, he hardened his voice. "If even one hair on one of their heads is harmed, I'll send up the alarm."

Everything depended on the lie. As long as the outlaws believed Tilly and the girls were his family, he had leverage.

The outlaw pressed a hand against his chest in mock outrage. "I'm not here to spoil your little family. Me and the boys only want what we deserve. Them Union pigs took everything. I figure they owe us."

Nolan gritted his teeth. A lot of men had lost their livelihoods to the war, but not everyone had turned outlaw. "That's the deal. The stagecoach drivers and the cavalry know who lives here. If something happens to one of us, they'll send in troops, and your plan is forfeit."

"You make a real good point, mister." Dakota Red grinned at his crew. "You got yourself a deal."

"The children," Tilly blurted. "I don't want them frightened any more than necessary. As far as they're concerned, you're only resting here for a few days. Nothing more."

Dakota Red ran his thumb along his bottom lip, his expression thoughtful. "You got an awful lot of demands considering you're not holding any of the cards."

"They'll give you away," she continued, her voice tremulous. "They're children. They can't keep secrets."

Nolan admired her quick thinking. He didn't want the girls living under the umbrella of fear any more than Tilly. They were an equal distance between both the river crossing and the cavalry fort. The travel time to each was an easy two days in the daylight. If he rode hard, he could make the trip overnight while the outlaws slept. But if he slipped out after dark, he'd be navigating without moonlight given the growing bank of clouds in the distance. He'd also be leaving Tilly and the girls alone with the outlaws if anything happened to him.

He narrowed his gaze at Charlie. Dakota Red appeared focused on the gold, and Snyder was too wary of the brothers to disobey orders. Charlie had him worried. The outlaw had a wild, reckless look in his eye, and he'd set his sights on Tilly.

Sensing the tension in the adults without understanding the reason, Elizabeth whimpered. Nolan cupped his hand around the back of her head, smoothing the fluff of curls.

"It's all right," he soothed. "I know where there's a whole mess of blackberry bushes."

"Boo-berry," Elizabeth declared.

"Yes. Boo-berries."

Dakota Red grunted. "Enough already. Get them young'uns out here and let me take a look at them."

Tilly shook her head and strained away.

Nolan placed his hand over her trembling fingers. "It's all right. Do as he says."

He appealed to her with his eyes, willing her to understand. The outlaws had them trapped. There was nowhere for them to hide. Sooner or later, the fugitives were going to find out about the girls. The fewer falsehoods he told now, the better chance he'd have for pulling off a deception later.

There was no way of explaining his plan to Tilly. She was terrified, and she had every right to be. He reached for her, then let his hand drop to his side. Elizabeth wrapped her small arms around his neck.

Tilly glanced between him and the tiny head resting

on his shoulder. She seemed to make some kind of a decision. Though her steps dragged, she made her way to the hotel and emerged a moment later with a bright, false smile on her face.

Holding each of the girls' hands in one of her own, she said, "Victoria and Caroline, these men are going to be staying in town for a few days. We don't want to bother them, so let's keep our distance, shall we?"

Caroline pursed her lips. "They can't stay in the hotel. I promised that mama raccoon no one would bother her."

Charlie turned his head and spit into the grass. "Is your young'un touched or somthin'?"

"No." Tilly glared. "A mama raccoon has taken up residence in the stove at the hotel."

The outlaw chortled and reached for his gun. "I'll make short work of that varmint."

"You can't!" Caroline shouted.

Dakota Red shook his head. "Don't go teasing the girl, Charlie. There's no reason we can't oblige these folks for their hospitality. Looks like there's a proper house next to the livery. No need to go bothering the wildlife."

"That's the undertaker's house," Nolan murmured beneath his breath.

Tilly's eyes widened. "You're joking," she whispered.

"Not at all."

"Serves them right." She grimaced, then raised her voice. "Why don't you girls return to Mr. West's, um, return to the relay station and we'll start dinner."

The two older girls exchanged a confused look, but dutifully followed orders.

Elizabeth strained toward her sisters and Nolan set her on her feet with a pat on her head. "Go with your sisters."

"Boo-berries."

"After dinner."

The toddler studied his face as though gauging his intent. Apparently satisfied he'd keep his promise, she ambled after the older girls.

Once they'd moved out of sight, Tilly set her jaw in the stubborn line he'd witnessed the previous day. He sensed she didn't like being given orders, which didn't bode well for the next few days. He'd have his hands full staying between her and the outlaws. If one good thing had come out of his time living in the camp, he'd picked up skills in dealing with folks who held all the power. Always let the man in charge believe he had his prisoners cowed. That way, he dropped his guard.

"There are five of us and only three of you," Tilly declared boldly. "You can't watch all of us all the time."

"I don't have to watch you." Dakota Red chuckled. "Neither you nor your husband is leaving without your young'uns, and there's no way them girls are getting very far in this terrain without horses. You follow what I'm saying? I don't have to keep watch on you, I just have to keep watch on the horses, and I've got all five of you wrapped up tighter than a beetle in a spiderweb."

Nolan's gut twisted. The outlaw had effectively snatched the last best chance of fetching help.

There was no way he was making the cavalry station or the river crossing on foot, which meant he'd best think of another plan. Quickly.

The girls disappeared into the relay station, and Tilly glanced in despair at Nolan. How were they going to survive the next few days? The girls would certainly give them away. How could she explain the situation without frightening them?

Charlie sidled closer, and nausea rose in the back of her throat. Her neck throbbed from his earlier vio-

lent behavior. He reached for her and she instinctively
launched herself at Nolan. His strong arms closed around
her, clasping her shivering body tight against his side.
The outlaw hadn't challenged the stagecoach man before,
and she prayed Charlie would keep his distance now.

"It's all right." The warmth of Nolan's breath feathered against her tangled hair. "You're safe. I won't let
him harm you."

Angry tears burned in her eyes. If she hadn't let her
curiosity override her good sense, she'd have been watching Elizabeth, and none of this would have happened.

At least her nieces were safe. For the moment.

Dakota Red gathered his men. "Snyder will follow
you two up to the house. The boys and I have a hanker-
ing for supper. Snyder will make certain there aren't any
weapons lying around. We wouldn't want the children
getting hurt now, would we?" He offered a toothy grin.
"I just need to speak with the boys for a few minutes.
You don't mind, do you? And if you do mind, I can always shoot you."

He took great amusement in his own macabre joke,
laughing until his belly jiggled. Tilly quivered and bur-
rowed closer to Nolan. When she realized she was clutching the stagecoach man with enough force to crush his
ribs, she started and pulled away.

He tightened his grip and spoke near her ear. "Stay
close. As long as Charlie is in view, we're madly affectionate. If he wants my cooperation, he has to know how
much you and the girls mean to me."

His cheeks reddened. "You know what I mean."

"I know."

She did understand. Perhaps because the situation
had turned dire, she was keenly aware of the stagecoach
man. His expression was grave, but she noted the rapid

rise and fall of his chest. When had her emotions gone topsy-turvy? She'd always assumed that she was the same person in any given situation, and that her inherent personality would surface under duress.

Yet here she was, cowering in the arms of a near stranger. She felt as though the outlaws had stripped away the thin veneer of her independence and exposed her weakness on a very basic level.

Tilly clamped shut her eyes. What was happening to her? The truth of her nature was disheartening. The woman she wanted to be wouldn't count on this man for protection—she'd take care of herself. Except she wasn't the brave person she'd thought herself. She was skittish and vulnerable, trapped between the outlaws and this quiet man.

Nolan's hands moved in soothing circles over her back, heightening her awareness of him. Shocked by her flare of unwanted longing, she glanced away. She mustn't read anything personal in his demonstrative actions. His caring was part of the act, nothing more.

As for her unexpected reaction, she was instinctively responding to his protection and his kindness. Wasn't she?

No matter her own pitiable weakness, she had others to think about. "I have to speak with the girls, make them understand without frightening them."

"We'll keep them separated from the outlaws as much as possible," Nolan said. "You'll keep them busy."

"How?" She tossed a glare at the outlaws' backs. "I suppose we could start by digging our own graves."

"Don't even tease about that. No matter what happens, we have to stay focused on surviving."

"All right then, but this town isn't exactly teeming

with activities. We can't exactly visit the mercantile and select ribbons from the general store."

"They're children. How much entertainment do they need?" The stagecoach man appeared perplexed. "Keep them busy however you keep children busy. They're your nieces, surely you know them."

Barely. Even when Walter was away at war, Eleanor had always hovered over the girls. She'd never trusted Tilly alone with them beyond an hour or two here or there. Tilly was never an authority figure to her nieces.

"I've only been watching them for a few days," Tilly explained. "And we've been traveling or packing for most of those."

"You were a child once. What did you do to keep busy?"

Tilly snorted. "Eleanor gave me chores."

"Then give the girls chores." He pressed two fingers beneath her chin and forced her to look at him. "Your nieces are counting on you."

She flashed a half grin. "I'd have them clean the relay station, but you've already scrubbed the wood grain from the floor."

Something flicked in his eyes, an emotion she couldn't read.

"I suspect they'll make another mess soon enough."

"You're probably right."

The girls were tidy. They'd grown up beneath Eleanor's guidance, after all, yet they still managed to create chaos with shockingly little effort.

Eleanor had always striven for perfection, while Tilly had been content with disorder. In her teenage years, her sister had once sent Tilly to bed without supper for failing to put away her stockings properly. Treating the girls in the same manner didn't seem right considering how much Tilly had chafed under Eleanor's strict rule.

"Hey," Dakota Red shouted. "You two quit your whispering."

Her anger rose up. She wasn't chattel to be ordered around.

"Get, woman," the outlaw ordered. "The boys and I are hungry. Until I'm certain you don't have any guns hidden around the place, the two of you stay together. Snyder will keep watch while you're cooking."

Tilly bit her tongue until she tasted blood.

Charlie crossed to his horse, making a deliberate show of brushing against her arm. Her flare of rebellion instantly died. Tilly shuddered and moved closer to the shelter of Nolan's arms. The mercenary part of her feared being alone with the fugitives—she feared being separated from Nolan's safety. Though she'd only known the stagecoach man for a day, they were banded together against the outlaws.

Their common enemy created an instant sense of union.

Her make-believe husband touched the spot where Charlie had brushed against her, as though erasing the mark of the outlaw. Their eyes locked and they both faltered for a moment. Her stomach did a little flip.

"Steady on, Miss Hargreaves." His gaze softened, and one corner of his mouth tilted up. "Wasn't Matilda called 'The Good Queen'?"

"You've studied your history."

"Only when forced. I'm certain your education is far more extensive. I grew up on a farm. I only attended school when I wasn't needed for chores."

Pressure built behind her eyes. This was the most he'd ever spoken to her. She hadn't realized until then how very much she missed conversation. In the years since the war, as her employment with her father's law practice had gradually dwindled, her circle of acquaintances had narrowed. As the men returned home, the ladies' war-effort committees had gradually disbanded. Her friends had drifted away, moving on with their lives, marrying and starting families.

Everything had happened so slowly, she hadn't realized until this very moment how isolated she'd become of late. How very lonely.

Nolan was staring at her, and his tiny quirk of a grin faded. "Tilly?"

He cupped her cheek and ran the ball of his thumb beneath her eye. "Don't give them the satisfaction of your tears. Men like that feed off others' weakness."

"I'm afraid of being caught alone with Charlie."

"I'll see that you never are."

"Thank you."

At the quiver in her voice, his hand glided down her cheek. He stroked the pulse throbbing at the base of her neck. "He won't touch you again. Not while I'm here."

A delicate shudder rippled all the way to her toes. He was staring at her with an intensity that made her breath catch. Any hint of his previous cajoling smile had vanished. She couldn't help but question what he was thinking. She sensed his inner conflict, and wondered at it. Her hand fluttered near his shoulder. She had an insane longing to caress him and comfort him, but she held herself in check.

One of the horses whinnied, and they jolted apart. The moment broken, Tilly glanced away. The wind caught her hair, whipping it across her face and eyes, obscuring her view of his expression. Had he been as affected by the moment as she had?

She'd consider the oddity of her reaction later, when they weren't in fear for their lives. This wasn't about feelings, this was about survival. Their pact was only temporary.

Nolan clasped her fingers and tugged her toward the relay station. His hand dwarfed hers, and the rough calluses on his palm chafed her skin. He caught her gaze and her heart kicked. She looked over her shoulder and caught Charlie following their progress, a speculative gleam in his beady eyes. She whipped back around.

Snyder grunted. "Let's go."

As far as the outlaws knew, she and Nolan were husband and wife. She'd been too stunned by Charlie's unexpected attack to refute his words, but Nolan had latched on to falsehood. He'd used the lie as a bargain, and he'd saved their lives, and her virtue, in the process. Though she wasn't adept at dealing with fugitives, she admired his ploy. He'd cleverly bargained his assistance for her safety and the safety of the girls.

Once inside the relay station, Snyder grabbed a heel of bread from the counter and bit off a hunk before wandering into the area containing the dining table. He didn't appear in any great hurry to start his search.

Nolan led her to the meticulously ordered kitchen. Another tidbit she'd discovered about the stagecoach man in the short time they'd known each other—he was neat. Obsessively so. Her father and Eleanor had shared the same trait. They obsessed over even the tiniest imperfection.

If growing up in a spick-and-span household had taught her anything, the two of them were bound to clash. Tilly had never been praised for her tidiness.

While Eleanor and her father had been obsessively neat, Nolan's living conditions were austere in the extreme. There were chalked outlines on the wall where the pots and pans had been arranged by size. Eleanor would probably swoon at the sight. An unexpected stab of jealousy focused Tilly's attention. Eleanor wasn't here. Eleanor was miles away, and Tilly had better keep her head clear. She'd already cost them with her inattentiveness.

Nolan lit the stove and adjusted the flame. "They'll expect the woman to prepare the food," he said. "Follow my lead and try and pretend you know where everything is located."

She looked heavenward. "You should know that I don't cook very well."

Another piece of domesticity she'd never mastered. Women's work was either frippery, like embroidering handkerchiefs, or tediously repetitious, like cooking and doing laundry. She hadn't the patience for either.

They'd employed a housekeeper off and on over the years, depending on the state of her father's law practice. That was another reason her volunteer work had dwindled. Since her father had to pay his current law clerk an actual salary, as opposed to Tilly's free labor, she'd once again taken over the role of housekeeper.

"I don't think they're expecting much in the way of food," Nolan replied wryly. "When Snyder is distracted, I'll slip into the bedroom and retrieve my gun."

"If he catches you retrieving a gun," Tilly whispered harshly, "he's liable to kill you."

A crash sounded and Elizabeth toddled from the bedroom the girls had claimed.

"Uh-oh," the toddler exclaimed ominously.

Victoria skidded from the room, Caroline close on her heels.

Caroline pointed. "It was her fault!"

"Was not." Victoria's lower lip protruded in an exaggerated pout. "She pushed me."

Tilly heaved a sigh. "What's broken?"

"Your looking glass."

Tilly scrubbed a hand down her face. "Never mind."

Of all the things that had gone wrong this day, a shattered looking glass was the least of her worries.

"Why don't you three wash up for supper?" she directed. "Stay out of the bedroom for now. I'll clean up the glass when I've finished with dinner."

She paused on an expectant breath, waiting for someone to protest. When Caroline merely shrugged, Tilly exhaled loudly. She silently praised the innocent acceptance of children. She and Nolan were treading through a minefield with this charade. Who knew what pitfalls they were bound to stumble over in the next few days? Her nieces hadn't questioned the fact that she was assisting Nolan with dinner, though he'd prepared the meals exclusively since their arrival.

She slanted a glance at Snyder, who'd been distracted by several burrs adhered to his canvas-clad calves. The men's escape must have led through tall brush. He twisted around, his attention focused on the stubborn spikes. Tilly edged toward the bedroom Nolan occupied. The outlaw grunted and straightened, abandoning the effort.

Panic tightened painfully in her chest. Her three nieces crowded around the wash bucket, laughing and splashing each other, their argument forgotten as quickly as it had flared. Pain throbbed behind her eyes. They had no idea of the danger, and she was determined to keep it that way.

Nolan's gaze darted toward the bedroom door at the opposite end of the relay station.

"You can't," she implored quietly. "It's too dangerous."

"We don't have any other choice. Dakota Red has us

trapped. He's right, we won't get very far without the horses."

"Then we'll help them. Once they have the gold, they'll leave us be."

Pity shimmered in his hazel eyes. "Sure."

Her heart sank. "They're going to kill us either way, aren't they?"

"Let's just get through tonight, we'll worry about the rest later."

He was backtracking on his words to keep her fears at bay, but she'd seen the truth in his expression. Once the outlaws had the money, their lives were forfeit. She glanced at the two long braids hanging down Caroline's back. For the first time in her life she was entirely free of Eleanor's authority and her father's disapproval, and all she wanted was to crawl back home. She'd been angry with her sister for treating her as though she was still a child, and here she was behaving like one.

Eleanor had always been stronger, but something had changed since Walter's passing. The facade of perfection had slipped, and her sister's fragility had unleashed a desperate terror in Tilly. It was a truth she'd been unwilling to face. If Eleanor wasn't the strong one anymore, where did that leave Tilly? As much as she chafed against her role in the family, at least she understood her place.

Victoria giggled and flicked water at her younger sisters. The juxtaposition of their innocence against the outlaw prowling the house was too much to bear.

Tilly's chest pounded like a kettledrum. "Where are those blackberry bushes, Mr. West? Are they close?"

"Out the back door, and straight ahead." He pitched his voice low. "You can call me Nolan when we're around the outlaws."

Her cheeks heated. "Of course. I keep forgetting."

She squinted through the window. The three girls would be away from the house, but still within sight. Nolan was correct, they needed distance between her nieces and the outlaws at all times.

She grasped a bowl from the counter and approached Caroline. "Gather as many berries as you can. Take as long as you need."

Once again Caroline shot her a speculative glance, but didn't question the orders. Tilly made a note to watch herself around the middle child. All of the girls were intelligent, but Caroline was the most like Eleanor, and Eleanor had always known when Tilly was up to something.

Once the girls were gone, Tilly and Nolan began the meal. Snyder skulked about the station, poking his nose in all the cupboards and stomping on the floorboards. He emerged from the first bedroom empty-handed, and she and Nolan exchanged an uneasy glance. The barren rooms gave little clue as to who occupied them.

Nolan started for the door, but Snyder blocked his path.

"You stay where I can see you," the outlaw ordered.

Nolan's concentration remained focused, and Tilly sensed he was weighing his options, deciding if he could challenge the man alone. She studied the scattergun clutched in Snyder's hands, then stared at her fingers. Nolan was the best hope for the girls. He was the only one who could truly protect them. He was the one the outlaws needed in order for their plan to succeed. Since she couldn't let him put himself in harm's way, she'd have to do this herself.

She wiped her hands on her skirts and straightened. "I can't work with my hair unbound like this."

She brushed past Snyder and marched toward the last

bedroom. Nolan's room. The room the outlaw hadn't yet searched.

Snyder grasped her upper arm in a viselike grip. "I like your hair just fine the way it is."

Tilly shot him a quelling glance. "I prefer my hair bound."

The painful hold on her arm eased. Snyder let her go and swiped at his mouth with his sleeve.

"Be quick about it, girlie. I'm hungry."

"I'll be quick as gunfire," she said over her shoulder.

If she wanted to live her life as a brave woman who wanted to live a purposeful life, then she'd better start acting like one.

Chapter Five

The shotgun layout of the relay station allowed Nolan to view all the exits. There were two rooms flanking the front entrance, which opened to the kitchen and dining room areas, and two rooms lining the corridor to the rear exit. He crossed the space and peered out the back door. The top of Caroline's head was visible behind a tangle of blackberry bushes. The girls laughed with each other, blissfully unaware of the tension brewing in the relay station.

The task should keep them busy for at least another thirty minutes, give or take.

He cast a glance at the door leading to his bedroom. How long did Tilly have before the outlaw grew suspicious? His gun wasn't exactly concealed, but he hadn't painted a bull's-eye on the barrel, either.

Snyder flopped onto one of the dining room chairs. He hooked his heel over the rung of a second chair, yanked the legs nearer, then propped his loosely crossed ankles on the seat. Nolan clenched his jaw. Bad enough the outlaws were forcing their participation in a heist before they murdered them, but they were a slovenly bunch of fugitives, as well.

The outlaw rested his shotgun across his lap and threaded his hands behind his head. The scattergun was an odd choice, but given the item was probably stolen, the selection made more sense.

Nolan ladled beans into a serving bowl, and the outlaw grunted.

"You always do woman's work?" the man sneered.

"With only the two of us running the station, we alternate tasks."

The outlaw grunted again, apparently satisfied with the answer. Nolan's gaze slid toward the partially open bedroom door. A thump sounded and Snyder straightened.

Nolan slammed down the coffeepot, pulling the man's attention from Tilly's activities.

"Why are you running with those two?" Nolan asked. "Seems like you're the sort of fellow who can take care of himself."

"I owe 'em for busting me out of jail."

"They're using you," Nolan said. "They'll kill you and take your share once they have the gold. They're brothers. They have no allegiance to you."

"Like you said, I'm the sort of fellow who can take care of himself."

The big guy was smarter than he looked. Still, it wouldn't hurt to sow the seeds of discontent now and again over the next few days. Anything the hostages could do to divide the men might ultimately aid in an escape attempt.

The gang had obviously been riding hard, and fatigue showed in the bend of Snyder's shoulders. His eyes drifted shut. Nolan gently set the stacked plates on the table, then wiped his hands on a towel. His nerves thrummed. Tilly was taking too long. Snyder was liable to wake and burst in on her at any moment.

He started toward the bedroom. The front door slammed open. Dakota Red and his brother stumbled inside, their arms wrapped around each other's shoulders, their faces flushed and their eyes glassy.

"Where's the woman?" Charlie demanded.

"Doing her hair or something," Snyder mumbled from his half slumber.

Charlie kicked the chair from beneath his heels, jerking the outlaw upright. "You're supposed to be watching them."

"I am."

Charlie slapped the back of the taller man's head. "I told you we shoulda left this big, dumb lug behind."

Snyder lunged upward but the quick tensing of Dakota Red's body had him checking his actions.

"Leave him alone, Charlie," Dakota Red snarled. "We need him. The next time he sleeps on duty, I'll wallop him myself."

"You say we need him." Charlie threw up his arms. "I say we can work this heist just fine on our own."

"Your last plan got us locked up in jail for fourteen months. I'm not swinging from a noose because you can't hold your temper."

The two men measured each other in silence, one deadly calm and sure, the other seething with barely concealed rage. Finally, muttering a vile imprecation, Charlie spun on his heel and stalked toward the partially closed door. The outlaw lifted his heel to kick the door, but the panel swung open before his boot made contact. The shock threw him off balance and he stumbled forward.

Tilly dodged his clumsy fall as she entered the room. Her face carefully impassive, she skirted past the prone man.

Charlie muttered another sharp curse, and Snyder chortled.

Dakota Red scowled at Snyder. "Don't rile him up. He's liable to shoot you, and I need a third man for this job."

The humiliated outlaw sprang to his feet and slapped his hat against his thigh.

Nolan frantically searched Tilly's face for any sign she'd had success in retrieving the gun, but he couldn't read her expression. She'd pinned her hair in place once more, appearing cool and composed. Only someone looking closely would see the way she clutched her fingers together, hiding the fact that she was visibly shaking. Apprehension crawled up his nerves. He'd try again for the gun later. Snyder must have forgotten he hadn't searched the room, because he didn't show any sign of moving from his perch at the table.

Tilly took in the tension flickering between the three outlaws and scooted nearer to Nolan. "I'm terribly sorry. I didn't see you there."

Aware the outlaws were monitoring their every move, he draped his hand around her waist and drew her near. She offered a stiff smile that might have passed as a grimace. Neither of them was particularly comfortable with the ruse, but until he thought of a better plan, they were trapped in the deception. The irony didn't escape him. He was an unlikely suitor even before the war. Women had mostly left him stammering and bashful.

Others in the prisoner camp had anxiously awaited letters from home, but his mother had died and his father didn't write well.

The perfumed letters caused the most ribbing amongst the men. Yet there was a melancholy edge in the prisoners' good-natured teasing. At the time, Nolan had been grateful he didn't have a sweetheart waiting for him. Anticipating the letters was agony, and receiving a missive was joy tempered with the sure knowledge of everything the men were missing. They were supposed to be grateful they were alive, and he was—other men perished by the hundreds each day. Except balancing on the cusp of living was its own torture.

Tilly slipped from his hold and patted his cheek, then ducked into the kitchen once more. Nolan touched the spot her hand had caressed. A simple gesture, the casual affection of husband and wife. He'd best follow her lead and stay on his toes, no matter how unnatural the actions.

As she sliced the loaf of bread he'd left on the counter, Nolan finished setting the table for the outlaws.

"Ain't you setting a place for yourselves?" Dakota Red inquired from his sprawl.

"We'll wait until you're finished," Tilly replied, her voice clipped. "The girls, remember."

"Ah, yes. Them girls who can't keep secrets."

She finished slicing the bread and carried the board to the table. Once she'd returned to the kitchen, she rinsed her hands and draped the towel haphazardly over the counter. Nolan automatically lifted the discarded item.

Tilly glared at him.

He glanced down.

She'd been covering the knife she'd used to slice the bread.

His ears burned.

He folded the towel in fours and rested the neat square over the knife once more.

She reached for the leather handle of the water bucket. "I'll be right back."

As she passed before the table, Charlie stuck out his booted foot and caught her ankles. She pitched forward and landed hard on her knees. The bucket shot from her hands and something skittered across the floor.

Rage surging through his veins, Nolan automatically reached for Tilly. Snyder squeezed his throat, holding him back.

"Well, well, well." Dakota Red stood slowly and crossed the room. "What do we have here?" He lifted the object from the floor, and the metal barrel of a gun glinted in the light of the kerosene lantern. "You're full of surprises, ma'am."

Tears of frustration sprang in Tilly's eyes, as much from the pain of falling as in losing the gun. They'd been watching her so closely, she'd thought she'd have a better chance of hiding the weapon outside. She hadn't counted on the outlaws' cruelty.

Charlie hooked his arm beneath her shoulder and hauled her upright. She cringed from the steely look in his close-set eyes, and braced for a cuffing.

"Teach him a lesson," Dakota Red declared.

"Him?" Tilly's eyes flew open.

The outlaw smirked. "Well, I can't hit a woman now, can I?"

Charlie wrapped Nolan's arm behind his back, and Snyder pounded him in the gut with a burly fist. Nolan paled and went to his knees.

The outlaw released her and Tilly rushed to his side.

Charlie grinned. "I knew you'd try something. Got anything else you'd like to tell us?"

He reached for Nolan and Tilly put her body between the outlaw and the prone man. "Nothing. That was the only gun."

"Why don't I believe you?"

"I don't care what you believe."

She reached for Nolan.

"I'm all right," he said, his voice strained.

He didn't appear fine as he staggered upright. His complexion was ashen, and his face was contorted in a grimace of pain.

Nolan declined her proffered hand. "I don't need your help."

Her fingers trembled. He might not need her help, but she needed his…desperately. The only other time she'd traveled outside of Omaha had been for Walter's funeral, and she'd had the guidance of her father. She'd thought Omaha slightly wild when compared to cities she'd read about back east. The gold-rush town of Virginia City had shattered her naive belief. She'd been shocked by the rough conditions and the hordes of dirt-covered men desperate for gold.

Eleanor had never voiced concerns over her living conditions, and Tilly hadn't pressed her sister. Being surrounded by these hardened men gave her new insight into Eleanor's challenges. Why hadn't her sister ever confided in her?

"Girlie!" Dakota Red shouted, a malicious grin slashing his craggy face. "The fellows and I have a powerful hunger. Fetch them vittles."

A filthy hand tugged on her skirts. She stepped away from Charlie's grasping hand, only to find herself bumping in to Snyder. The burly man laughed and plucked at her sleeve.

"Got any more guns hiding in there?" he demanded.

She dodged his grasp, her eyes flashing with anger. Charlie halted her exit, splaying his arms and grinning as though this was all some sort of game to him. She whipped around and discovered she was trapped. Panicked, she was near to crying. She set her jaw, refusing to shed a tear. Charlie seemed to feed on her desperation and fear. She wouldn't break down. Nolan had warned her. If she broke down, they'd have her.

Nolan straightened, one hand braced against the table, the other clutching his ribs. "You know the deal. Leave her be."

An insane gratitude swept over her. Though her independent spirit rebelled against cowering behind the stage-coach man, survival took hold. At this moment, she had no other choice except clinging to the safety he provided.

Charlie threw back his head and chortled. "Your man has some fight."

"We need him, Charlie." Dakota Red's expression was a frigid as a winter wind. "Stay away from the woman."

"She ain't worth it anyway," his brother spat out. "She's plain as a fence post and she's got hips like a buffalo."

Outraged, she cocked her palm. In a flash Nolan caught her wrist. Blinking rapidly, she lowered her hand. If she struck Charlie, he'd be forced to strike back, hard, or risk losing face in front of the other men.

Lifting her chin, she moved away, refusing to let the outlaws see the devastation Charlie's words had wrought. She was plain, and she'd always had more curves than the other ladies. Having her faults displayed before the other men smarted. Who was she kidding? Nolan's opinion was the one that mattered most to her. She snuck a look at him from beneath her eyelashes. His expression was dark and unreadable.

"Git, woman," Dakota Red ordered once more. "She don't need to be pretty to make supper."

The outlaws grumbled at giving up their game, but when Tilly hastily set the beans and bacon on the table next to the bread, they shrugged and relented. She returned to the kitchen and scooted nearer to Nolan.

"Are you all right?" she asked in a hushed tone. "How are your ribs?"

"Good," he replied, his voice strained. "Nothing to worry about."

"I'm so sorry."

"Woman," Charlie hollered. "Fetch me more water."

Tilly ground her teeth and turned away from Nolan. He caught her hand, his gaze fierce.

"We have to see this through," he whispered. "Do you understand? Don't let them get to you, or they'll kill us all. They'll try and get under our skin to keep us off balance."

Her face burned. He knew. He knew she was humiliated. At least he hadn't tried to appease her with lies, and for that she was grateful.

She'd rather have his anger than his pity. "I understand."

"Charlie has to look tough for the other men. The best way to make himself look big is to belittle someone smaller than him. We're caught in the middle, that's all."

"I said that I understand, and I do," she said through clenched teeth.

Nolan pressed a kiss against her temple.

Her whole body quivered. She leaned into his touch, then caught Charlie staring at them. The affectionate gesture was obviously for his benefit.

Tilly moved away. Her looks weren't what gave her worth.

The outlaws ate the simple meal with gusto, nearly emptying the pan of beans before the girls arrived with the berries. With her nieces present, the icy knot of fear settled in Tilly's chest once more. She directed the girls inside with a nervous grin, admonishing them to wipe their feet. Best to keep everything as normal as possible.

Elizabeth had purple stains covering her mouth and the front of her dress. "Boo-berries."

She approached the far end of the table and held out a handful of smashed purple. "Want?"

Dakota Red drew his chin toward his chest and angled his head with a shake. "You keep 'em. Let's go, boys." He pointed one gnarled finger in Tilly's direction, his mouth set in a grim line. "Remember your young'uns the next time you want to try something. You got me?"

She suppressed a shiver of fear. His threat was obvious. "I understand."

Gracious. She was beginning to sound like a parrot, chirping the same phrases over and over again.

"Me and the boys will be keeping a tight watch on the horses," he continued. "You play along real nice like we asked, and everything is going to be fine. You got that?"

Tilly gave a hesitant nod.

"Glad we came to that agreement. We'll just search the place again. Even though you've given us your word."

The outlaws tore up the entire station looking for hidden weapons. They emptied all the drawers, moved all the furniture and tapped on all the floorboards. During the search, Tilly kept the girls busy with baking a batch of blackberry muffins.

Victoria glanced up at a particularly loud thump. "What are they doing? What's taking them so long?"

"They lost something. They're trying to find it."

"Mama said if you put your stuff away when you're done, you don't lose things."

"She's right. But I don't think they're interested in your mother's advice right now."

Once the outlaws were satisfied, they left to tend their

horses. Snyder took a seat outside the front door, and filled his pipe bowl with tobacco.

After the excitement of the afternoon, the rest of the evening passed in relative monotony. Only the faint stench of pipe smoke kept Tilly on edge. As much as she and Nolan struggled to present an air of normalcy, the danger was ever present. With each tick of the clock the tension took its toll, gradually draining her body and soul of energy. Tilly fed the girls and had the three wash up for bedtime.

Caroline stifled a yawn behind her fingers. "What time will the stagecoach come by tomorrow? I'm ready to see Nanny and Poppy."

"About that." Tilly tugged her lower lip between her teeth. "Nolan thinks the next stagecoach might be too full. If that's the case, we'll have to stay another day or two."

Caroline shrugged. "All right."

Tilly breathed a sigh of relief at her easy acceptance of the lie. The next few days were going to be a trial. Tonight she needed rest.

After they'd finished cleaning up the broken looking glass and preparing for bed, the three of them stretched out on the mattress in the main bedroom. Tilly pulled the covers up to their chins, and they each said a quick prayer. Caroline and Victoria prayed for their mother's safe travels, and Elizabeth prayed for a puppy.

Caroline rolled her eyes. "You're never getting a puppy. Mama doesn't like dogs. She says they're messy and they shed hair. She says dog fur is disgusting."

Elizabeth set her chin in a stubborn line. "I pray."

She stuck out her tongue for emphasis.

Caroline swiped at her sister and Tilly lunged between

them. "No fighting. Elizabeth can pray for whatever she wants. No hitting each other at bedtime."

Her nerves were stretched too taut for this sort of the nonsense. Thankfully, the two scooted away from each other. The girls chatted and their animosity quickly dissipated.

Pausing at the door, Tilly blew each of them a kiss. Their eyes drifted shut and she lingered in the doorway. She'd missed them terribly over the past few years. She hardly knew Elizabeth, who'd been an infant when her parents moved to Virginia City.

Victoria and Caroline had been just as precocious at that age. They'd played games and she'd read them books. They'd taken endless walks around the neighborhood. Traveling with them brought back fond memories of all the fun they'd shared.

She'd only have a few weeks with them before she left for New York. Her eyes burned. She hadn't considered how much she'd miss them. Especially now that she'd gotten to know them once more. Her heart heavy, she turned away.

She discovered Nolan with his forearms braced on the table, his hands fisted before him. His attention seemed to be turned inward. He didn't even flick a glance in her direction.

She rested a hand on his shoulder. "You should eat something."

His eyes glittered with shadowed emotion. "I could say the same of you."

At the mention of food, her stomach rumbled. She hadn't realized until that moment how little she'd eaten. Though the outlaws had left the "family" mostly to themselves throughout the evening, she'd been too worried and nervous to eat.

"Apparently, it wouldn't hurt for me to miss a meal or two," she said with a wan smile. "I have hips like a buffalo, remember?"

"You're plenty beautiful, and they all know it. Even Charlie. Especially Charlie." She started to turn away, but he caught her hand. "Don't let them bother you. Don't you see? They're breaking us down, searching for our weaknesses. Don't listen to the lies. Don't give them the satisfaction."

That first day, she'd mistaken Nolan's silence for disinterest. His quiet manner disguised an intense watchfulness.

A melting warmth flowed through her. She'd been invisible for most of her life. She'd been invisible next to Eleanor's beauty and accomplishments. She'd been an invisible member of her father's working staff. For the first time in her life, she felt as though someone was actually seeing her, and not comparing her to something better.

Of course he wasn't comparing her to anyone else—they were trapped in a deserted town. She mustn't let herself read something more in to his concern. He was a kind man showing his good nature. She wasn't special. Everything had turned to chaos, and her feelings were wrapped up in the dangerous situation the outlaws had created.

She'd never been much for childish fantasies. She knew the ways of the world. She wasn't as beautiful as Eleanor. She hadn't done her father proud by marrying one of his law clerks. Instead, she'd tried to be one of those law clerks. She'd discovered just how useful her services were to her father once the men came home from war.

Lightning flashed outside the window, and a sudden burst of rain pattered against the glass windowpanes.

"We should talk about what's going to happen tomorrow," Nolan said.

"Not here."

Tilly cast a nervous glance at the door behind which the girls slept. If there was one thing she recalled from growing up, she and her sister had eavesdropped on more than one conversation to the complete ignorance of her father.

She tiptoed to the front door and angled her body. Snyder had slumped over, his pipe cold. He snored softly. The front awning didn't offer much protection, and he'd be soaked to the bone soon. She let the door shut quietly behind her. Though it went against her natural Christian charity, she couldn't bring herself to be concerned over the outlaw's comfort.

"Out back," she whispered.

Nolan followed her to the tiny back porch and together they huddled beneath the narrow overhang. He rubbed his bruised ribs.

"I'm so sorry," Tilly said. "About what happened with the gun. They were watching us too closely. I thought if I could hide the gun outside, near the well, you'd have a better chance of retrieving it without them noticing. It was a foolish idea."

"It wasn't a dumb idea. You couldn't have known what Charlie would do."

"I think he plays the fool on purpose." Despite the patter of rain, fireflies dotted the inky blackness. They sparkled over the tangle of blackberry bushes, the thorn-covered branches little more than dark shapes in the moonless night. "But he's always watching us, isn't he? He keeps track of everything."

"Yes. Both him and his brother. Nothing gets past Dakota Red."

"How do you think they crossed the river?"

"I don't know. Maybe they crossed at night. Maybe they slipped out when the cavalry wasn't watching. I've never put much stock in Captain Ronald's leadership abilities."

"He didn't seem so bad."

"Maybe."

"Why don't you like him? The captain?"

Nolan heaved a sigh, wincing at the movement. "He reminds me of someone."

The silence stretched out for so long, she thought he'd finished speaking.

"Captain Ronald reminds me of someone I knew during the war," Nolan said at last. "Not in looks, but in attitude. The man I knew was charming and slick, but that part of his personality was an act. He was a cruel man. Sadistic in his punishments."

"That must have been horrible."

"It was a long time ago."

"Suffering seems to shorten the distance to our memories, don't you think?"

"I suppose. We all suffered during the war, in one way or another."

A pang of sadness settled in her chest. "I lost my cousin. We were the same age. We'd practically grown up together. How about you?"

"Most all the boys I went to school with lost their lives. I lived in Virginia. On the border. The war hit our town fast and hard. There isn't much left of where I grew up."

His voice was flat, yet she sensed a deep undercurrent of grief despite his emotionless recounting. "That must be difficult," she replied.

"I don't think about it much."

A gust of wind blew of smattering of rain beneath the eve. Tilly shivered and crossed her arms over her chest.

"Wait here," Nolan said.

He disappeared inside and returned a moment later with a canvas coat, then awkwardly draped the material over her shoulders.

"Thank you," she murmured.

She tugged the collar tighter around her neck. Though early summer, the rain had dropped the temperature.

"What are we going to do tomorrow?" she asked. "The driver will know that we're not married."

"I've been thinking about that. The outlaws have to stay out of sight, which gives us the advantage. You hang back with the girls, and I'll search the stagecoach. I'll see if I can get a message to the driver."

"Is that wise? What if you're caught?" She glanced at his stomach, flinching as she recalled Snyder's punishment. "The girls and I need you."

He extended his hand and cupped her cheek. "Don't worry, nothing will happen to me."

She caught the slight cadence in his voice, and her eyes narrowed. There was something about his bearing that nagged at the edges of his consciousness. She recalled his slight flinch when she'd mentioned the war, and understanding finally dawned.

He was Southern.

She'd simply assumed he'd been on the northern side of the border, because that was what she wanted to believe. For a moment her mind rebelled at the thought. She'd resented the war, and the men who'd started the fighting. Selfishly, she'd resented the glimpse of a different life she'd been given. She begrudged having that chance stripped away.

Her nerves grew taut. The men holding them hostage

were Southern, as well. They wanted what was coming to them, they wanted revenge on the Union army. Where did Nolan place his loyalties? Did he want his due, as Dakota Red had declared? If the outlaws forced him to choose, where would Nolan place his loyalties?

Yet he could have turned on them in the very beginning, and he hadn't. There was no reason for him to switch his loyalties now.

As though seeking to form some sort of connection beyond the fear they shared, assuring herself of their shared allegiance, she placed her hand over his. They stared at each other for a long moment. There was so little she knew about this man. That first day she hadn't given him much thought. He'd been a part of the passing scenery, someone she'd leave behind and never see again.

The outlaws had forced them into contact. The arrival of Dakota Red had changed the relationship between her and the stagecoach man. They were irrevocably united by the dangerous events. Even if she never saw him again after tomorrow, she sensed they'd always be linked by the events that had brought them together.

A second later he jerked away. She dropped her arm to her side, the warmth of his hand lingering on her fingertips.

"Whatever happens," he said, "we'll have to work together to stay alive."

"I want to help, but I don't know how I can."

"Keep your eyes open, watch every move they make, and we'll take our chance when we see it. We wait and we watch. In my experience, the more time a prison guard spends with a prisoner, the more he relaxes. That's what we wait for. We watch for them to make a mistake."

"You said, 'in my experience.'" Her natural curiosity

rose to the surface. "What sort of experience have you had with prisoners and guards?"

"Nothing of importance. Just, well, just trust me."

She knew instinctively that he was lying. He'd said the words too quickly, too easily. She recalled the tales of Andersonville and the other prisons in the South. The idea of someone living under those conditions sickened her. Yet certainly things had been different in the north? More humane. Either way, he clearly wasn't interested in pursuing the subject, but his rebuff only raised her curiosity. All at once she was eager to know more about this man, more about his experiences and his life before Pyrite.

Tilly took a step back and squinted into the darkness. There was a flaw in his plan that neither of them had addressed.

"What if the gold is on the stagecoach tomorrow?" she asked. "What then? We have to at least consider the possibility."

"I hadn't thought that far ahead." Nolan ducked his head. "If you and the girls have a chance to escape, take it. I can look out for myself. If that happens, I'll buy as much time as I can for you."

Though he hadn't said the words, the undercurrent of his meaning was obvious. He'd sacrifice himself for them. Her chest tightened. What sort of man sacrificed himself for strangers? A good man.

Ceaseless worry had taken its toll, and her head throbbed. She rubbed her temples. "We can only pray."

"Yes."

The rain grew heavier, chasing away the fireflies. She gazed sightlessly into the distance, unexpectedly soothed by the relentless patter. "Are you scared?"

"Yes."

The breath whooshed from her lungs. "Thank you."

"For what?"

Her eyes burned. "For being honest. I'm scared, too."

"I should have told you to run as soon as I saw those men," he said. "I should have done something sooner."

"We wouldn't have gotten far. You did the right thing. You were outnumbered. The girls and I didn't exactly help. Miss Elizabeth is as slippery as a buttered pig sometimes."

He chuckled, the sound hollow and humorless. "Not to mention her insatiable taste for blackberries."

"I don't know how Eleanor has managed all these years."

Tilly scrubbed at her face. Taking care of the girls these past few days had given her a new appreciation for the challenges Eleanor faced, especially now that she was widowed. Her sister was always so brisk and efficient. Did she ever have doubts?

Nolan crossed his arms and leaned his shoulder against the railing post. "Your sister is fortunate to have your help."

Tilly snorted. "I doubt Eleanor would agree with you."

Despite the odd juxtaposition of her worries, she couldn't shake the truth that had been nagging at her since her arrival in Virginia City.

Nolan frowned. "I don't follow."

"Eleanor is perfect. I have never lived up to her standards."

"No one is perfect. Everyone fails at something. Failure is simply the law of humanity."

"That almost makes it worse, you know?" Tilly unleashed the truth she'd been avoiding on some level her whole life. "Because if someone as perfect and accomplished as Eleanor fails, how does someone like me stand a chance at succeeding?"

Chapter Six

Nolan flipped open the cover of his watch and checked the time. With the arrival of the next stagecoach, all their lives hung in the balance. If he gave in to the fear, he'd be lost. Instead, he channeled his emotion into a cold, focused rage.

Beneath the watchful gaze of Dakota Red and his two cronies, he hitched the team for the change of horses. The bugle call sounded, and he returned the signal with a slight change in the cadence. It was a small thing, but if he added several of them together, the driver might get suspicious.

He adjusted one of the buckles and surreptitiously checked his pocket. He'd written out a note. Delivering the message was a long shot, but had to grasp any opportunities that were presented, however slight.

Dakota Red hooked his leg over the stall door and perched on the top rung. "Did I ever tell you that Charlie was a sharpshooter?"

"Nope," Nolan replied shortly.

"Considers himself one of the better shots this side of Ohio."

"You don't say."

"He's got his rifle trained on your woman."

Nolan tensed. "I see."

"I thought you might. The next hour is going to be special for you and me. We're building trust, you and I. The kind of trust I don't have with them other two fellows."

Nolan slanted a glance at the fugitive. "Isn't Charlie your brother?"

"We have the same father, yes. Which makes us kin, but I don't trust ol' Charlie as far as I can see him. That boy has a wild head on his shoulders. Sometimes he's as calm as a church on Sunday, other times he's as wild as a mountain pass in spring."

"Then why do you run with him?"

"The same reason I busted Snyder out of jail. Sometimes a fellow needs someone who ain't afraid of bending the law. A fellow in my position needs someone who ain't afraid to make the hard choices. Like following through on a promise to kill a woman if I give him the signal."

"You've made your point."

The outlaw leaped from his perch and slapped Nolan on the shoulder. "I like you. You seem like a real honorable fellow. What are you doing out here in the middle of nowhere?"

Nolan's suspicions flared. The outlaw was testing him, but he didn't know why. "I have my reasons."

"Couldn't figure you out at first. I mean, your wife ain't much to look at."

Anger simmered beneath the surface of Nolan's feigned calm. "I knew you were stupid, I didn't know you were blind, too."

"Don't get your back up, let me finish. I couldn't figure out what Charlie was looking at, but she grows on you. Those eyes are real pretty, and her hair is nice."

"Not another word about my wife," Nolan replied, his voice husky with barely suppressed rage.

"You're not much for talking, are you?"

"Nope."

The rumble of hoofbeats ended their conversation.

Grateful for the distraction, Nolan slapped the reins against the horse's rumps and drove them from the side of the livery to the middle of the street. As the Concord rounded the last bend, he caught sight of the driver, and his spirits lifted.

Rintoon was one of the best mule skinners in the territory. He was ramrod-thin and carried his lanky body in a rolling gait, as though his joints were only loosely connected within his slim frame.

The old mule skinner was as tough as leftover stew meat, and wouldn't be easily fooled by lies. The trick was delivering his message without alerting one of the outlaws. Charlie was sitting on a hair trigger, and Nolan wasn't risking Tilly's life. He understood full well what these men were capable of, and he wasn't pushing them.

When Rintoon drew up his team, Nolan called, "Where's your outrider?"

The driver jerked his thumb over one shoulder. "Busted his arm two stops back. I'm looking to pick up Bill for my next run."

Nolan rapidly calculated the meaning of that seemingly innocuous statement. If Rintoon was traveling without an outrider, this wasn't the stagecoach carrying the gold. Captain Ronald wasn't real smart, but he wasn't an idiot, either. He'd never send the gold unaccompanied.

Nolan considered his options. Setting his plan into motion was going to be tricky, but at least they weren't confronted with the more immediate problem of what happened after the gold was lifted.

If Nolan failed to deliver his message, he and Tilly had another day or two to plan an escape.

"Sorry to hear about your outrider," Nolan said. "Bill's a good man. He'll do you right. You carrying passengers?"

"No passengers today, just mail."

Nolan's tension eased another notch. Not even Captain Ronald would ship the gold on a stagecoach without a guard. Another reason to assume this wasn't the right coach.

Nolan quickly scrambled for his next move. Since Rintoon was vulnerable without an outrider, enlisting his help would be suicide for the driver. And if the tough mule skinner caught wind of their circumstances, he was liable to try something foolish and get himself killed.

"What's for supper?" Rintoon called. "Let me guess. Boiled beans, bacon and bread."

"Yep."

"We should call this stop the three Bs. You oughta get yourself a woman up here to do a little cooking."

"About that." Nolan kept his expression neutral, and sketched a glance at the livery door. Dakota Red was too far away to hear their conversation, but he wasn't taking any chances. "I've got passengers staying here for a few days."

Rintoon hoisted his eyebrows in question. "How'd that happen?"

"Long story."

"I'll bet."

Nolan didn't provide an explanation, and the crusty old mule skinner didn't ask. That was the benefit of dealing with some of these old-timers. They weren't much interested in anything beyond their next meal and their next paycheck.

The two set about switching the teams. Once they'd finished, they started for the house.

Rintoon paused at the corral. "Them your horses?"

"Yep."

Any explanations he made would only make the man more suspicious.

"You oughta feed them animals more," Rintoon said. "They're showing ribs."

Nolan grunted his reply. He and Rintoon had always gotten along well, and the mule skinner knew that Nolan cared for his animals. There was always hope that he'd put the pieces together later, and realize something didn't fit. Lengthy explanations only drew attention to discrepancies, and it was too soon for Rintoon to know all the details. The old man might try something foolish. The less said, the better.

They stepped inside the relay station, and the driver caught sight of Tilly.

Rintoon quickly doffed his hat. "Ma'am."

Nolan's suppressed fury sparked to life once more. She was frightened, but putting on a brave face. He didn't know how anyone could think she was plain. She had thick lashes over her bluebell eyes, and an expressive sweep to her brows. Her wardrobe wasn't inspired, but she was traveling, after all. Nothing unusual in that.

Her gaze flicked between him and the mule skinner, and Nolan set his jaw, giving only a slight shake of his head. Relief flitted across her face. The girls had been directed to stay away from the house while the stagecoach came through town. They hadn't blinked at the terse order. The girls appeared well conditioned to stay out from under foot. Another piece of information that led him to believe Tilly's sister might not be as perfect as Tilly suspected.

Aware that Snyder was ten feet away in the bedroom, listening to their every word, Nolan carefully considered his explanation. "Tilly will take care of your lunch today."

"Pleasure to meet you, ma'am."

Nolan strategically dropped a pan during the driver's reply. Snyder would assume they knew each other already. They'd practiced a few responses if the driver's conversation turned personal. Since Rintoon often regaled Nolan with tales of his past exploits, their plan was to keep the mule skinner busy telling his tall tales.

Nolan ladled himself a long draw of water, then swiped at his chin with his wrist. "Tilly has never heard the story about the time you wrestled that alligator in the everglades, Rintoon. She'd enjoy hearing every detail, wouldn't you, Tilly?"

"Every detail," she replied weakly.

"Don't disappoint her," Nolan continued, suppressing a grin. The story grew longer with each retelling. "Especially the part when your partner nearly got his leg bit off—"

"Hold your tongue," the mule skinner interrupted with a wide grin. "Don't tell her all the best parts of the story afore I get to them."

"I wouldn't dream of it."

Though he was reluctant to leave Tilly alone, Nolan had to search the stagecoach for the benefit of Dakota Red. He doubted the outlaws would follow his logic about the unlikelihood of a gold shipment on such a poorly guarded route.

"I saw a loose spoke," Nolan said. "I'll tighten that for you."

"No need to work alone," Rintoon said. "I'll help when I finish here."

"It's no bother. I've got extra time, and I know Tilly is looking forward to your story."

"Suit yourself."

Nolan shot Tilly and encouraging smile on his way outside. Charlie whistled softly. The outlaw had perched in a tree, and wasn't bothering to conceal himself. Nolan slashed his hand across his throat, and Charlie sank back into the shadows. The outlaws' plan of escaping unnoticed was forfeit if they gave themselves away before they stole the gold.

Dark clouds had gathered, blotting out the sun. The wind blew in fits and starts, bending the tops of the cottonwood trees. The rumble of thunder drifted from the west. Nolan picked up his pace. They didn't have much time before the storm broke loose.

With Dakota Red hiding in the livery, Nolan made a point of searching every inch of the stagecoach. Much as he'd suspected, there was no sign of the gold. He gave a signal to Dakota Red, and made his way toward the relay station.

Tugging his gauntleted gloves over his wrists, Rintoon met him halfway. As they passed behind the stagecoach, out of sight of Dakota Red and Charlie, Nolan slipped his hand in his pocket and palmed the note he'd written, then held out his hand. Rintoon gave his arm a quick pump and slapped Nolan on the opposite shoulder.

The note flitted gently to the ground. Nolan froze. Though he'd written his plea in thinly veiled code, referencing bits of the stories Rintoon had told over the years, he didn't want the outlaws finding the note before the driver.

Rintoon stooped and retrieved the folded paper. "This yours?"

"No, uh, you must have dropped it."

The driver stretched out the arm holding the paper and squinted. "Some of the mail musta gotten loose. It sure ain't mine. I don't read."

Nolan blanched. "You don't read?"

"Funny, ain't it?" Rintoon grinned, revealing a gap where his eyetooth had once been. "I deliver thousands of letters each year, and I can barely read my own name."

He stuffed the folded piece of paper in his pocket.

Nolan's stomach knotted. His clever plan wasn't quite so clever after all. If someone else read the message, they'd have no idea of the deeper meaning.

Only Rintoon could decipher the code. "Don't let me keep you."

Matching the driver's relaxed grin, Nolan circled around the stagecoach. If he delayed any longer, he'd only incite Dakota Red's curiosity. His plan was dead in the water anyway. He'd have to regroup, and decide how to alert Bill when he came back through on the stage-coach returning to Virginia City.

Rintoon took his seat once more, and gathered the reins in his gloved hand. "You all right, West? Seems like something is bothering you."

Hesitating, Nolan fought against the temptation. He could signal the man, but Dakota Red was an ever-present danger. Nolan risked Rintoon's life, as well as the lives of Tilly and the girls. Rintoon was the oldest driver on the trail. They were outnumbered and outgunned. He'd take the chance on himself, but he couldn't risk having the older man getting caught in the cross fire.

"Not used to having company, is all," Nolan said. "You know how it is."

"Can't say that I do." The stagecoach driver propped his elbows on his bent knees, the reins slack. "You oughta get outta here once in a while. It ain't natural for a fellow to live all by his lonesome."

"I do all right."

"Suit yourself. But if you ever find yourself down around Omaha, I've got a spread on the outskirts of town. Come on by for a visit."

"Will do."

"I doubt you will. I've seen your kind before. Once a fellow stays away from folks too long, he can't go back. Mark my words, if another fellow moves within a mile of you, you'll pack and head farther west." He gestured toward the relay station. "That little lady is real nice."

"She sure is."

"A lady like that needs to be near people. She needs to live near a town, where she can visit with other ladies. I've seen women go loco out here. The wind and the loneliness drives 'em crazy."

Nolan sobered. "She's going to New York City. She wants to help the war widows and orphans."

"That's good. A lady like that deserves more than what this sort of life can offer. I know. I'm speaking from experience."

"I understand what you're saying. You don't have to worry about me."

Rintoon gathered his reins. "I'm not worried."

Nolan glanced behind him. This was his last chance. "Don't forget—"

Except Rintoon had already released the brake and fixed his attention on the horizon. There was a schedule to keep, and a good driver never lost sight of the time. Mud splattered from beneath the wheels and the carriage rumbled by.

Nolan's stomach clenched. This chance was gone. He'd try again with the next driver. If they lived that long.

At least for today, the worst of the danger had passed.

"Mr. West," a small, panicked voice called. "Mr. West, come quick. We need your help."

Nolan caught sight of Victoria dashing toward him, her braids flowing behind her.

"What is it?" He searched her for signs of injury. "What's happened? Are you hurt?"

"I'm fine. It's Caroline. We can't find her. She's lost."

Tilly paced before Elizabeth and Victoria. "How long has Caroline been missing?"

"We were exploring the town." Victoria wrung her hands. "We were staying away from the relay station, just like you asked."

Nolan flashed his palm. "With limits, of course. I don't know which buildings are safe."

"No limits." Victoria shrugged. "Aunt Tilly didn't say anything about limits."

Tilly pinched the bridge of her nose. "Obviously we need to discuss a few rules for the next time you three explore the town. Right now, designating blame isn't helping us find Caroline. When was the last time you saw her?"

"I hungie." Elizabeth pouted. "Boo-berries."

"No boo-berries." Tilly pinched harder, she was losing her mind and adopting Elizabeth's speech patterns in the process. "No *black*berries until we find Caroline."

The toddler's lower lip trembled.

"Don't worry." Tilly patted Elizabeth's head. Surely Caroline hadn't gone far. There wasn't much of the town, which meant there weren't many places to get lost. "We'll find her. She couldn't have gone far."

Drawn by the commotion, Dakota Red sidled over. "What's going on over here?"

Tilly and Nolan exchanged a glance. The outlaws were bound to figure out something was wrong sooner rather than later.

"We've lost one of the girls," Tilly said. "Have you seen her?"

"Which one?"

"The one that isn't either of these two." Tilly rubbed her eyes with her knuckles. "Who did you think?"

The outlaw scowled. "Don't get lippy with me, missy. I ain't seen her."

His derisive tone only intensified her annoyance. She was tired, hungry and sick of being afraid all the time. "Then I suggest you gather your men and help us look."

Nolan touched her sleeve, and she was immediately contrite. If she didn't control her emotions, she'd get them all killed.

The outlaw rested his hand on his gun belt. "You better find her quick. Me and the boys are fixing to eat."

"I, ah, I can't prepare lunch until she's found."

Tilly needed to appease the men, not antagonize them. When this was all said and done and they were caught, and surely they'd be caught, she hoped they'd have to spend years in a jail cell.

"That ain't how this works, lady." Dakota Red clicked his tongue. "You find the kid, or give up the search and fix supper. I'm not a nursemaid. I didn't lose her, you did."

Wonderful. Even the outlaws were critiquing her guardianship. She might as well leave for New York the minute she was free. There was no way Eleanor was ever going to let her see the girls again.

Tilly lifted her nose. "There's no need to point fingers."

"Caroline can't have gone far." Though still light out,

Nolan lit the lantern he'd retrieved from the relay station. "If the three of you were exploring the town when she got lost, that's where we'll start. Tilly, Elizabeth and Victoria can search the buildings on the north side of the street, I'll search the south side of the street. Holler if you find something."

Tilly gave a curt nod. His calm, efficient attitude kept her focused. There was no point in panicking. They'd find Caroline. At least Eleanor wasn't here to voice her disappointment. She'd immediately bring up the dog Tilly had lost when she was ten after leaving the gate open. That was the last dog the Hargreaves family had owned.

This was far graver than losing the family dog. Tilly flinched. She'd lost her niece.

She motioned for Victoria. "The sooner we start, the sooner we'll find Caroline."

"Don't worry," Nolan said. "We'll find your niece. She probably doesn't even know she's lost."

His kindness had her eyes burning. "Thank you."

If he knew her history with family pets, he might not be as optimistic.

Elizabeth wrapped her arms around Nolan's leg. He gently extracted himself and took her pudgy hand. "I'll take Elizabeth, and you take Victoria."

"Isbeth go with No-wan."

The toddler had taken a shine to the stagecoach man. Though Tilly couldn't help her twinge of jealousy, Elizabeth's preference wasn't entirely unexpected. He *had* provided a nearly endless supply of blackberries.

Before Tilly turned away, Nolan cupped the back of her head and pressed a quick kiss against her temple. "She'll be fine."

The gesture was so quick, she might have imagined it. Aware that Victoria and Elizabeth were staring curiously at her, she cleared her throat and crossed the street. The heels of her boots sank in the soft soil, and she caught the sound of rushing water. Had the Niobrara ever flooded? They'd crossed a couple miles upstream, and she'd kept her eyes shut tight during the whole journey.

The ferryman kept grumbling that he'd never seen the river this high. The trip had taken the combined efforts of the ferryman, the driver and the outrider to control the float against the rushing tide.

The town hadn't been around long enough to show signs of past breaches in the natural levies between here and the river. The Missouri River near Omaha had flooded often enough, and the result was devastating. At least there were no watermarks on the abandoned buildings—a good sign.

She shook off the disquieting thought. They'd had enough misfortune already.

Since the mother raccoon was still nesting, she decided to check the hotel first. She'd seen Caroline sneaking scraps out of the kitchen, and it didn't take a genius to figure out where she was taking them.

The empty restaurant was oddly ghoulish. A drinking glass and an empty bottle, both covered in a layer of dust, had been inexplicably abandoned on the floor. A smoky mirror set in an elaborately carved frame hung over an empty space that might have once held a buffet. Round tables and overturned chairs were scattered throughout the space.

The empty room gave her the same icy chill as the rest of the hotel—as though all the residents had simply vanished. Surely there was some sort of organized effort in closing down a business? Yet the town exodus appeared haphazard and chaotic. Leaving everything behind was a far messier business than she'd imagined.

Victoria wrote her name in the dust covering a table-top, then giggled. "This place would make Mama crazy. She dusts twice a week."

"She and Mr. West would get along like a house on fire."

Tilly peered into the kitchen. The raccoon remained safely ensconced in the stove. Fish bones carpeted the floor near the opening. The raccoon was obviously supplementing her diet from the nearby river. At the scuttle of claws against iron, she and Victoria scooted through the door that led to the barbershop. This building had been gutted. Save for the sign out front, there was no indication that the bay had ever housed a barbershop.

Stepping outside once more, she considered the next storefront. The sign read Pyrite Trading Company. She pushed open the door and grimaced.

"You had better wait here, Victoria," Tilly said. "This building doesn't look safe."

In the last building on the row, a tree had fallen through the roof. Months of water and snow damage had left the inside a shambles. Light showed through the enormous holes in the roof, and debris littered the rotted floorboards.

"Caroline," Tilly called. "Are you in here, Caroline?"

She hesitated on the threshold. There was too much debris to see clearly. What if Caroline had fallen behind one of the overturned shelves? Or worse.

Tilly tugged her lower lip between her teeth and carefully tested a floorboard with her toe. The wood creaked and groaned, but held firm. Feeling more confident, she stepped into the dimly lit space. Overturned, empty shelving blocked her path.

"Caroline!" she called. "Say something if you're in here, Caroline."

A thump sounded, and Tilly jumped. Her heart pound-

ing, she skirted around a pile of overgrown brush inside and peered deeper into the dimly lit interior of the
building.

She took a few more cautious steps, assessing the
floorboards with her toe before planting her weight. "Is
that you?"

Something fluttered, and she sucked in a sharp, frightened breath. The next instant the floor gave way beneath
her feet.

Chapter Seven

Tilly's stomach dropped and her body plummeted. Feathers beat against her face, and a bird cawed. She shrieked and flailed her arms, catching herself on the jagged floorboards. With her shoulders and arms clutching the edge of the break, her legs dangled beneath her. As Tilly clawed for purchase, the frightened bird escaped through a hole in the roof.

Victoria peered through the open door. "Are you all right, Aunt Tilly?"

"Fetch Mr. West," Tilly shouted. "Quickly."

She strained her head, seeking a better glimpse of the gaping hole beneath her. If she lost her grip, how far did she have to fall? Her fingers slipped, and she focused on holding herself aloft. She'd rather not find out the hard way.

Screeching and cawing, the displaced bird danced along the edge of the hole in the roof above her.

Tilly grimaced. "I'm the one who should be angry. If you hadn't made a bunch of noise, I never would have investigated this part of the building. This is all your fault, really."

The bird quieted, pecking its beak a few times before flying away.

Moments later, Nolan appeared in the doorway, a dark shape against the sunlight streaming through the open door.

"Don't come any closer," Tilly ordered. "The floor won't hold us both."

Nolan paused. "Hang on."

"That was my plan."

Victoria appeared behind him. "Will Tilly be all right? What about Caroline?"

"Elizabeth, stay back," Nolan ordered. "Victoria, will you fetch me another lantern from the livery? We'll finish searching for Caroline after we help your aunt Tilly."

Tilly moved her hands for a better grip. Though her instincts urged her to flail her legs, she found if she kept still, her arms weren't quite as strained. Nolan stretched out on the floor and crawled deeper into the building. The rotted boards groaned beneath his weight.

"Stop!" Tilly ordered.

At least ten feet separated them. Squinting, he peered through the floorboards.

"I can't see anything," he said. "This building doesn't have a basement. You must be hanging over a sinkhole caused by all the rain. If that's the case, it's not a good idea to let go."

"A sinkhole? How deep is a sinkhole?"

"Deep," he replied ominously. "I'm coming closer."

"Don't! You can't fall. We need you."

"We need you, too," he answered somberly.

Their gazes met and caught. Her whole body trembled. Tilly pointed her toe and stretched out one foot. She sensed she wasn't far above solid ground, but she was too frightened to release her hold. Her arms strained and the rough splinters in the broken floorboard dug into her hands and the edges of the broken wood pressed against her armpits.

She pulled with all her might, struggling to drag herself over the edge. The rotted wood splintered, and she immediately stopped.

Flat on his stomach, Nolan scooted toward her.

Tilly frantically shook her head. "We'll both fall."

"Your hold is slipping. If the floor sags, I'll stop."

Her desire for rescue warred with her fear that the water-damaged floor would collapse, dropping them both into the unseen abyss below her.

She sought a better look and lost the grip with her left hand. She felt as though she might pull her right arm from the socket if she held on longer. She shut her eyes and braced for a painful landing. Nolan grasped her wrist, holding her steady.

Her eyes flew open.

"I've got you," he said.

Victoria returned, a lantern held above her head. "I'm back. I need some matches."

Nolan moved and Tilly's heartbeat quickened. "Don't let go."

"I'm not letting go. I'm reaching in my pocket for some matches."

"I'm not supposed to play with matches," Victoria declared, a note of petulance in her voice. "You said so."

"We'll make an exception. Just this once."

A delighted grin spread across her face. With a scratch of flint that spoke of practiced ease, Victoria lit the wick and replaced the glass chimney. Nolan grasped the handle and swung the light around.

"I have to come a little closer," he said.

"Be careful."

"I will."

The floorboard strained and creaked. Tilly attempted to look over her shoulder.

"Look at me," Nolan said. "Don't look down. Just keep looking at me."

She gave a hesitant nod.

When he'd breached the distance, their faces were mere inches apart. Tilly stared into his eyes, willing herself to remain calm, willing her arms to remain strong.

With a better vantage point, he dangled the lantern beside her. Inching closer, he pushed up on one elbow and glanced down. The grip around her wrist tightened.

Her stomach plummeted.

"How bad—"

The edge of the floor gave way, ripping the words from her throat. She barely had time to register the terror before her feet struck solid ground. As though in slow motion, Nolan fell before her. Since he'd been lying down, he hit the ground with the full length of his body.

A sickening thud sounded.

She immediately rushed to his side. "Are you all right?"

He groaned. "Told you. The fall wasn't that bad."

"Don't joke until I know that you're all right. Can you move your arms and legs? Does your chest hurt?"

"I was wrong." He grunted and flopped onto his back. "This building does have a space under the floorboards."

She studied their new surroundings. "Well, if you're not hurt, we'd best see about finding Caroline. These buildings are dangerous. Someone could get hurt."

"I think someone did get hurt," Victoria offered helpfully from her vantage point above them. "Mr. West doesn't look so good."

"I'm not hurt," Nolan insisted. "I'm simply catching my breath."

"Are you certain?" Tilly asked. "You're awfully pale."

"Nothing to worry about."

"You probably shouldn't lie on the ground like that. You'll catch your death in this mud." She glanced around their surroundings and shuddered. "Who knows what else is hiding in here?"

Nolan righted the lantern at his side. "We're so close to the river. They didn't lay foundations beneath these buildings. The ground must have been too soft. They've placed footings instead."

"Fascinating." Her boots were rapidly sinking in the soft muddy earth. She tipped back her head and stared at the sky, which was visible a story and a half above, through the broken roof. "If we don't get out of here before the rain starts, we're going to need a boat."

She reached for Nolan, slipping on the muddy floor.

He struggled upright, his hand wrapped around her upper arm for support, a speculative gleam in his eye. "Miss Hargreaves, you are a genius."

There was no time to ponder Tilly's brilliant deduction. With Caroline still missing, Nolan hoisted himself onto the splintered floorboards. His canvas pants caught on a jagged edge, ripping the material apart along the seam.

He assisted Tilly and protectively covered the hole in his trousers. She caught sight of his maneuver and quickly glanced away.

Victoria raised her hand.

"What is it?" Tilly asked.

"I think I know what happened to Caroline."

Nolan whipped around. "Is she all right? What happened?"

Victoria tugged her lower lip between her teeth. "You better see for yourself."

Nolan exchanged a confused look with Tilly. "Lead the way."

After the horror of seeing Tilly nearly plunge to her death, discovering Caroline had locked herself in the abandoned jail cell paled in comparison.

Tilly pressed her palm against her forehead. "Victoria, why didn't you tell us immediately?"

"Because one time Elizabeth got lost in the park. Mama was so excited when we found her that she forgot to be mad. I figured if you were worried first, then you'd forget to be mad."

"While I understand your reasoning," Tilly said, "in the future, let's not dillydally."

Victoria scuffed the floor. "All right. The door is stuck tight."

Both Tilly and Nolan yanked on the bars, and they both came to the same conclusion: The door was stuck tight.

"Caroline seems fine for the moment," Nolan mumbled. "I, uh, I need a minute. I'll be right back."

Tilly glanced at the place where his fingers clutched the fabric of his trousers together, and didn't argue.

Changing from his filthy clothing went quickly. Scrubbing the mud from beneath his fingernails took longer. Three times he turned to leave, and three times he found himself back at the wash bucket. Only when his skin turned pink and raw was he able to return to the jail.

The first time he'd entered the building, he'd been panicked about Caroline and had barely glanced around. This time he took in his surroundings.

Ancient and faded Wanted posters hung haphazardly, offering rewards for men who were probably dead or jailed already. A map covered the opposite wall, the ink stained and blurred from a leak in the roof that had dripped down the paper. In the center of the room, the ceiling pipe had come loose from the top of the pot-bellied stove, and a pile of ash had formed beneath the separated chimney.

Caroline reclined on the rusty springs of a cot, the back of her head propped against the wall, her hands threaded over her stomach. She caught sight of Nolan and offered a cheerful wave.

"Hello again, Mr. West."

"Hello again, Caroline."

No one appeared angered by his lengthy delay, which only increased his guilt.

"Victoria was telling me about what happened to Aunt Tilly," Caroline said. "I almost hid out in that building, but I was afraid of the critters. I think there was a bird nesting somewhere in there."

Tilly rolled her eyes. "Yes. There was most definitely a bird nesting in the Pyrite Trading Company."

"Did you figure out how the door became stuck?" Nolan asked.

"Apparently they were playing hide-and-seek. The jailhouse was the perfect location for hiding. Caroline slipped inside, and now the gated door won't open."

Though Tilly's hem was blackened nearly to her knees, and dirt streaked her arms and face, she appeared singularly unconcerned by her appearance.

Shame tightened in his chest. He'd left Tilly muddy and bruised and Caroline trapped in the cell for longer than necessary because of his selfish urges. Recalling Tilly's near miss, a helpless rage built inside him. The harder he tried to fight his urges, the harder they fought back.

"At least you had the sense to clean up." Tilly glanced at her filthy hands and grimaced. "I'm going to rinse off my hands. I'll change later, if you don't mind the filth."

"I don't mind."

He'd been raised a Southern gentleman, he'd fought a war as a Southern gentleman, but no gentleman would behave as he had.

He wasn't a man with good sense; he was a man who couldn't control his own compulsions. An admission of his flaw welled up from his soul and hovered on his tongue. He swallowed hard and tried to force out the words. He was a man of inexplicable impulses. He was a flawed man who didn't know how to fight the urges that overwhelmed him.

How could he explain to someone else what was wrong with him when he couldn't even explain the weakness to himself? Tamping down his frustration, he drew a deep breath and steeled himself. Another few days, and he'd be alone again. He needed the solitude to heal.

"This day has turned into quite an adventure," Tilly said. A ghost of a smile drew the edges of her mouth upward. "I think Caroline was actually enjoying the peace and quiet until her sisters stormed in."

"She appears remarkably unconcerned with her fate." Nolan cast a sidelong glance at the trapped child. "She's not scared or hurt?"

Though she'd seemed fine when he made his hasty exit before, he hadn't exactly waited around to find out for certain. He'd been too focused on his own needs.

"She's being quite brave," Tilly said.

"I'm fine," Caroline added cheerily. "I've never been locked in a jail cell before. I can't wait to tell Mama."

"Your mother is going to throttle me," Tilly grumbled. "She's never been overly confident in my abilities."

Caroline giggled. "Mama told us all about the time you decided to run away from home. She said you made it all the way to the end of the lane before you got too scared and came running home. She said that you cried for an hour."

"How nice of your mother to share that experience." A flush of color crept up Tilly's neck. "There was a very large, very frightening dog lurking at the end of that lane. I had every right to be afraid."

Yanking hard, Nolan tested the jammed door. The corner had wedged into the rotted wood floor, and the tip was solidly imbedded. He kneeled and studied the latch.

Tilly leaned over his shoulder. "Is it locked or something?"

He turned his head toward her, and his gaze landed on her parted lips. "It's not locked, it's stuck," he said, his voice thick. "The structure of the building has shifted. When the door closed, the corner dug into the floor. We'll have to dig it out."

In order to distract his attention from the slight flush of color on her cheeks, marred only by a streak of dried mud, Nolan mentally ticked off the array of tools he'd need from the livery.

She hoisted an eyebrow. "You know, we have the perfect men for this problem."

"I don't follow."

"Who better to break someone out of jail than a bunch of outlaws?"

Nolan straightened and dusted his hands. "I'd rather keep that as a last resort."

"Agreed. But keep in mind we may not have a choice."

She tilted her head. "Are you all right? You look a bit peaked today."

"Tired, is all."

"I don't think any of us are sleeping well."

He hadn't slept more than a few minutes at a time since the arrival of Tilly and her nieces two nights ago. Though he'd attempted to keep his routine as normal as possible, he felt the pull of the nightmares, and he was worried about frightening his unexpected houseguests.

As long as he kept to his routine, he was largely in control of his disquiet. Except his routine had been completely disrupted these past few days, and the changes were taking their toll on his endurance. Tilly didn't understand why their presence was disruptive, and there was no way of explaining without admitting his own instability.

She kneeled beside him. "Where can we find some tools for a jailbreak?"

He retrieved the pristine handkerchief from his breast pocket and gently dabbed at the spot of mud on her cheek. She gasped and scrubbed at the spot with her fingers.

"Did I get it?" she asked. "I must look a mess."

"Let me."

He finished cleaning the spot, and his gaze dropped to her lips once more. His heartbeat quickened and his breathing turned shallow.

A tumult of conflicting emotions warred within him. He was drawn to her, and yet he wanted to run from the terrifying longings she stirred inside him. She evoked yearnings he'd never felt before, and couldn't act upon. He couldn't drag anyone else into his waking nightmare. Maybe in a few years, when he'd overcome the impulses, and the nightmares abated.

He'd never been an extraordinary man, even before

the war. He'd been a simple farmer like his father before him. Yet he mourned that simple man—the man he'd been before the war.

He folded his handkerchief in a neat square and replaced the material in his pocket.

Her expression softened. "Are you certain you're all right? You have an odd look in your eyes."

"What kind of look is that?"

"Troubled."

He rubbed the bridge of his nose with a thumb and forefinger. She was far too perceptive. In that instant he understood why Bill had confided in her. There was a sense of peace and belonging about her. Her forthright manner invited confidence.

When he'd seen how she affected Bill, he'd vowed to keep a barrier between them. He'd been too late from the beginning. She'd already stolen past his defenses, and he vowed to redouble his efforts. The less she knew about him, the better. He didn't want her looking at him as though he was a madman.

"I'll cut the door free," Nolan said, his voice harsher than he'd intended. "The wood of the floor is soft, shouldn't take too long. I'll fetch my saw."

"I'll go along."

"I can manage."

"I know you can manage, but I want to fetch Caroline some water and a snack."

"Yes. Of course."

"All right, girls." Tilly clapped her hands, gathering their attention. "Be good while we're gone. One crisis at a time, if you please. My nerves can only handle so much. We'll be right back."

"Mama says her nerves are shot, too," Caroline said

from the cell. "How come your nerves don't last when you're an adult?"

"You'll understand when you're older."

"I hate that answer."

Tilly sighed. "Your present circumstances should offer a clue."

"You mean parents can't keep their nerves healthy because kids are always getting into trouble and stuff?"

"There's much more to it, but that's a good place to start."

Nolan smothered a grin.

Tilly patted both Elizabeth and Victoria on the head. "Stay out of trouble."

Together Nolan and Tilly walked the length of the street toward the relay station. They parted when they reached the livery.

As Nolan entered the darkened barn, Dakota Red jerked upright from his nap on a hay bale.

"What's going on?" He mumbled, his eyes only half-open. "What are you doing, stagecoach man?"

The outlaw blindly waved his gun and Nolan ducked.

"Put down that gun, you fool. You'll kill me."

"Don't sneak up on a man if you don't want to die. Whaddya doing in here?"

"We've found the lost girl. She's gotten herself stuck in the old jail cell. We need some tools."

"Tools? I ain't giving you no tools. How do I know you won't try and use them against me? You could murder me while I sleep."

"Then don't sleep." Nolan gritted his teeth until his jaw ached. "Someone has to free the girl from that jail cell. It's me or you. Your choice."

"Watch your attitude, boy." A vein throbbed in the outlaw's forehead. "You've been doing real well up until this point, stagecoach man. Remember how I said that we'd be building trust? This is another opportunity for you and me. You can fetch your tools, but if you abuse my goodwill, I'll let Charlie shoot you between the eyes like he's been itching to do. You follow me?"

"Yep." Nolan swallowed back his pride. Antagonizing the outlaw only meant Caroline would be trapped longer. "I'll just be about my business."

Dakota Red leaned back against the hay bale once more, tugging the brim of his hat over his eyes. "Make it quick."

Nolan quickly fetched what he needed and left the outlaw to his slumber. Tilly waited for him near the double doors, her arms laden with a basket and a blanket.

A storm rumbled in the distance.

"I heard what that outlaw said to you," she declared. "I hope all three of them rot in jail. Dakota Red is a bully. If he didn't have that gun, he'd be nothing more than a nuisance. I bet you could sock him good."

Her confidence in his ability bolstered his male ego. "Maybe."

A light misting of rain peppered their cheeks. Tilly swiped at the moisture. "I've never seen this much rain in my life. Has the river ever flooded?"

"I don't know. I've only been here a year."

The spring had been unnaturally wet, blanketing the countryside in emerald green. While he'd explored other areas of Nebraska, none had quite the same feel as the Niobrara River Valley. Though the sand hills had their own unique beauty, they were nothing but stark, rolling hills. The Platte River Valley was drab and uninspiring, endless prairie flatlands with a few trees breaking up the barren, unrelenting horizon.

The Niobrara Valley, in contrast, was lush and rolling, with secluded valleys and knots of cottonwoods. Not long after the turn of the century, Meriwether Lewis and William Clark had camped near Old Baldy and captured a prairie dog for President Jefferson. Over the past year he'd poured over reprinted copies of their journals, fascinated by their travels.

Tilly marched down the street, her long strides matching his. Everything about her was graceful and efficient, with a minimum of adornment. Yet there was a spark in the details—the contrasting red calico of her yellow dress, the long braid wrapped around the simple knot at the base of her neck, her vivid eyes the color of a Virginia bluebell.

They reached the jail and she pushed open the door. The air was dank and he kicked a loose brick before the door, propping it open for a breeze.

The children had trampled through the mess, leaving sooty footprints across the floor. There was no pattern to the steps—the trails crisscrossed and doubled back on each other, some faded and some dark. His skin crawled. Nolan backed toward the exit. Perhaps he could retrieve a broom and a dustpan.

Tilly grasped his sleeve. "Don't lose your nerve now. Left to my own devices, I'm liable to bring the building down around us."

She trekked through the ashy footprints and he trailed behind her, missing the worst of the dust.

The sheriff's office was the same as any other he'd seen over the years. A front room for the sheriff to drink, smoke and gossip with the townfolk, and a back room that held the jail cell.

Elizabeth and Victoria sat crosslegged outside the bars. Caroline sat on her knees in the enclosure, her arms before her, her hands limp.

Elizabeth playfully poked a stick through the bars.

"Stop this instant," Tilly shouted. "What on earth are you doing?"

"She's a bear," Victoria said, affronted. "We're pretending like she's a bear in a cage."

"Well that's no way to treat a bear *or* your sister. Find another game."

"She doesn't mind."

"*I* mind." Tilly planted her hands on her hips and scowled. "You are not allowed to poke each other with branches. Even in jest."

"You're not as fun as you were when we started this trip."

"You have no idea."

Victoria tossed aside her stick and curled her fingers together. "This place is filthy."

"Agreed," Tilly replied. She pinched the edges of a dented spittoon and tossed it aside. "Every building in this town is a disaster. Apparently the inhabitants simply dropped their belongings and fled. I guess people don't care about leaving a good impression when they're abandoning a town."

"Mama cared," Victoria said. "She cared about leaving a good impression. Mama said she was leaving the bank a clean house."

"The bank?" Tilly asked. "I think you mean the people buying your house."

"Mama hates the bank. That's all I know."

"If cleanliness is next to godliness, your mother is seated at the right hand of the Lord, that's for certain."

Carolina and Victoria giggled.

Tilly grasped the bars and poked her nose through the opening. "Just a little while longer, Caroline. Don't worry. We'll have you out of there lickety-split."

Nolan shook off the past and focused on the current situation. Not only did Caroline seem unconcerned by her confinement, but she also appeared to be enjoying her role as the center of attention. With two siblings, no doubt the opportunity was rare.

Caroline folded her hands over her stomach. "Did you bring some water?"

"Yes. And some sandwiches. We'll make a party of your entrapment." Tilly dug through her basket, retrieving the wrapped lunch. "Mr. West has an idea on how he can free you."

"Let's see." He rubbed his chin with a thumb and forefinger and made a show of considering the situation. "I have some dynamite back at the house."

Blanching, Caroline shot upright. "Isn't that dangerous?"

Victoria giggled.

"He's teasing," Tilly said. "You're teasing, aren't you?"

Mostly. Dynamite would definitely bust the lock. If it had been him trapped in the cell, he'd take the option immediately. He couldn't stomach confined spaces.

"I'm teasing," he said.

The mere thought of being trapped sent his heart hammering in his chest. He covered his unease by studying the spot where the bars had jammed into the floorboards. Sweat slicked his palms and he set down the pry bar. The metal was stronger than the floor, which meant he might be able to force them loose.

He braced the bent tip on the bar, then leaned back, levering his weight against the action.

For the next fifteen minutes, he attempted to pry free the door without success.

Tilly studied her nails. "Can't you simply unscrew the hinges or something?"

"They're welded shut. It's not good for business if you can simply unscrew the hinges."

"I suppose not." She tossed him a withering glance. "Do you need a break? I've brought a sandwich for you, as well."

"I can't take a break until Caroline is free."

"Sure you can."

Her casual acceptance of the situation baffled him. "I'll have to cut through the floor. That could take hours."

"All right."

"Didn't you hear me? She'll be trapped in there for hours."

"She's got food, she's got water and she's got company. She'll survive for a few hours."

The second year of his confinement, a prisoner in their barracks had struck a guard with a rock. In retaliation, their meager rations had been halved. Close to starvation, he'd slipped beneath the fence and stolen slop from the kitchen refuse. His transgression had cost him a lengthy stay of shackled, isolated confinement. He didn't know how long they'd kept him in that tiny box—he'd lost all track of time and place.

Sweat beaded on his forehead. "I can't be here."

As casually as he could muster, Nolan strode past the curious stares of Tilly and her nieces. Once outside, he hung his head and took several deep, heaving breaths.

A moment later the door opened beside him.

"Mr. West," Tilly called. "Is there anything I can do to help?"

He fisted his hand against the chipped paint exterior of the jail and straightened. "I need a different tool."

Anything to buy himself some time before going back inside. The mere idea of being confined behind the bars sent his skin crawling. He loathed feeling like this—helpless and frustrated by impulses he didn't understand. He'd never had these troubles before the war. While he'd never had much affection for small spaces, he'd been able to overcome the difficulty. Since his time at Rock Island, the fear left him vulnerable.

"You needn't be ashamed, Mr. West," Tilly said. "Lots of people are claustrophobic. Thankfully, Caroline isn't one of those people."

"My fears shouldn't matter. I'm not the one locked inside there."

"I'm terribly frightened of heights. When someone else approaches a precipice, my hands sweat and my heart pounds. Even if I'm nowhere near the edge myself, watching the other person breach the distance is frightening."

"You don't need to placate me."

Her sympathy only exacerbated his shame. He should be stronger.

"Why don't you stay out here for a few minutes? Breathe the fresh air and don't think about closed spaces. I'll keep the girls busy. Everyone has something that frightens them. My father's cousin is frightened of horses. She fell off a horse as a child, and she doesn't ride. I think that's why she lives in New York City. She can walk everywhere. Every family has an eccentric member."

He was about to take over the role in his family, an idea that was far from comforting. "My aunt Vicky has fifteen goats."

"That doesn't seem odd."

"She dresses them on holidays."

"My point exactly." Tilly grinned. "Every family has an eccentric member."

Anxiety knotted his stomach. He didn't want to be the "Aunt Vicky" in the family. The person that folks talked about with a mixture of amusement and pity. He'd rather live in solitude than suffer that fate.

"I'm all right," he said. "I can finish. As soon as I'm done here, I have to prepare for the next stagecoach."

"The next stagecoach." Tilly blanched. "I just realized something."

Immediately concerned, Nolan straightened. "What?"

"For all we know, Eleanor might be on the next stagecoach," Tilly said. "She doesn't know what's going on, which means she's liable to get us all killed!"

Chapter Eight

Tilly paced behind Nolan, carefully avoiding the growing pile of sawdust from where he was cutting through the wood.

Mindful of the girls, she chose her words carefully. "Eleanor has only just lost her husband this past year. What will we do if she passes through town before the other, you know, um, package we're supposed to be looking for?"

"What package?" Victoria asked.

"Mr. West is anticipating the arrival of a gold package."

Tilly hadn't considered that Eleanor might be boarding a stagecoach as they spoke, anticipating a reunion with her daughters. Just what they needed—Eleanor stumbling into town and discovering her girls were being held hostage by a group of outlaws.

"We're going to take this one day at a time," Nolan said. "One stagecoach at a time, one trapped little girl at a time. Right now, our job is freeing Caroline. Then we'll worry about dinner, then we'll worry about this evening."

"But what about—"

"One foot in front of the other, one step at a time.

That's the only way we're going to survive. We have hours to worry about tomorrow."

"You're right." Her eyes burned. "I'm sorry."

"Don't be sorry. This time next year, you'll be living in New York City. You'll be saving widows and orphans by the dozens, and this will be an exciting story you tell over dessert and coffee."

"I hope so."

"I know so."

"Let's try the pry bar again," Tilly said. Anything to get her mind off the thought of Eleanor. "I'll add my weight and we can push together."

Despite the decay, the floorboards were proving remarkably difficult to saw through. The awkward angle wasn't helping Nolan's efforts.

Nolan took one side, and she positioned herself on the other. Together they bore down on the board. The bars slipped an inch before jamming again.

Tilly wiggled her fingers through the narrow opening. "That didn't help much."

"The building has settled more than I thought. The corner is really jammed. This is going to take more of an effort."

Studying the problem, she frowned. "Let's approach Snyder. He's the most amiable. I'm guessing he was the muscle behind the breakout anyway."

"It's his muscle I'll be needing."

Nolan was reluctant to ask for the outlaw's assistance, but he conceded they needed help. "Let's go."

They discovered the outlaw brushing down one of the stolen horses. After explaining the situation, Snyder rubbed his chin.

"I'll see if I can help you, but they make those cells hard to bust out of for a reason."

"How did you break out of jail?" Tilly asked.

"We used the birdcage."

"The birdcage?"

"Charlie had this birdcage in his cell. He used to tell folks there was a bird inside. The guards let him keep it, because they figured he was loco. Then one day, he tells this guard that he's got to give the cage to his brother. When the guard opened the door, Charlie clobbered him on the head."

"Oh, my." Tilly pressed her fingers against her lips. "Clearly, that's not going to work in our situation."

"Charlie unlocked all the other fellows." Snyder resumed the vigorous rubbing of his chin. "He figured that having all those fugitives on the run would make it harder to catch us. He was right."

"Clever," Tilly said weakly.

Fifteen minutes later, with both Snyder and Nolan straining with effort, Caroline was freed from her temporary prison. Snyder collapsed on a bench and grinned, clearly relishing his role as the hero of the situation.

After a moment he appeared to gather himself. He stood and offered a gruff, "Don't bother me again," before storming out.

Nolan shrugged. "At least he helped."

Victoria had spread out a blanket over the dirty floor, and she and Elizabeth sat across from each other.

When Victoria caught sight of the open cell door, her face fell. "Aw, shucks. I was just fixing to have a pretend tea party."

"We can have a celebratory pretend tea party." Tilly reclined on the edge of the blanket. "I'll have a pretend scone with my pretend tea."

A crack of thunder rattled the building, shaking dust from the eves. The girls shrieked and huddled together.

"Back to the relay station," Nolan ordered gently. "This ceiling offers about as much protection as a sieve. The tea party will have to move."

Moving quickly, they gathered their supplies. The girls dashed ahead of them, giggling and splashing through the gathering puddles. Nolan held the blanket over Tilly's head as they hurried back to the relay station.

The meager cover offered little protection, and she was soon soaked through to her skin. They splashed through puddles and moisture settled in her boots. The girls quickly outpaced them.

Sheets of rain swept over their heads, and he prodded her to the side of the street, where they ducked beneath the sheltering eves of an abandoned building. The wind whipped the trees, tearing at the branches. Nolan lowered the blanket and shook off the moisture.

"We'll wait here until the rain lets up," he said.

A leaf had caught in his hair. Tilly raised up on tiptoes and plucked it free. The serrated edges of the leaf caught in his hair, and she placed a steadying hand on his shoulder.

Their faces were inches apart, and his gaze grew intense. She wasn't quite certain who closed the distance between them. Their lips touched and heat flared between them. His hand slipped over her shoulder, caressing the nape of her neck. She wrapped her arms around his waist and pressed closer.

Emboldened by his response, she angled her head, increasing the contact between them. She felt him tremble against her and her stomach fluttered. A gust of wind sent a smattering of rain over them, but she barely registered the discomfort. His heady scent surrounded her, a mixture of leather and coffee.

Thunder crashed and they both started, then separated. His eyes were wide and dilated and his breathing was almost as harsh as her own.

She touched her lips in wonder.

He raked his hand through his hair. "We should go."

Her emotions reeling, she blindly took his hand. He sheltered her with the blanket once more and they dashed the distance.

She reached for the door but he caught her arm. "I'm sorry. I shouldn't have. We shouldn't have."

"But—"

"I've got chores. I won't see you tonight."

He was gone before she could say more, her words lost in the clatter of rain beating against the building.

She touched her cheek with trembling fingers. He'd felt it, too. He must have. Something had changed between them, and there was no going back.

Nolan stayed away from the relay station until the outlaws finished dinner and stumbled down the stairs. He watched as they made their way across the rain-soaked ground. There was no avoiding the inevitable. He'd kissed Tilly. Or she'd kissed him. He wasn't really certain. She certainly hadn't resisted. Neither had he.

He couldn't help the flare of masculine pride. What man wouldn't want the attentions of such a vibrant woman? The next instant, reality struck. He couldn't bring anyone into his world. He couldn't subject another person to his rigid routines and his obsession with cleanliness and order.

Despite his good intentions, the feel of the soft hair on the nape of her neck lingered on his fingertips. He rubbed them together, as though imprinting the memory into his very skin.

In the time he'd lived with his father immediately

following the end of the war, he'd taken to obsessively counting the number of plates in the cupboard. He didn't know why. He only knew he had to count them, and then count them again. He'd seen the mingled look of disgust and disappointment in his father's eyes.

Don't let anyone else see you doing that, his father had said. *They'll think you're mad.*

Nolan took a deep breath and entered the station. He'd act as though nothing had happened. He suspected Tilly would do the same. They'd met under extreme circumstances, and her emotions were heightened. If Caroline hadn't taken ill that first day, he doubted Tilly would have remembered his face, much less his name.

The realization left him with an odd pang of regret.

He opened the door to cries of distress.

Victoria and Elizabeth were engaged in an angry tug-of-war over a rag doll.

"Mine!" Elizabeth sobbed.

The older girl put her weight behind the next yank, ripping the doll from the toddler's fingers. "No, mine!" she shouted.

Tilly came from behind the kitchen table. Tendrils of damp hair clung to her cheeks, and she swiped at the sweat beading her forehead.

"Stop it, both of you. Those men ate all the food and I've got to prepare a second dinner. I don't have time for your fighting. Can't you simply get along?"

She caught sight of him and a pleased grin lit her face.

"Nolan. How are you?" Sounding breathless, her hand fluttered before landing on her hip. "I meant to ask if you were hungry. Are you hungry?"

Elizabeth broke into loud, hiccupping sobs, saving him from having to reply.

"Mine!" the toddler repeated.

Victoria set her lower lip in a stubborn pout. "You always take my things. You're a baby."

"Not a baby!" The toddler took a swing at her sister. "You baby."

Nolan kneeled between them. "That's enough, you two."

Victoria hugged the rag doll to her chest. "I wish Elizabeth was a boy. Because a brother wouldn't take my dolls."

He smothered his chuckle with one hand. "Brothers are annoying in other ways."

Elizabeth threw her arms around him and clasped her fingers behind his neck, sobbing into his shoulder.

Tilly flashed a grateful smile. "Thank you. They've been arguing since we returned from the, uh, from the jail."

Her lips parted and her nostrils flared. Neither of them moved for a moment, though a delightful blush stained her cheeks.

She was remembering.

Their gazes caught and held and her eyelashes fluttered. His gaze dropped to her lips before he forced his gaze away. So much for pretending as though nothing had happened. There was an intimacy between them now, a familiarity that would be impossible to ignore. Especially considering the close quarters and their precarious situation.

Caroline touched his shoulder. "I can make Elizabeth a doll," she said quietly. "That way she has her own, and won't take Victoria's."

"That's a very generous offer." He held Elizabeth away from him. "Is that all right with you?"

The toddler blinked, the tears on her lashes glistening in the light from the kerosene lanterns. "My doll."

Caroline twirled a length of her hair around one finger. "I have some cloth and a sewing kit, but I don't have any yarn for the hair. You'll have to wait for that."

"Isbeth doll."

Elizabeth faced Victoria and stuck out her tongue.

Nolan frowned. "Be nice, or Caroline won't make you a doll."

The defiant tongue immediately retracted. "I good."

Nolan gathered the outlaw's discarded dishes. His brief relief at a small victory quickly faded, and his frustration simmered as he considered his supplies. He was well stocked for one man, but he hadn't prepared for a relay station overrun with people. If the coach containing the gold didn't come through town by the following week, they'd have to send for more supplies, which was bound to attract notice.

Though he usually assisted with cleaning the kitchen after supper, the girls and Tilly made another batch of blackberry muffins. The sisters laughed and giggled, their earlier animosity forgotten.

Despite their obvious joy, his head throbbed. The outlaws had littered the floor with food. Snyder had left a larger halo of crumbs than Elizabeth. Because of the constant rain, dirty footprints marked nearly every inch of the floor. He hadn't oiled the harnesses that day, and Dakota Red had prevented him from moving the horses to the upper pasture. The outlaw feared he had an ulterior motive for the transfer.

Near as he could tell, the girls were using every pan in the kitchen for their muffins. A bowl hit the floor, raising a plume of flour dust. The pounding in his temples grew more intense. For the past year, he'd spent nearly all of his time alone. He'd probably spoken more words in the past two days than he had in the past two years.

The sudden jolt from solitude to being surrounded by constant commotion was jarring. Not to mention his unexpected attraction to Tilly had him wrapped up in knots.

She stifled a yawn behind fingertips purpled from berry juice. "It's been an eventful day," she said. "I'll see you in the morning."

Nolan glanced into the kitchen and back at her. "Aren't you going to clean up?"

"Tomorrow."

"Tomorrow?" His left eye twitched. "The kitchen is in a shambles."

"It will still be in a shambles in the morning."

"Breakfast will be late."

"I'm not overly concerned with ensuring a bunch of murderous outlaws are fed on time."

Bowls and spoons were stacked haphazardly in the dry sink, flour footprints tracked across the floor. She'd tossed the leftover muffins together and draped a towel over the heap.

Nolan rubbed the back of his neck. He was exhausted. He hadn't slept a full night in days. Fatigue had wormed into his brain and strangled his emotions.

"Good night," he said, his tone clipped.

Tilly tilted her head at the abrupt response. "I promise, we'll clean up our mess in the morning. I'm exhausted."

She appeared undecided, then yawned once more and turned away. Her steps dragged and her shoulders drooped. He shouldn't be angry. The fault was his. Leaving a mess for a few hours was hardly cause for panic.

Fearful of waking the girls, who were liable to create another catastrophe, Nolan silently scrubbed the kitchen. He arranged the muffins in a pan, and neatly folded a towel over the surface. He scrubbed the dirty dishes, wiped down the counter, replaced all the clean dishes in their designated locations and alphabetized the cooking supplies once more.

When he'd finished the kitchen, he set to work on the rest of the living spaces. Even with a limited amount of luggage, the three girls created an alarming level of mayhem. When he'd finished sweeping and dusting, he methodically wound each of the timepieces located in the relay station.

When the clocks chimed three in unison, he stepped back and surveyed his work in the dim light of the kerosene lantern. Every surface gleamed.

He had restored order.

For however long his work might last.

Both physically and mentally exhausted, he collapsed on the cot in the third bedroom of the relay station. Threading his hands behind his head, he crossed his ankles. He'd done it. He had restored order.

He could sleep in peace.

Chapter Nine

The shouts woke Tilly. They were muffled, but distinctly troubled. Flipping off the covers, she swung her feet over the side of the bed. Groggy and not quite alert, she fumbled for the lantern at her bedside and clumsily lit the wick.

She slipped on a shirtwaist and grimaced at the dress she'd tossed over the foot of the bed. The hem was torn and muddied, and she doubted the outfit was salvageable. Her wardrobe was never going to survive Pyrite at this rate.

Her feet bare, she padded past the girls' room. The sliver of light from her lantern revealed the girls positioned three across in the enormous tester bed. Elizabeth, sucking her thumb, was tucked in the middle. Rain pattered against the roof and the air was heavy and loamy, scented with summer leaves and freshly turned earth.

The stifled mutterings became more insistent, and she cautiously nudged open the door of the third bedroom.

"Mr. West," she whispered. "Are you all right, Mr. West?"

A thump sounded.

She swung the door wider, and her knees weakened.

Nolan was sprawled on the floor, his back to her. Had something happened to him? She frantically searched the empty room. No outlaws sprang from the shadows. She hesitated before stepping across the threshold, but she couldn't leave him laying there if he'd been hurt.

Taking a cautious step, she stretched out her arm. The mutterings quieted, and she paused. Perhaps he'd simply had a nightmare and tumbled to the floor. She'd done the same as a child. Either way, she couldn't leave until she was certain he was uninjured.

She nudged his shoulder. "Mr. West."

In a split second, pandemonium erupted. With a blood-curdling roar, Nolan surged upright, pitching her backward. Thrown off balance, she tumbled into an ungainly heap just inside the door. The lantern in her hand pitched sideways and died, plunging the room into darkness.

He came alive with the ferocity of a cornered animal, his fists and elbows flailing wildly. She scrambled backward and her hand slipped on a loose rag rug. With a sickening crack, her temple slammed against the door frame.

"Get off me!" Nolan bellowed. "Get off."

Nausea roiled in her stomach and she pushed away, desperate to escape his fury. He stumbled upright, towering above her in the shadows. Tilly groped for the doorway and her hand met with solid wood. In her confusion, she'd scuttled away from the exit, cornering herself.

Her breath came in shallow gasps and she stilled her lungs, afraid to move, afraid to breathe. The floor groaned ominously beneath his weight. She cringed, bracing for a blow.

"I told you!" he shouted hoarsely. 'I told you what would happen if you touched me."

Several flashes of lightning in rapid succession illuminated the room. The stagecoach man's eyes were wild and unfocused. He was looking at her, but she sensed he wasn't seeing her.

"I'm sorry," she gasped, huddling deeper into the corner. "P-please."

She didn't know what she was begging for, only that she desperately needed to release him from his fugue of rage.

At the sound of her voice, he jolted. "What happened?"

His rage instantly dissipated, leaving his expression wan and confused.

Her whole body sagged. Her voice must have awakened him from whatever sleeping nightmare had taken hold of him.

"I-it's me, Tilly," she stuttered.

He stumbled backward and raked his hands through his hair. Something warm and wet trickled against the side of her cheek and she tentatively touched the spot. Gasping, she yanked her hand away, then gently probed the growing lump on the side of her face. She'd have quite a shiner in the morning.

Nolan staggered a few steps and collapsed on the edge of the low mattress. With a groan he hung his head and laced his fingers over his crown, letting his elbows roll forward. For an agonizing moment they sat in silence.

She cocked her head, listening for the girls, then heaved a sigh of relief. They hadn't woken. Although how anyone could sleep through Nolan's awful shout, she'd never know. A cold shiver rippled through her. She'd never heard such terror. Such desperation.

Keeping her gaze fixed on Nolan, she warily fumbled for the lantern in the darkness and righted it. Thankfully, the splashing oil had doused the wick before anything had caught fire.

He lifted his gaze, his eyes bleak. "Why are you here? Did something happen?"

Another streak of light from the storm revealed his disorientation, and he fumbled for the candle at his bedside.

"No." Tilly brushed at her skirts, shaking herself from her stunned inaction. "I heard something. I came to check on you."

"You shouldn't have done that."

"I couldn't very well ignore you."

A scratch and a hiss sounded. Keeping her face averted, Tilly scrambled upright. She felt her way along the wall, her movements stiff and awkward.

"Why were you on the floor?" he asked, his voice shaky.

She sensed by his voice he was coming out of his stupor, shrugging off the sleep and trying to piece together what had happened.

"Did I push you?"

"It was nothing." She cringed at the hitch in her voice. "I slipped."

Though she desperately wanted to mitigate the circumstances, there'd be no hiding the bruise in the morning. Judging by the moisture trickling down her neck, the wound needed tending.

His candle threw her misshapen shadow against the wall, and her pulse quickened. She mustn't let him see her face. Right now she wanted to hide back to her room, and forget any of this ever happened. Quickly. Before he saw the damage.

She might have made her escape, but she was too unsteady on her feet, her balance reeling from the blow. The moment she stumbled, he was at her side.

There was no hiding.

She turned her face. "It's nothing."

She watched in growing dismay as the awareness of what had happened struck him. His face crumbled and he tentatively reached out one hand, then stilled, as though he couldn't bring himself to touch her.

Nolan remained silent for a heartbreaking moment, his expression stricken. When he spoke, his voice was no more than a whisper.

"What have I done?"

"Nothing," Tilly replied. "You did nothing. I told you, I slipped."

Nolan couldn't move. He couldn't breathe.

Blood trickled down her face from a growing bruise. Was she lying? Had he struck her? He was still half-asleep, his thoughts sluggish. He glanced at his hands, at his knuckles, nearly collapsing in relief to find them uninjured. The next instant despair took hold once more.

Whether or not he'd touched her, he was at fault for her injury. As he'd feared, his nightmares had returned.

She touched his sleeve, her eyes full of pity. "You should sit."

Her kindness woke him from his torpor. "I'm not the one who needs tending."

The next hour passed in a haze. Someone lit lanterns. It might have been him. He couldn't remember. He retrieved bandages and alcohol from a box he kept beneath the sink.

Tilly remained still beneath his ministrations. He dabbed at the blood oozing from the wound. She winced and hissed a breath.

"I'm sorry," Nolan murmured.

"It's all right," she whispered in obvious deference to the sleeping girls. "It was an accident."

He'd meant that he was sorry for the pain of the alcohol, but this was as good a time as any to apologize.

"Truly. I'm sorry."

"What happened? What were you dreaming about?"

"I don't remember."

"You don't remember, or you won't tell me?"

"It doesn't matter why," he said. "Nothing will change what happened."

"You're Southern, aren't you? You fought for the South."

He paused, then heaved a sigh. "Yes. I fought for the Confederacy. How did you know?"

"You still have the barest hint of an accent."

"I didn't realize."

"I doubt most folks would notice."

"You did," he said. "You noticed."

"I have an ear for that sort of thing." She touched the spot on her head and winced. "Where did you serve?"

Guilt twisted his gut. He wanted to leave. He wanted to retreat deeper into the wilderness, but he couldn't. He had to stay. He had to protect Tilly and the girls. He had to protect them from the outlaws and from himself.

"I didn't kill your cousin," he said. "If that's what you're worried about. I served in two battles before my unit was captured. I spent the rest of the war in the Rock Island prisoner camp."

"There was so much death and loss, what's the point of blame? We're all to blame." She caught his gaze. "I've never heard of Rock Island. Where was that?"

"Far from here. Prisoner camps rarely make the news when battles are being fought."

"Is that what you were dreaming about? Were you dreaming about the camp?"

"Yes."

"What was it like? I've read about—about Andersonville."

Nolan snorted. "We didn't have conditions nearly as bad as what those boys faced. I'm ashamed of my fellow Southerners for the atrocities."

"Still, being held prisoner must have been awful. Suffocating."

Suffocating. Even as he rolled the word around in his mind, the walls seemed to close in on him. The camp had been a confinement, but he'd never realized, until she said the word, how stifling his time had been.

She touched his sleeve and he jerked away.

"I'm sorry," she said. "Maybe if you talked with someone about what happened, the nightmares would fade."

He stared at the cut marring the side of her face, along with the red splotch, which would soon purple and bruise. What was the point of talking?

"I don't need your pity."

Her gaze dropped, and she stared at her clenched fingers. "I'm sorry. I didn't mean to pry."

"There's nothing to apologize for," he said, instantly remorseful. "No one else should have to know what happened. Especially not someone like you."

"A stranger?" she asked, clearly hurt.

"Someone who still has hope in the future. You shouldn't have to know what happened to us."

She clutched his fingers, looking down. "What happened to you? I want to know. You need to tell someone."

He almost didn't hear the noise, a slight sniffle. It was faint, so faint he might have mistaken it for something else, until he saw the single tear splash against her wrist.

Something inside his chest seemed to fracture. "I'm sorry. Truly, I am. I'll sleep in the livery from now on. I can't risk hurting you again, or one of the girls."

"It's not that," she said, her voice watery. "I'm not worried about you hurting one of us. What happened was an accident. I know better than to disturb you when you're sleeping now. I'm sad because I feel guilty. There were times when I didn't want the war to end. I was helping with my father's law practice. I knew once peace was declared, and the men came home, that I'd have to quit. I wanted that job even though I knew people were suffering and dying, people like you, but I couldn't stop those thoughts. I enjoyed the work. I was good at what I did."

He brushed the hair from her forehead. "No one ever lost God's love for having a selfish thought. You didn't want anyone to suffer and die, you wanted to continue the work you enjoyed. There's nothing wrong with that. A person can have those two thoughts in their head at once. You could want the war to end, and still want to keep doing the work."

She sniffled. "I never realized how much guilt I've been carrying. Working for the widows and orphans society was the perfect solution. I could be helpful, and I could atone for the guilt."

"We'll survive this, and you'll be stronger. You'll live in New York, and you'll help all the widows and orphans you can find."

"Will we? Will we survive this?"

"You have to believe. Sometimes, the only thing we have left is hope."

The door to the girls' bedroom swung open. Knuckling her eyes, Elizabeth padded into the room in her nightgown.

"Thirsty," she declared.

Tilly held out her hand. "Come along. Let's fetch you a drink of water."

Elizabeth tilted her head and pointed at Tilly's forehead. "Ouch. You have an ouch."

Nolan's hands quaked. He'd done that. He might not have laid a hand on her, but her injury was his fault.

"Yes," Tilly replied easily. "I have an ouch. Now let's fetch that water."

Elizabeth crossed her arms and vigorously shook her head. "No-wan help."

Tilly rolled her eyes. "You've obviously become her favorite."

"Here." Nolan extended his arm and she grasped his index finger. "I'll fetch you some water."

The child's unwavering trust in him was humbling. She'd been born after the war. She'd only lived in a time a peace. Would that all children could know only settled times.

Tilly glanced down the corridor to the front door. "They really aren't worried about us escaping, are they? They haven't even bothered to stay awake during their watch."

"They keep a tight hold on the horses. That's all they need to do."

"Shh." She held a finger before her lips. "I think there's someone outside."

Anxiety thrummed along his nerves. "Which one is it? Snyder?"

She crept toward the door. He handed Elizabeth her cup of water and followed Tilly, then pushed her back and out of sight. He didn't trust anyone at this point.

"It's not one of the outlaws," she said. "It's too dark to see, but I think it's one of the cavalry men."

The outlaws always set a watch, though they often dozed through their duties. The purple fingers of dawn crept along the horizon. Nolan caught a glimpse of a familiar animal. While it was too dark to make out the man, he recognized the horse.

A jolt of pure relief flooded through him.

The horse belonged to Lieutenant Perry—the one man he trusted.

They were saved.

Chapter Ten

A flash of lightning threw the rider into focus, exposing the distinctive gold braiding on the man's hat.

Tilly's heart soared. "We're rescued."

Elizabeth blinked. "Rescued?"

"Nothing. Never mind, dear. Off you go to bed. You've had your water."

"I awake."

"It's too early to be awake. Don't disturb Victoria and Caroline."

Tilly quickly hustled the toddler back into bed with her sisters.

"Wait here," Nolan ordered. "I'll direct him around back. He doesn't know the outlaws are here. Otherwise, he wouldn't be riding past the relay station. Anyone could spot him. If they recognize his uniform, he's a dead man."

"Be careful," Tilly said.

He tugged his collar over his neck, set his hat low on his forehead and dashed into the rain. He caught up with Perry and waved him toward the relay station. The two men gestured back and forth in the rain. Unable to see clearly, she scrubbed at the windowpane.

When they finally circled the house, she grasped a

lantern and dashed for the back door, then ushered them inside.

The cavalryman touched the brim of his hat. "Officer Perry, ma'am, at your service. Nolan says you've had some excitement."

"Come inside, Lieutenant." Tilly stepped aside to let the men pass. "We'll have to speak softly. There are children sleeping."

The lieutenant met her gaze and his eyes widened. "You've been injured, ma'am."

"It's nothing." She gingerly touched her cheek. "An accident. I'm sure it looks worse than it actually is."

Nolan flushed and looked away. Tilly's heart went out to him. She hadn't considered how she'd explain her injury without making Nolan feel worse than he already did. She'd simply avoid the subject whenever possible.

The lieutenant inclined his head. "My sympathies on your misfortune. I'm relieved the injury doesn't pain you."

He was shorter and stockier than Nolan. A thick beard covered the lower half of his face, making his age difficult to discern, though she guessed he was in his midtwenties. His pale blue eyes flashed in the light of the lantern. He wasn't as handsome as Captain Ronald or as rugged as Nolan. Though not unattractive, there was nothing particularly noteworthy about him. He was the sort of man one passed in the street without a second glance.

The three of them made their way to the kitchen and took seats around the table.

She offered the lieutenant a towel and he blotted the rain from his face and hair.

"How did you and your children come to stay here, ma'am? I was given to understand this relay station never housed overnight guests. Everyone in these parts knows that Mr. West is a bit of a recluse." The lieutenant winked at her. "I'm certain your delightful countenance swayed him."

"Actually, my niece became ill, forcing our stay."

"Your niece? Then you're not traveling with your husband?"

The lieutenant glanced around, as though searching for her phantom spouse.

"I'm not married, Lieutenant."

An enormous grin split his face. "This is growing more interesting by the moment. You wouldn't have a cup of coffee for a man who's been riding in the rain, would you?"

"I've just set the pot to brew."

Tilly took an immediate liking to the man. He was friendly without the forced charm of Captain Ronald. The lieutenant's pleasant demeanor was genuine, while she'd sensed the captain's flattery was practiced.

"The coffee should be ready shortly."

The lieutenant threw one arm over the back of his chair and followed her progress. "Where do you hail from, ma'am? If you don't mind me asking."

"Omaha."

"Fine city."

Nolan cleared his throat. "If we're done with the pleasantries, we have more important problems to discuss." He leaned forward and clasped his hands before him. "Where's the rest of your unit? I can't believe the captain let you travel alone. Especially under the circumstances."

"Just me, I'm afraid. With Dakota Red on the loose, we're spread thin. The captain has everyone watching the other side of the river, but I spotted smoke yesterday on the south bank, and decided to cross."

Tilly checked the pot and adjusted the flame higher on the stove. "Smoke? I didn't see anything, did you?" She directed her question toward Nolan.

He shook his head. "I didn't see anything. Then again, we were both distracted looking for Caroline."

"True."

The lieutenant glanced between them. "Someone made camp north of here. I decided to have a look. Turned out it was a band of Indians."

Tilly jolted, and accidentally touched the side of the coffeepot.

She yelped and quickly retracted her hand.

The lieutenant hastily stood. "Are you all right, ma'am?"

Tilly squeezed the blister on her index finger. "I'm fine. I was surprised, that's all." She'd been so worried about the outlaws; all her other fears had paled in comparison. "Indians? Are you certain? Are we in any danger?"

Nolan snorted. "Any more danger."

"Not at all," the lieutenant replied smoothly. "I'll explain everything over a cup of coffee."

Once the coffee had percolated long enough, she grasped the handle with a folded towel, then hooked her fingers around three mugs before rejoining the men at the table.

"It's the Ponca tribe," Lieutenant Perry said, accepting a mug. "They're peaceful. Nothing to worry about. As long as we leave them alone, they leave us alone."

Tilly secured the lid with one hand and poured coffee into the lieutenant's cup. "Isn't it dangerous, traveling without a companion in this area?"

The lieutenant cradled his mug with both hands and leaned back in his chair. "The captain couldn't spare any more men, and he figured I was on a fool's errand anyway. But I had to see for myself. We've been staked out across the river for two days, and we haven't seen any indication of the outlaws. It's as though they've vanished. We finally decided they must have moved on, but the captain wanted to stay another day. I was desperate for any sign of them. Folks don't simply disappear. After I realized I'd been chasing a dead end, I kept traveling as long as the moonlight held. I thought I could beat the storm, but it caught up with me. I figured I'd better settle in here overnight. Nolan always has extra room."

"The smoke might have been a dead end, but your hunch was correct," Nolan announced grimly. "Dakota Red, his brother, Charlie, and a third man have been holed up in Pyrite for two days."

The lieutenant jerked upright. His coffee sloshed over the side of his cup, and he winced, shaking the scalding liquid off his fingers. "I don't understand. We've had men watching the river crossing since the escape. There's only one ferry between here and the village of Yankton. They sure didn't swim across. The current is too strong."

"I don't know when they crossed, but I'm guessing they were already on this side of the river before the patrol came through town on Tuesday. Maybe they slipped across during the night. Doesn't matter now. They're here."

The captain glanced between Tilly and Nolan. "You two are blessed to be alive."

She circled the table and rested her hand on Nolan's shoulder. "We're alive thanks to Nolan's quick thinking."

"He's a good man."

The lieutenant's attention lingered on where her hand was touching Nolan's shoulder. She flushed and moved away.

"He's the best man in the area," the lieutenant said. "Where are the fugitives now?"

"They're staying in the house next to the livery. The old undertaker's place."

"Fitting." Lieutenant Perry tugged on his gauntleted gloves. "I have my rifle and a sidearm. If they're all in the house together, the two of us can ambush them. We'll use the element of surprise to confuse them."

Nolan raked his hands through his hair. "How many men are watching the river crossing right now?"

"I don't know. As I said, we're spread thin. The captain has been switching out the patrols with the men keeping watch. Could be two men, could be a dozen or more. Depends on the time of day, and what else is pulling them off watch."

"Fetch the extra men, and then come back."

"I can't do that. I can't leave a woman and children alone with those outlaws."

"If we ambush them and we fail, we'll be far worse off. All of us."

"True. But it doesn't sit right with me, abandoning you like this."

"Leave me your sidearm. You have the rifle. If something goes wrong before you return, I'll try and hold them off for as long as I can."

"You won't be able to hold them off for long." The lieutenant reluctantly handed over his sidearm. "You've only got six bullets."

"Six?"

"Remember the steamship that sank? That boat was ferrying all of our supplies. The ammunition is rationed until the next shipment."

"Six bullets are better than nothing."

"Don't do anything foolish until I return." The lieutenant finished off his coffee and stood. "By the time I fetch help, it'll be sundown at least."

"Sundown is better. Take the old buffalo trail. The path is longer, but you won't be seen." Nolan hesitated. "There's another thing. It's only a hunch, but keep your eye on the captain."

"The captain?"

"Don't you find it odd that the outlaws were able to make it across the river as easily as they did?"

The lieutenant gave a negative shake of his head. "Surely you don't suspect the captain of aiding outlaws?"

"Enough gold will make a man do peculiar things. Maybe he'd rather live like a king somewhere far from here."

Understanding spread across the lieutenant's face. "I should go. The quicker I fetch help, the better. I'll keep my eye on him. If he refuses to help, I've got men I trust. Men that will help me even if the captain refuses."

"Good. That's what we'll need."

"Isn't that too dangerous?" Tilly asked. "You can't leave yet. Not in this weather. We can hide his horse away from town, at least until the sun rises."

"Don't worry about me, ma'am." The lieutenant's teeth flashed in the dim morning light. "I've been scouting this part of the country for the past year. I know where I'm going."

Tilly appealed to Nolan for help. "Can't you talk some sense into him?"

"He's right. We're taking a big risk right now. Those men will be up any minute. They might even be awake now. The sooner he leaves, the better."

"All right," Tilly reluctantly replied. "Promise me that you'll be careful."

"I promise."

Nolan held up one hand. "Stay here. I'll check on Dakota Red." He stepped outside and returned quickly.

"There's movement at the house. Snyder is getting up for the day. You'd better go."

They went outside. The lieutenant mounted his horse and touched the brim of his hat. "Y'all sit tight, and I'll be back with help by sundown tonight. We'll set up watch at twilight, and make our move around nightfall. It'll be safest that way. If you sight one of our men, don't be alarmed."

Tilly pressed her hand over her chest. "I'm so grateful for your help. I'm ready for this to be over."

"We'll get 'em, I promise you that. Keep out of their way today, and act as though everything is normal. The less suspicious they are, the better."

As his shadowed form faded into blackness, her feet remained rooted to the spot.

"Don't worry," Nolan said. "Tomorrow this will all seem like a bad dream."

Tilly unconsciously touched the side of her head. "I'm ready to wake up from this bad dream all together."

"He's a good man."

"I'm sure you're right," she replied absently. "I'm grateful he came through town when he did."

"He admires you."

"I don't understand."

"You could do worse for a husband."

The words took a moment to sink in. Her stomach dipped. Nolan was letting her know that her attentions toward him were unwanted. He obviously regretted his actions. She didn't know why he'd kissed her, and she probably never would.

She lifted her chin a notch. "Good night, Mr. West."

She didn't need a husband and she certainly didn't need the stagecoach man's pity.

* * *

As the morning progressed, there was a festive mood in the air. Tilly and the girls slept later than usual and prepared breakfast. She poured streams of batter into the griddle, forming letters, then ladled more batter in a circle over the letters. The technique allowed their morning flapjacks to be emblazoned with each of the girls' initials, much to their delight.

The slight bruising on her temple left Nolan unable to fully enjoy the idea of their impending rescue, but their buoyancy was infectious. He dug into his pancakes, inordinately pleased that she'd given him a stack with the letter *N* in darkened batter.

He finished his chores and skirted past the outlaws, who were engrossed in a card game on the front porch. Though the men had grown more lax since that first evening, true to their word, they never left the horses unprotected.

They moved the animals into the barn each evening, and Snyder or Charlie slept by the door.

The wind stirred the trees, and he studied the branches. How long before the lieutenant mustered a rescue? The sooner his guests were out of danger, the better.

Anticipation of their impending freedom kept the exhaustion from his sleepless night at bay.

As though sensing the mood of the adults, the girls were full of restless energy. Nolan scrounged some flat steel tire rims from replacement wagon wheels, and they rolled them through the center of town. Laughing and giggling, they challenged each other to see who could make their rings roll the farthest.

He returned to the relay station to clean up the kitchen, and stopped short inside the door. Every surface gleamed.

Tilly splayed her arms and smiled. "You'll notice all the pots and pans are in their proper places."

"You didn't have to do that."

"I did. I'm sorry I left such a mess last night. In all the excitement, I forgot to thank you for cleaning up."

"I didn't mind."

"I did. This is your home, and I know you like things neat. It was terribly rude of me to leave a mess."

"You were tired."

"Yes, but that's no excuse." She lifted a stack of towels. "Look. I folded them each exactly the same size. All the edges are even."

Nausea roiled in his stomach. "I don't know what to say."

He certainly hadn't done a very good job of hiding his compulsions. She'd noticed everything. All the pots were hung in their places; all the jars were lined by height. The plates were even stacked in neat, even-numbered piles.

She scrubbed at a smudge on the counter. "There. It's perfect. Now you have no excuse."

"Excuse for what?"

"You have no excuse not to come with the girls and me. We have a special adventure planned, and we need your help."

She motioned him to follow her outside, where the girls waited. "We're going down by the river. We're looking for something."

"What?"

"You have to wait. It's a surprise."

He plastered a disinterested look on his face. "I'll stay behind."

"You can't. The girls are already looking forward to their surprise. You can't let them down."

He had no excuse to stay. Nothing. Tilly had scrubbed

the surfaces and left everything neat and tidy. He had no excuse. No excuse except that he was a coward.

He was supposed to be healing in solitude. With the arrival of the girls, he'd lapsed. Worse yet, his compulsions were spreading to his houseguests.

She tilted her head, a crease between her brows, her bluebell eyes troubled. "What's the matter?"

"I don't like surprises."

"Then you've never been surprised by me."

His heart sat heavy in his chest. She'd surprised him at every turn, and that's why he feared her. She brought vitality to his life and created shared, life affirming experiences. She'd brought light and love to his shadowed world.

And what had he brought her?

She'd spent the morning arranging the pans by size.

They were unequal partners. She brought joy, and he brought nothing but his obsessive need to control his environment. She had everything to offer, and he had nothing to give.

Though he was looking forward to his solitude once more, he'd miss them when they were gone.

No surprise there.

Chapter Eleven

The girls giggled. Tilly shot them a quelling look.

Nolan frowned at her. "What are you looking for?"

"We'll tell you when we find it."

Holding hands, the two oldest sisters skipped ahead. Elizabeth struggled to keep up, but soon fell behind. The toddler plopped onto her bottom in the center of the path and burst into tears.

Nolan kneeled beside her. "Why don't you walk with me instead?"

Elizabeth eyed him warily. "They bad."

"Yes. They are very naughty for running ahead and leaving you behind."

The toddler stretched out her hands and flexed her fingers. "Up."

Nolan hoisted her into his arms. "Do you want to make them jealous?"

"Uh-huh."

"Then I'll make you taller than both of them. You'll be the tallest sister in the family."

He hoisted her onto his shoulders. She squealed in delight and grasped the brim of his hat, crumpling the leather.

Beside him, Tilly grinned. "She's very fond of you."

Nolan returned the smile. "I didn't have siblings growing up. I admit that I'm sometimes dismayed at the amount of fighting they do."

"I can assure you, the fighting is perfectly normal. My sister and I fought quite often. She's five years older, and inevitably won the argument. She has a spotless memory. It's terribly annoying having an argument with someone who has such excellent recollection of events."

"That doesn't seem fair."

"I think she resented me. She was an only child for five wonderful years, and received all the attention. Then I was born, and our mother died shortly afterward. You know, until now, I hadn't really thought of how Eleanor must have felt when she was five. She lost her mother and received a squalling infant sister in return. That must have been very confusing at five years old."

"That's hardly your fault."

"No, but it's a sobering thought. For her, I must have been a reminder of our mother's death."

She paused in the center of the path. As a child she'd visited a secluded garden built in the center of the city. Opening the gate had transported her into an entirely different world. The unexpected view had given her a new perspective on the world around her. From then on, she'd always had a curiosity about what was hidden behind each corner.

Thinking about Eleanor as a child gave her that same feeling. As though she was opening a door to a world she'd never seen before. A world she'd never imagined. A world she'd taken for granted.

"Aunt Tilly," one of the girls shouted from farther up the path. "Aunt Tilly, we've found the perfect tree!"

Tilly skipped ahead while Nolan and Elizabeth followed behind.

She paused and stared at a large cottonwood perched on the banks of the river, then planted her hands on her hips. "This is perfect."

"Perfect for what?" Nolan asked, catching up to her.

"For a swing, of course. We'll need a rope and a wooden plank for a seat. Do you think you can help us?"

Tilly couldn't help her stab of pride. The idea was inspired. The activity would keep the girls busy while they waited for the impending rescue. Though she was grateful the cavalry was near, she wasn't confident in Captain Ronald's abilities. Nolan didn't like the man, and she trusted his instincts. The safety of the girls was their greatest concern.

They were also remarkably astute for their ages. If she didn't find a way of distracting them, they'd immediately sense the unease among the adults.

"I can help," Nolan replied. "But I'll need some assistants."

Victoria's hand shot into the air and Caroline followed suit.

"Me! Me!" they both shouted.

"All right," he said. "I have two helpers."

"Me, too, me, too!" Elizabeth, still perched on his shoulders, slapped her hands against his hat. "I help."

"I have three helpers. Let's go back to the livery and gather our supplies."

As they passed the undertaker's house, whoops and hollers drifted through the open windows. Shouts of anger soon followed. Tilly and Nolan exchanged a look. Judging by the few words she could make out, someone had lost a great deal of money in cards.

Caroline glanced in the direction of the commotion. "When will those men be leaving?"

"Soon," Tilly said. "Very, very soon. Until then, remember what we talked about. Stay far away from them."

All three girls nodded solemnly.

The reminder of the men put a temporary damper on the festivities, but as soon as they gathered their supplies, the mood lightened once more.

They retrieved a broken floorboard from the abandoned building where Tilly had fallen. The girls crowded around as Nolan cut and sanded the edges, then augered holes in the sides for the rope.

Victoria rested her chin on her hands. "Why do you have chalk marks everywhere?"

"So I know where my tools belong." Nolan glanced up. "Then I don't lose things."

"Mama is like that. She's always hollering at us to put things away."

Caroline giggled and shook her index finger, planting her opposite hand on her hip. "That's not how you stack your blocks, girls. Largest to smallest."

"Quite right." Victoria mimicked her sister's posture. "We can't leave the house until everything is spotless."

Caroline sobered. "Which means we rarely get to leave the house."

"Papa managed to leave the house every day," Victoria said. "I think that's why he spent so much time at the mine, because he could never make things good enough for Mama."

Busy with knotting the rope around the wooden seat of the swing, Tilly listened to their chatter with half an ear, then slapped her hands on her knees and stood. "Come along. We mustn't speak of your mother that way." She lowered her voice. "Does she make certain your stockings are separated by color?"

The girls eagerly nodded. "Yes. She's terribly cross if we don't."

"Do you know how I solved that problem? I insisted on only wearing black stockings. Summer, winter, spring and fall. I would only wear the black stockings. That way, I didn't have to worry about sorting them!"

The girls giggled.

Nolan followed their exchange, an odd expression on his face.

"Is everything all right?" Tilly asked.

"Almost finished." He tightened the first knot in the rope wrapped around the wooden seat and straightened. "The swing is almost ready."

"We should make a picnic lunch," Caroline said.

"Absolutely," Tilly agreed. "We'll need a blanket and a basket. We'll have a proper picnic."

"I'll get started with hanging the swing," Nolan said. "You four can catch up."

Tilly paused. Though reluctant to separate, she didn't see any harm in letting Nolan proceed ahead of them. "All right."

Elizabeth shook her head. "I go with No-wan."

He reached for the toddler's hand. "I don't mind. She can walk with me."

"All right," Tilly said. "The rest of us will fetch lunch and catch up with you two."

He hoisted the coil of rope over his shoulder and tucked the wood plank beneath his arm. Elizabeth clutched the fingers of his free hand. Tilly smiled indulgently. He was growing accustomed to Elizabeth's childish affection.

She recalled the odd look on Nolan's face and stopped in her tracks. She mentally slapped her forehead. They'd been joking about Eleanor's mannerisms, the same mannerisms Nolan shared. No wonder he'd been quiet. They'd been mocking him right in front of his face.

She vowed to be more careful in the future. From what she recalled growing up, Eleanor couldn't change even if she wanted to. Her sister liked things a certain way. There was nothing wrong with that. Tilly vowed to be more understanding of her sister...and Nolan.

With renewed determination, she set off to prepare their picnic lunch.

She'd simply be more careful in the future.

Her footsteps slowed, and her enthusiasm waned. However much future they had together.

Elizabeth pointed. "What that?"

"That plant is called goldenrod," Nolan said.

The ditch along the stagecoach path leading to the river had filled with rainwater, giving rise to a plush blanket of prairie grasses near the edges. Wildlife and plants flourished in the ideal conditions.

"What's that?"

"That's a bullfrog. There are always more bullfrogs when there's been a lot of rain."

"Why?"

"They like the rain."

Oddly enough, her incessant chatter and questions took his mind off the nagging sense that he was forgetting something important. He'd struggled with the affliction in the past. When he kept to his routine, the feelings didn't bother him as much. Since the girls had arrived, he was constantly on edge, with an undercurrent of anxiety constantly nipping at his heels.

He didn't know what to make of the children's earlier discussion. They loved their mother, but they recognized her faults. This morning Tilly had cheerfully cleaned the kitchen to his standards. How long, though, until he drove her away? The girls had spoken innocently, but even they had sensed the tension their mother's obsessive tidiness had caused.

The anxiety was a constant companion, as though someone had wrapped a band around his throat. If the girls were not here, he'd return to the relay station and count his tools, then oil the harnesses. The monotonous labor didn't loosen the band, but the work distracted him, and that was enough.

When they arrived by the river's edge, Nolan climbed the tree they'd chosen earlier. He braced his hand on the branch and stared across the valley. Was the cavalry crossing the river yet? Anticipation built in his chest along with a nagging sense of unease. He'd rather be acting than sitting around and waiting for a rescue.

He caught sight of Elizabeth below and the tension eased. Keeping the girls busy while they waited was a noble cause. They were smart and perceptive. They sensed something was wrong with the adults without fully understanding the cause.

He was grateful Perry had trusted his instincts and gone against the captain's directive. Their options were growing more limited by the day. Nolan grasped the rope and rigged the swing before shimmying down once more.

"Me first!" Elizabeth demanded.

"You're first," he agreed.

By the time the picnic lunch arrived, Elizabeth had gotten the hang of swinging. Her two sisters skipped down the path, each of them dangling a bucket from one hand.

They caught sight of Elizabeth's merry swinging and paused.

"I'm next!" they both shouted in unison.

"I said it first," Victoria insisted.

"Did not." Caroline's lower lip protruded. "I said it first."

Tilly, a blanket clutched beneath her arm, sighed. "You know the rules. Stone, paper, scissors. Best two out of three wins."

The girls grumbled before dutifully facing each other.

Pounding one fist into the opposite palm, they said in unison, "Stone, paper, scissors, shoe."

On the last word, they each presented their hand in either a fist, a flattened palm, or a scissor.

After three rounds, Caroline emerged victorious.

Victoria scuffed the ground. "She always wins."

"She does not *always* win," Tilly said. "It simply feels as though she always wins."

"Same difference."

Tilly rolled her eyes. "You will *all* get a turn. Mr. West and I will keep track of the time. Everything will be fair."

She spread the blanket on an area of flattened grass, swept her skirts aside, then sat. Victoria huffed and plopped beside her aunt.

The girl scratched her cheek. "Why do those men staying at the undertaker's house think you two are married?"

Nolan's heart slammed against his ribs. "Did you tell them any different?"

"No. I heard them talking. They were calling Aunt Tilly your wife. I just wondered."

"Well, uh, you see," Tilly stuttered. "It's a long story."

"Is it a boring story?"

"Extremely boring and extremely long."

"I thought so." Victoria wrinkled her nose. "Adult stories are always boring."

"In the extreme." Tilly flashed Nolan a relieved glance

over the girls' heads. "It was better for us if we let those men believe that Mr. West and I were married."

"I understand. Mama said it was better for us if the merchants in town thought Papa's mine had gold."

Tilly's expression grew speculative. Nolan scrubbed his hands down his face. The sooner they were rescued, the better. He didn't know the extent of Eleanor's misfortunes, but the glimpses the girls had let slip painted a grim picture of her circumstances.

Plucking at the corner of the blanket, Tilly pursed her lips. Eleanor was keeping secrets from her family. From what he'd gathered, Eleanor took great pride in appearances. Snippets of conversations he'd had with Tilly drifted through his recollections.

Eleanor was perfect.

If Tilly had been given the role of rambunctious younger sister, then Eleanor had been given the role of perfect older sister. Their father had reinforced their positions in the family with his words. Old habits were hard to break.

Nolan collapsed back on his elbows. The girls took turns swinging. When they'd exhausted their interest, they grasped the leftover length of rope. With Victoria and Caroline holding each end, Elizabeth jumped rope. The older girls circled the rope slowly in deference to her younger age.

When the sisters were fully distracted, Tilly crossed her arms over her chest. "I can't believe Eleanor never said anything to me about what was happening. She made all of us believe she and Walter were doing well. The more I hear from the girls, the more I realize that she was lying to us all along. She didn't trust me with the truth."

"She didn't trust your father, either."

"She didn't trust any of us. We might have done something. We might have helped." Tilly pressed her index fingers against her eyes. "We fought before I left with the girls. She was acting particularly atrocious, even for Eleanor."

"I suspect that admitting the truth would have damaged her pride."

"Perfect Eleanor isn't quite so perfect."

"Yes."

"But none of this is her fault." Tilly made a sound of frustration. "Walter was the one who dragged them to Virginia City in the first place. His greed led to their downfall." She jerked her chin over one shoulder. "Nothing good comes of people searching for quick riches. Greed will land those three in jail soon."

"Perhaps Eleanor is jealous of you."

"I sincerely doubt that," she scoffed. "Eleanor takes every opportunity to remind me of my faults."

Elizabeth managed two jumps before the rope caught on her ankles. With a merry laugh, she skipped out of the jump rope.

Caroline sang, "'As I went down to my grandfather's farm, a billy goat chased me around the barn. It chased me up a sycamore tree, and this is what it said to me—I like coffee, I like tea, I like Aunt Tilly to jump with me!'"

Laughing, Tilly stood and doffed her bonnet. "Go slowly, I haven't done this in years."

After a few rounds of watching the circling rope, she gathered her skirts to one side and hopped inside the swinging rope.

Victoria danced on the balls of her feet without losing her time. "My turn to sing a song. 'Benjamin Franklin went to France, to teach the ladies how to dance. First the heel, and then the toe, spin around and there you go.'"

With one hand raised for balance, and the other holding her skirts aside, Tilly hopped to the rhythm of the song before jumping out once more.

"Your turn, Caroline," she said.

For the next twenty minutes, the three of them took turns jumping in and out of the game, exchanging places. Overhead, the sky darkened. Lightning flashed, illuminating the clouds. Nolan kept one eye on the sky. There was a good chance the storm would drift north. If not, their plan was in jeopardy. Crossing the river in good weather was dangerous. Navigating the rapids in a thunderstorm was suicide.

Tilly laughed and stumbled toward the blanket. "I'm exhausted. I can't go on anymore."

"Ah, c'mon," Caroline chided. "We've hardly even begun."

"Yeah, Aunt Tilly," Victoria said. "We once played for three whole hours without stopping."

Tilly held up her hands. "I'm not a little girl anymore, I don't have your stamina."

"What does that mean?" Victoria asked.

"It means I have to rest." Tilly collapsed back on her elbows. "I forfeit my turns."

Nolan glanced at Tilly's profile. She watched the girls at their game, and indulgent smile stretching across her face. She appeared relaxed and at ease, hopeful for the rescue ahead, and he couldn't bring himself to point out the weather. There was no point in ruining her afternoon with pointless worry.

She hadn't bothered to replace her bonnet, and sunlight glinted off her chestnut strands. Though fashion favored a pale complexion, he much preferred the way the sunlight bronzed her cheeks and freckled her nose. Her chest rose and fell from her exertions, and his gaze skittered away from the sight.

Nolan plucked a slender blade of prairie grass near the edge of the blanket. "I don't ever remember having that much energy."

"They're quite resilient, aren't they?" She lowered her voice. "What do you suppose will happen tonight?"

"The outlaws don't see us as much of threat, and we'll use that to our advantage. The lieutenant will ensure the relay station is protected. I'll join the men while you and the girls stay inside and take cover. That way, if anything goes wrong, you're well away from the danger."

She collapsed onto her back and crossed her arms over her chest. "I cannot wait for this to be over."

He glanced at his watch and realized he'd forgotten his afternoon chores. Not once in the past year had he strayed from his rigid schedule. Though a part of him wanted to leap up and complete the tasks, he fought the urge. While the weather might prevent an ambush this evening, there'd be ample opportunity for Captain Ronald and his men to launch a rescue tomorrow.

He'd be back to his old, familiar routine in no time. The same chores, the same counts, the same checks of the locks. A sudden sense of melancholy filled him.

Tilly caught his gaze. "Something has been bothering me. When we were searching for Caroline, and I plunged through the floorboards, you said I was a genius. What did you mean?"

"You mentioned a boat. Dakota Red knows we can't escape on foot, but we can escape by boat down the river."

"Except we don't have a boat."

"That's not precisely true. We have a boat, but it's not seaworthy. I was planning on doing the repairs before Lieutenant Perry arrived. Now that he's coming back with a rescue party, we won't have to take such drastic measures."

"I'd rather not risk a trip on a rickety boat with the girls."

"We won't have to. The cavalry will come for us. You'll be home soon."

She threaded her fingers behind her head. "I'm sure you're anxious to have your home back."

"It'll be quiet, that's for certain."

He couldn't lie. He didn't want them to leave. His time as Tilly's make-believe husband was coming to an end. She'd been cool to him since he'd mentioned the lieutenant's suitability. He should be grateful. She'd gotten the hint. He didn't have to worry about ruining her life the way his own had been. Their presence had shined a light on all the reasons he'd chosen to live in solitude.

Everything that had happened over the past few days had supported that decision. He still wasn't fit for regular company.

He'd go back to the way things were before.

A knot of regret settled in his chest. Except he had a feeling things would never be the same again.

Chapter Twelve

Lightning flashed, illuminating the bedroom. Tilly groaned and rolled over, tugging the pillow over her head. A booming crash of thunder rattled the windowpanes. For the past hour, the storm had been unrelenting. She might have slept through the constant flashes, but the earth-shaking thunder was unavoidable.

There'd been no sign of Lieutenant Perry or his men. Dinner had come and gone. The sun had set, and the clouds had obscured the stars. Her mood had deteriorated with each passing hour.

Nolan had finally urged her to bed. He'd assured her that the weather was preventing a rescue attempt. He'd assured her that the cavalry would try again tomorrow. She wasn't certain if he was assuring her, or himself.

A door creaked and she bolted upright. Her heartbeat quickened. Had the cavalry decided to brave the weather anyway?

A braided head poked around the corner. "Aunt Tilly, Elizabeth is scared of the storm," Victoria said.

Caroline appeared behind her sister.

Tilly swung her feet over the edge of the mattress.

Victoria clutched her hands together. "Aunt Tilly, I'm afraid of the storm, too."

A flash of lighting threw the room into relief, immediately followed by another crash of thunder.

Victoria jumped and dove onto the bed, Caroline at her heels. Tilly snatched her wrapper from the post.

"I'd best check on your sister."

She pushed open the door of the girls' bedroom and discovered Elizabeth sound asleep in the center of the mattress.

She bolstered a few pillows around the sleeping toddler and returned to her room. The clock chimed the five o'clock hour, and her heart sank. Their chances of being rescued safely diminished with each bell toll. Since they'd lost their first opportunity, would the men try to attack during the day?

Though she was frightened of the impending violence, the waiting was driving her mad.

Straightening, she considered how to distract her nieces. "Since it's almost sunrise, why don't we dress and make a special breakfast? I noticed the bread is running low, so we'll start by making a fresh loaf."

Having something to do energized the girls, and they dashed away, returning shortly with their faces washed and their clothing donned. Tilly peeked at Elizabeth once more, and decided to let the sleeping child remain in bed. No sense in all of them dragging around that afternoon.

Though she'd never been particularly adept at making bread, there was something relaxing about kneading dough and watching the loaves rise.

She'd finished setting out her supplies when the front door swung open. Nolan stood on the threshold, rain dripping from the brim of his hat.

She quickly ushered him inside. "You're soaking through."

He glanced into the kitchen and raised his eyebrows. "The girls are up early."

"The storm."

He lifted his hat and raked his hand through his hair. "I think you and the girls should stay close to the relay station today. If the captain is smart, he'll wait until evening when the weather is clear enough to make an attempt at a rescue. But just in case he decides to make a daylight attack, we should stay inside."

"If this rain doesn't let up, there's not much we can do outside anyway."

Nolan replaced his hat. "If I see anything, I'll let you know."

"You should stay." She prodded him inside. "We're making breakfast. We figured since everyone was up already, we might as well do something useful."

"I should go. I need to keep watch."

"If the cavalry hasn't come by now, they're not coming anytime soon." Thunder crashed above them, rattling the dishes she'd set on the counter. "There'll be nothing to see in this rain. You might as well sit out the storm with us."

He hesitated. "I have chores."

"Suit yourself."

"My chores could probably wait. Until after the storm."

"I won't twist your arm."

A knock sounded on the back door.

Tilly clutched her throat. "The lieutenant is here."

The outlaws never knocked. They came and went as they pleased, acting as though they owned the place.

Her heart soared. "That's our help. It has to be."

"Stay behind me," Nolan ordered. "I'm not taking any chances."

He angled his body and opened the back door. A man in blue cavalry pants brushed past him. He wore an overcoat against the rain and a hat pulled low over his eyes.

He lifted his head and Tilly gasped. "Captain Ronald. You came!"

Stomping his feet, the captain glanced up. "If I had known you'd be this happy to see me, I'd have checked on you five yesterday."

"Checked on us?" Tilly's euphoria lowered a notch. "Where are the rest of your men?"

"Back at the fort. I sent my scout ahead, but I wanted to stop by Pyrite and see how you were holding up."

"Then you haven't spoken with Lieutenant Perry?"

"No." The captain shrugged out of his coat and rainwater pooled on the floor. "Lieutenant Perry is on leave. He won't be back for another month."

Tilly's confusion grew. "But I don't understand. The lieutenant was supposed to deliver a message."

Her stomach knotted. Nothing made sense. The lieutenant hadn't mentioned he was on leave. A small enough oversight. Perhaps this was simply a misunderstanding or a break in communication. Had Perry and the captain crossed paths without realizing they'd missed each other?

Nolan grasped a handful of the captain's shirt and shoved him against the wall. "What's going on? I want the truth."

"Have you gone mad?" The captain brought up his hands and shoved Nolan. "What's gotten into you?"

"I think the other man already delivered his message," a small voice said.

The three adults turned toward the speaker.

Victoria's cheeks pinkened at the attention and she went silent.

Tilly strode across the room and draped an arm around

her niece's shoulder. "You're not in any trouble, but I need you to explain."

"The man who came by before, he was speaking with Dakota Red."

Tilly felt as though all the air had been sucked out of the room. "Are you certain?"

"Yes. I'm certain. You and Nolan woke me up that night with your talking. I saw the man's horse, and I watched him from the window."

"It was raining that night. Are you certain you know what you saw?"

"Fairly certain. He was speaking with someone, and it wasn't you or Mr. West, because you two were still inside. The first man left. Then Nolan came outside and the second man followed him inside. You three talked for a while, and then he left."

Lieutenant Perry had betrayed them. He'd been in league with the outlaws all along. That was the only explanation for his actions.

"We're not being rescued." Tilly's hand flew to her mouth, and she collapsed onto a chair. "Help isn't coming."

Nolan staggered backward and raked both hands through his hair.

"Hold up." The captain yanked his shirt, straightening his wrinkled collar. "What's going on here? What are y'all talking about?"

"Where's your horse?" Nolan demanded.

"Hitched to the front post. Where else would he be?"

"Did you see anyone else when you rode through town?"

"No. No one."

"There's no time to explain," Nolan said. "Put your coat back on, we have to hide your horse."

"I'll follow along for now," the captain said. "But you owe me an explanation, and that explanation had better be good or I'll speak with your superiors at the Pioneer Stagecoach. If you're yanking my leg, you'll be manning a station in the Mojave Desert."

"That would suit me fine," Nolan replied grimly. "Follow me."

The back door burst open.

Caroline shrieked.

The two men turned toward the front entrance, and the second door slammed open. From opposite ends of the house, Dakota Red and Charlie stalked toward each other, effectively blocking the exits, keeping them all trapped.

Captain Ronald reached for his sidearm. A gunshot sounded.

"Too slow." The outlaw chortled.

A plume of smoke drifted from the barrel of his gun.

The captain grunted and lurched to one side. He slid down the wall, his legs stretched before him, his right hand clutching the wound on his leg.

Tilly shoved the girls behind her and backed them toward the kitchen. Nolan stood before them, his arms splayed, shielding the girls as best he could with his body.

A heavy thud sounded.

Dakota Red chuckled, a low menacing sound that sent shivers snaking down Tilly's spine. Victoria whimpered and Tilly tightened her hold.

"It's all right. I promise. It will be all right."

She didn't know why she said the words. Clearly, nothing was all right. Caroline trembled violently and Victoria sobbed. The acrid stench of gunpowder filled the air. Tilly glanced toward the bedroom door, searching for Elizabeth. There was no way the toddler had slept through the commotion.

"What do we have here?" The outlaw chortled. "I only seen one horse. You traveling alone? And don't lie to me, or I'll know."

"I'm alone," Captain Ronald gasped, his voice strained. "But you already knew that, didn't you?"

"Yeah. I watched you ride in. You're just the man I wanted to see. When is the gold shipment coming through town? I'm tired of waiting."

"Friday," the captain wheezed.

"We've got ourselves a real problem. One of you is lying. The stagecoach man says there ain't no coach scheduled on Friday. You're telling me there is. Which one of you should I kill for trying to fool me?"

Charlie grasped Nolan's upper arm and yanked him forward. "Let's shoot this one. I never did like the way he looked at me."

"No!" the captain shouted. "He's not lying. The regular stagecoach is coming through tomorrow. On Friday, there will be an unscheduled coach. We figured it was safer if no one knew about the extra shipment."

Charlie kicked aside the worktable and grinned. "Come out, come out wherever you are. I guess we won't be needing you folks anymore."

Tilly blanched and hugged the girls tighter. Nolan lunged for them and Charlie's gun cocked, halting his motion.

"We still need them." Dakota Red waved his gun in their direction. "We need a clean getaway. I want a head start on our escape. The more miles we put between us and this town, the better. That's what got us caught the last time. We stick with the original plan. The stagecoach man and his wife will keep everything looking normal. We unload the shipment during the change of horses, and no one is the wiser. By the time they discover the gold is missing, we'll be long gone."

Nolan pushed the girls behind him, and Tilly scooted to his side, blocking the girls' view of the wounded man in the center of the room. The captain clutched his leg, and blood oozed through his fingers.

"He's bleeding," Tilly said. "Let me help him."

"He's going to die sooner or later," Dakota Red snarled. "You're wasting your time."

"I can't watch him suffer."

Nolan gave her waist a reassuring squeeze. "Let her help."

"It's your time to waste." Dakota Red said.

Tilly gathered her nieces. "Come along—you two wait in the bedroom and watch Elizabeth."

None of the outlaws protested as she led the sisters away from the violence. The girls perched on the edge of the bed. Blurry-eyed, Elizabeth stuck her thumb in her mouth. This time Tilly didn't scold her.

She kneeled before them. "I promise you, everything will be all right. I need you to stay strong for a few minutes, and take care of each other. Can you do that? Can you take care of each other?"

The three of them nodded in solemn unison.

"Good girls. I'll be back soon. Stay in here until I come for you."

"Is that man going to die?" Victoria asked, her face stricken.

"I hope not. I'm going to do everything I can to help him. You girls can offer up a prayer."

She dropped a kiss on each of their foreheads and gathered a handful of linens, then took a fortifying breath before exiting the room.

The captain's complexion had gone ashen, and his lips had taken on a bluish tinge. Tilly rushed to his side.

Charlie had Nolan's arm wrapped around his back, the gun barrel pressed against his forehead.

"Be quick, girlie," Dakota Red ordered. "As soon as you're finished, we'll leave. I need to make certain the captain isn't in any shape to cause us trouble."

She kneeled beside Captain Ronald and he slumped onto his back. The captain had a small wound on the front of his thigh, and a much larger exit wound in the back. At least she didn't have to dig out the bullet. Her hands shaking, she ripped the linens into several strips, then wrapped them around the captain's leg.

"Hold on here," she requested gently.

The captain placed his fingers over the binding, and she knotted the length over his fingers. He slid his hand free and she quickly tightened the knot. Blood oozed from the wound.

Her stomach pitched and nausea rose in the back of her throat. She'd never had much tolerance for this sort of thing.

Gathering herself, she added two more layers of bandages. By the time she'd finished, a dark red blotch had oozed through the binding.

"He's no threat," Nolan said. "He needs stitches and rest. Leave us alone so that we can attend him."

"He needs to answer my questions, first." Dakota Red loomed over the prone man. "First you need to tell me why you've been prowling around all by your lonesome. Seems like you don't trust your men to do their jobs."

"I don't," the captain groaned. "We've been watching the opposite side of the river for two days solid, and we didn't see you cross. The only sign of an encampment had been abandoned. You hadn't gone north, which meant you must have gone south. Since we were watching the crossing, I figured someone helped you."

"You're a real clever fellow. Too bad you ain't gonna live."

"Stop it!" Tilly demanded. "Just stop it! I won't have you threatening this man. He's wounded. He's no danger to you."

"Your gal has some sass." Dakota Red chortled. "Fine, little lady. We'll let you play nursemaid to the man until he dies on his own. That wound will probably turn septic in these conditions."

"You've done your damage," Nolan said. "Leave us."

Dakota Red stifled a yawn. "Even if you run, you ain't getting far with a wounded man and three children. Y'all are too softhearted to leave each other behind. That's gonna get y'all killed."

"Too stupid, more like." Charlie pointed the tip of his gun at the ceiling. "Ain't none of them going nowhere, and Snyder has the next watch." His beady eyes narrowed. "I'm getting some shut-eye."

They were a pitiable group. Exhausted, bedraggled and wounded. There was no need for the outlaws to fear them.

The men tramped out, and Nolan and Tilly assisted the captain to his feet.

"Let's get you into a bed before you collapse," Nolan said.

Tilly strained beneath the man's weight. "I only know how to embroider. I don't know if I can sew his wound."

"Don't worry, I do."

"You do?"

"We didn't get much medical attention as prisoners of war. We learned to do for ourselves."

"I'll help." Tilly offered. "I can do that much."

The captain staggered. "I'll be fine. No need to put yourselves out on my account."

"You'll be fine, all right," Nolan said. "After we get you in bed and stitched up."

This time the captain didn't argue.

Together they led him into the last unoccupied bedroom of the relay station and hoisted him onto the mattress. Tilly helped with removing his jacket, then excused herself.

Giving Nolan time to attend the man, she returned to the girls. "You'll need to say in here a little longer, all right? Then you can leave. I have to clean up a few things."

"The blood?"

"Yes."

There was no use lying. The older girls had witnessed everything.

"Why did those men shoot that officer?" Victoria asked.

"It was an accident."

Victoria sat up straighter and folded her hands in her lap. "I'm the oldest. I'll be in charge. I'll help watch Caroline and Elizabeth."

"I don't need watching," Caroline huffed.

Tilly pressed a hand over the painful ache in her chest. "You three will look out for each other. You've done exceptionally well already, but you'll have to be brave awhile longer. I have to assist Nolan while he cares for the captain. I need you three to get along. No fighting. Agreed?"

"All right," Caroline reluctantly conceded.

"That's the spirit," Tilly said. "Try and sleep if you can. Tomorrow is going to be another long day."

Caroline slumped against the headboard. "I want to go home."

"Me, too," Tilly replied weakly. "Me, too. Nolan and I working our hardest to get us home soon."

After kissing each of them on the forehead and tucking them back into bed, she quietly shut the bedroom door behind her.

While Nolan prepared the captain for stitches, Tilly gathered towels and scrubbed at the floor. Not wanting the girls to see the mess, she stuffed the towels in a hamper. Considering there was no one coming to rescue them, there'd be time enough tomorrow for the washing.

She returned and discovered Nolan setting out his supplies. Blood oozed from the wound on the captain's leg, and she grimaced.

Averting her gaze from the sight, she threaded the needle Nolan had finished sterilizing with the flame from the kerosene lamp.

"I can do this part, at least," she said.

Nolan poured antiseptic on the wound and the captain hissed out a breath.

"Easy there." The captain grimaced. "You don't want to kill me tonight and save Dakota Red the pleasure tomorrow."

"Let's save the gallows humor for another time."

The captain's gaze flicked toward Tilly. "My apologies, ma'am. I'm accustomed to the company of men."

"I don't mind a little gallows humor. Whatever takes your mind off the pain."

"You're a kind woman."

Tilly's cheeks flushed.

"How long until your men come to look for you?" Nolan asked. "Any chance they'll get here before Friday?"

"That's the hope. If my men follow orders, they'll send out a search party today or tomorrow, give or take. I've been splitting my time between the fort and the men on lookout. Which means they may not realize I'm missing right away."

"Traveling alone was stupid," Nolan said. "You should have known better."

"I know, but I didn't know who I could trust."

"There's no need to assign blame," Tilly admonished. "The captain was doing what he thought was best."

Nolan scowled. "He knows what he's done. He knows he put us all in danger."

"Nolan!"

The captain held up a weak hand. "Mr. West is right. I behaved foolishly. I acted on my own."

"How many men are guarding the shipment on Friday?" Nolan asked.

"None."

A muscle ticked in Nolan's cheek. "None? What fool sends gold through this territory with no escort?"

"I'm sorry," the captain was ashen, his voice barely more than whisper. "There isn't a stagecoach coming through town on Friday because there isn't any gold."

Chapter Thirteen

Nolan felt as though the floor had collapsed beneath him. "What do you mean there's no gold?"

"The whole thing was a trap," the captain replied. "I thought it was you. I thought you were helping them."

Nolan rubbed the back of his neck. "You were wrong."

"I know that now."

Tilly handed over the needle. "We'll sort this out while you stitch up the wound. The captain has already lost too much blood."

Nodding grimly, Nolan accepted the needle and thread and began stitching. "You're fortunate the bullet went clean through your leg."

"I don't feel fortunate."

"What gave you the fool idea that I was involved?" Nolan demanded. "Let me guess—the lieutenant planted the idea."

"Lieutenant Perry encouraged my thinking, that's true. But there were other things that made me suspicious. No one in their right mind would man this station all alone. No one lasts out here for more than a few months. You did. You also took over the post the same month Dakota

Red and his brother were jailed in Yankton. When they broke out, the trail was leading directly to you."

"The trail led to the river." Nolan snorted. "I just happened to be on the other side. Did you really think I'd shelter a bunch of outlaws with a woman and three children staying at the relay station?"

"That's when I started second-guessing myself. We'd already set the plan in motion, and if you weren't involved, there would have been no harm done." The captain gripped his leg above where Nolan was stitching. His knuckles whitened and he pursed his lips. "There was no way you'd let a woman stay here if you had something planned. I figured you'd either caught a bad break, or you were innocent."

Tilly tore off another strip of bandages. "I can't believe you were suspicious of Nolan."

She gave his arm an encouraging squeeze, and his chest swelled. Her faith in him was heartening.

"He was the obvious choice," the captain said.

"When did you figure out that you wrong?" Nolan asked. "Before or after Dakota Red shot you?"

"About the same time."

"That's comforting."

"Look, I'm sorry. I was focused on you, but then we lost sight of Dakota Red. People don't vanish around here. There were no hoofprints, no signs of an encampment, nothing. I knew they couldn't cross the river without someone helping them. I figured I'd check on you. I figured even if you'd thrown in with the outlaws, you couldn't shoot me in front of the woman and her nieces."

"At least you had that much faith in me."

Nolan motioned for Tilly to finish tying up the wound. She wrapped more bandages around the captain's leg, then she stepped back and planted her hands on her hips. "What now?"

"I don't know," Nolan replied. "We're on our own. I don't know where the lieutenant has gone, but he sure didn't go for help."

Tilly crossed her arms and tapped her foot. "I didn't think our situation could get any worse, and yet it has. The captain is wounded and we're waiting on a shipment of gold that's never arriving."

"Yep." The captain struggled to sit upright. "I'm real sorry, ma'am. I never once suspected Lieutenant Perry would do something like this. He helped those outlaws across the river right under my nose."

"You're certain your men aren't looking for you?" Nolan hooked his arm beneath the man's shoulder and helped him to recline against the headboard. "Will your scout come back for you?"

"Eventually. With the weather, he'll probably figure I stayed overnight. He won't send out a search until tomorrow evening at the soonest."

"Unless Lieutenant Perry tells him not to search," Tilly said. "He's been keeping the cavalry away from town this whole time. He's not going to stop now."

"I'm not counting on a rescue," Nolan said. "With Perry in the area, who knows what he's telling the rest of your unit. For all we know, he's taken charge."

"I hadn't considered that."

"We have to assume that Tilly is right. He'll find a way to sabotage any rescue attempt. He's still thinks there's gold."

"I'm no help in this condition." The captain pressed the heel of his hand against his forehead. "What do you suggest?"

"We float out of here. They're keeping watch on the

horses. The girls will slow us down on foot, and you sure aren't going to make it very far without a horse. Our only choice is the river."

"You have a boat?"

"There's a boat that needs repairs in one of the barns near the edge of town. It's small, but it'll hold the six of us. I need at least a day to make repairs."

"How long before the outlaws notice you're up to something?" the captain asked. "Too risky."

"You can help us, Captain Ronald," Tilly said. "You can stay with the girls. You can keep watch on Dakota Red and the others. I'll work on the repairs with Nolan."

Nolan wiped his bloodied fingers on a towel. "I can't involve the girls."

"They're already involved," Tilly said. "What do you think will happen when the stagecoach fails to appear on Friday? We're all dead. You said as much yourself. Help isn't coming, and neither is the gold. We're on our own."

"All right," he conceded. "You've made your point. We need to start as soon as possible. First, we need a plan. I need some tools from the livery, which is risky. Dakota Red keeps track of what I take. He's not very worried about us escaping, but he's smart enough to protect his own hide."

Tilly paced the narrow space beside the bed. "We'll fetch the tools and erase the chalk marks. I doubt any of the men will even notice they're gone."

The captain frowned. "Chalk marks?"

"Never mind." Tilly flapped her hand. "It's a long story. But Nolan's organization will help us tremendously. Dakota Red keeps track of the tools by the empty chalk marks. As long as we're careful, he'll never be the wiser."

"We also need a distraction," Nolan said. "If we're

spending too much time in one building, they'll grow suspicious."

"They hardly pay any attention to us these days. Mostly they play cards or drink or sleep."

"What happens when they run out of whiskey?"

"That shouldn't happen for a while. Snyder found a stash in the saloon." Her cheeks were flush with excitement. "We simply need to outsmart them, which shouldn't be too difficult. With the girls' help, we'll track their movements. As long as we stay one step ahead of them, they'll never figure out what we're doing."

"You've convinced me, but I still don't like the idea," Nolan said. "Clearly we need the help of the children for this plan to work. Call them in."

Tilly stepped out and returned with the girls a moment later.

She kneeled before them. "We're going to play a game."

"Like tag?" Victoria asked.

"More like hide-and-seek," Tilly said. "Nolan needs to fetch some tools from the livery without the men staying in town noticing."

"Like taking a piece of cake without Mama finding out."

"Exactly!" Tilly exclaimed. "Cake is the perfect solution. We'll bake a cake for the outlaws. While I'm delivering the cake, Nolan can fetch his tools, and no one will be the wiser."

"How can we help?" Victoria asked.

"You can keep watch. We'll need to keep track of their movements."

"That shouldn't be hard," she said. "If they're not here or in their house, then they're at the livery."

"Which makes your job easier."

"That's all well and good for you people." Captain Ronald pressed a hand against the wound on his thigh. "How can I help?"

"You can help by keeping an eye on the girls while Nolan and I are working on the boat."

"All right," the captain grumbled. "But I feel as though I should be doing more."

"You should be resting. We need you strong for the escape."

Nolan exchanged a glance with Tilly. Their plan would work. It had to, because they were fresh out of other options.

Tilly and the girls gathered their supplies and baked a lopsided cake.

Tilly licked her thumb and studied their achievement. "It's not pretty, but it tastes good."

She transferred half of the cake to another plate, and wiped off the counter.

With the help of the girls, in another twenty minutes, she had the kitchen gleaming. Nolan returned from assisting Captain Ronald, and his eyes widened.

"Wow. You girls were busy."

"I know you don't like a mess, so we cleaned up."

He blinked. "You did this for me? Why do you care?"

"Because you care, and this is your home." She grasped the plate and presented their lopsided cake. "What do you think?"

"I think you're a genius."

She flushed beneath his praise.

"We're ready. Caroline has been keeping watch on the outlaws, and they're all playing cards in the undertaker's house. I'll deliver the cake while you retrieve your tools from the livery. The girls will keep watch. If one of the outlaws leaves the house before me, signal Nolan."

"How do we signal him?"

Victoria raised her hand. "I can start a fire."

"No!" Tilly placed a hand over her chest. "No fire. That will, um, that will take too long and it's far too dangerous. Instead, one of you can yell, 'Olly, olly, oxen free.' The men will think you're playing a game."

Victoria's shoulders drooped. "All right."

"Good. Let the games begin."

Elizabeth crossed her chubby arms and pouted. "I go with No-wan."

"Not today," Tilly said firmly. "You can stay with Captain Ronald, or you can go with your sisters."

A frown puckered her brow. "I stay."

Captain Ronald sighed. "Don't worry. I'll keep an eye on her."

"Be good for the captain," Tilly ordered. "Or no cake after supper."

Elizabeth's gaze flicked between the counter and the captain. "I be good."

"I thought so."

Tilly gathered herself. "Let's go."

With a firm grip on the plate, Tilly led the girls across the street toward the undertaker's house. She climbed shallow stairs to the front door and gave a firm knock.

A moment later, Charlie answered.

"Whaddya want?" he demanded.

Tilly wrinkled her nose at the acrid scents of pipe tobacco, whiskey and unwashed male. "We've brought you some cake."

"Huh?" He scratched behind his ear. "You trying to poison us or something?"

Tilly glared at him. "No. I am not trying to poison you."

"You take a bite."

"Who is it?" a voice called from the recesses of the house.

"They brung us cake," Charlie shouted back.

Tilly broke off a large chunk and stuffed the piece in her mouth. "There," she said, her voice muffled over the bite. "Are you happy? We aren't poisoning you."

Dakota Red appeared behind his brother. "Let her in, Charlie. I'm hungry."

Tilly carefully stepped over the heap of garbage blocking the corridor. The stench of smoke grew stronger and she stifled a cough. The dining room table was littered with empty bottles, discarded drinking glasses, playing cards and plates full of ashes.

Loath to touch anything, she tucked her elbows against her sides. "I've brought cake."

"Set it on the table," Dakota ordered, the chewed stub of a cigar protruding from his mouth. "Only half? Where's the other half?"

"The girls are eating the other half."

"Next time, bring the whole cake. I don't like sharing."

Tilly plastered a grin on her face. "Certainly." She hoped they spent a good long time in jail when this was all over. "I'll see you men at supper."

She slid the plate over the clearest spot on the table— a pile of discarded playing cards.

Carefully picking up her steps over the rubble, she made her way toward the door. Her heart pounded so loudly against her ribs, she feared they'd hear the racket. She sincerely hoped that Nolan had had enough time to acquire the tools he needed, because she couldn't stomach the stench in the house any longer.

They'd have to burn the building to the ground at this rate. There was no other way of cleaning out the filth. A mouse scuttled along the wall, and she shrieked and scooted away. If they had to distract the men with dessert in the future, she was leaving the cake on the porch stoop.

Once outside, she paused at the bottom of the steps. Gripping the railing, she bent at the waist, then took a few heaving breaths of fresh air.

She straightened and turned, but a hand caught her around the wrist.

Charlie loomed over her. He bent forward and she strained away, her back dug into the railing.

The outlaw leered. "Ain't you got something else for good ol' Charlie?"

Nolan dropped the tools and wiped the sweat from his brow. He'd loaded up his supplies and scrubbed away the chalk marks. Since the barn was on the opposite end of town, he'd sprinted the distance.

The girls jumped rope in the center of the street between the livery and the stagecoach relay station.

Halfway back to the station, he heard the call. "Olly, olly, oxen free!"

After hollering their warning, as agreed upon in advance, they dutifully dashed toward the safety of the relay station.

Nolan broke into a sprint again.

Charlie had Tilly bent over the railing.

Nolan added a burst of speed and launched himself at the outlaw. Caught by surprise, Charlie lost his balance. The two of them tumbled onto the street. Charlie came up swinging. Nolan ducked the first blow. He let the second blow catch him in the jaw. Charlie paused to savor his hit, and Nolan used the distraction to his advantage.

He caught Charlie beneath the chin with a left hook, then pummeled him with his right fist. The outlaw lurched and collapsed backward on the stairs.

Snyder and Dakota Red rushed through the doorway.

From his slumped position, Charlie yanked his side-arm from his holster. "That's it, stagecoach man. Now I'm going to kill ya."

A strange calm descended over Nolan. There was no-where to run, nowhere to hide. He'd faced death more than once in his life, and he was ready. He prayed Charlie only wounded him. Nolan still had Tilly and the girls to think about. Either way, he was ready to face his fate.

As Nolan braced for a bullet to rip through his flesh, Dakota Red kicked his brother's hand. The gunshot sounded and Nolan flinched. The slug whizzed past his ear. A second later the gun skittered across the porch, out of reach of Charlie's seeking hand.

Enraged, Charlie clawed toward his weapon. He'd nearly wrapped his fingers around the barrel when Sny-der wrestled him back.

Tilly rushed over and patted Nolan's chest. "Are you hit?"

"No. The bullet went wide."

The full realization of his near miss had yet to set in, leaving him in numb shock. In his mind he replayed the moment Charlie's finger tightened on the trigger. He'd nearly lost everything.

Tilly collapsed against him, and he buried his nose in her hair.

"Let me go." Charlie struggled against Snyder's hold. "Or I'll kill you both."

"Stop it!" Dakota Red ordered. "Stop right now."

Charlie stilled.

"You're a fool," Dakota Red snarled. "You're going to

ruin everything. Quit messing with that fellow's wife, or he's going to kill you. And I'm going to let him."

"You're going to let him kill me, huh?" Charlie swiped at the streak of blood on his chin. "I suppose you think he's more important to the plan than me."

"Yes, you idiot, he is more important to the plan than you. Near as I can tell, you're becoming a liability. I'm done serving time because of you and your fool stunts."

Tilly trembled against him and Nolan grasped her hand. "Come along. Let's leave them be."

"Not so fast," Dakota Red called from the porch. "How's that cavalry man doing?"

"Not good," Nolan replied. "He's lost a lot of blood. I'm not certain if he'll live through the night."

"If he dies, haul him down to the river and toss him in. I don't want him stinking up the place."

"Whatever you say."

Tilly grimaced and Nolan placed a hand on the small of her back. "Don't listen to him," he whispered. "They're trying to scare us."

"They're doing a good job."

"Let them fight amongst themselves."

He guided her away from the outlaws and led her toward the abandoned hotel, then shut the door behind them.

She covered her face with her hands. "Those men are awful. They're going to kill us when they discover the truth."

"At least we know for certain the cavalry isn't coming."

"How?"

"Dakota Red must know that no one is watching the ferry crossing anymore. He wouldn't have told us to dump Captain Ronald in the river if he thought the cavalry might spot him."

Her expression shifted. "You're right."

"I'm guessing Perry already called off the watch."

"Were you able to retrieve the proper tools?"

"I've got everything we need. The girls did well this afternoon. They signaled as soon as you walked out of the house."

Her shoulders sagged. "I'm glad."

Nolan touched her hair. "I didn't think Charlie would try anything with the other men around. We'll have to figure out another way to distract them in the future."

"The longer this goes on, the bolder he gets. He followed me outside. I'm worried about the next two days. They're getting restless and desperate. The place is an absolute pigsty."

"We stay with the plan. We let them think the captain is knocking at death's door. That will make our escape easier."

Tilly's expression turned wry. "For a deserted town, this place sure is getting crowded."

"No kidding."

"Your plan is going to work, right? It has to."

"It'll work."

A sense of foreboding descended over Nolan. While some of them were bound to escape, there was no way this ended well for all of them.

After facing Charlie's bullet, he was more than ready to make whatever sacrifice was needed to save Tilly and the girls.

He'd always wondered why he survived the war when so many other died. Now he had an answer.

Chapter Fourteen

For the first time in days, the sun peered through the clouds. In order to distract the girls, Tilly set up a tea party in the abandoned town square. They rummaged a table from the hotel, and brought supplies from the relay station.

Once they'd set the table with a cheery cloth and chipped cups and saucers, they searched the surrounding area for wildflowers. They gathered daisies, black-eyed Susans, camphor and purple chicory.

Caroline put together an arrangement in an empty milk bottle. Tilly set the second half of the lopsided cake in the center of the table near the flowers.

The four of them took their seats around the cheery setting.

Victoria grinned. "Mama never does things like this."

"Your mother is a very practical person," Tilly said, shaking out her napkin. "I'm not certain tea parties in the outdoors are very practical."

Elizabeth forked a piece of cake and scattered crumbs down the front of her pinafore. Caroline grimaced and Tilly shot her a quelling glance.

"We're here to have a little fun. No criticizing each other."

"Yes, Aunt Tilly," Caroline grumbled.

Elizabeth took another messy bite and Caroline grimaced, but remained silent.

Tilly raised the chipped teacup they'd scrounged from the abandoned restaurant. "To your mother."

The girls raised their glasses in unison.

After taking a sip, Victoria reached for her slice of cake. "Mama cries a lot."

"I think she misses Papa," Caroline said. "I miss Papa, too."

Tilly slumped in her seat. She hadn't been very charitable in her thoughts about Walter recently, but he was the girls' father, and they loved him. Eleanor had loved him, as well.

Walter might have made some mistakes in his life, but he'd left behind a beautiful family. Perhaps Eleanor hadn't been hiding her situation from Tilly out of spite, perhaps she'd been trying to protect her children from the truth. The girls deserved to remember him fondly.

"What do you miss most about your father?" Tilly asked.

"He let us do things that Mama didn't approve of," Victoria said. "He took us places Mama wouldn't take us."

Caroline giggled. "Do you remember when he took us to the dancing hall? There were velvet drapes on the windows and a crystal chandelier. There was a man practicing his piano, and Papa made him stop singing the words."

Tilly raised an eyebrow. The song must not have been suitable for young ears. "That sounds like fun."

"Mama met him on the front porch with her finger

waving," Victoria said. "I don't think she liked that he took us there."

"No harm done." Tilly refilled her tea from the coffee pot they'd repurposed as a teakettle. "I'm sure the velvet curtains were very pretty."

Elizabeth held up her empty plate with both hands. "More."

"All right, one more piece," Tilly said. "But that's all."

Elizabeth eagerly accepted the cake and shoveled a piece into her mouth.

Caroline shooed a fly from their flower arrangement. "I miss Mama. When will we see her again?"

"Soon," Tilly replied. "Very soon."

Lying to the girls sent her head throbbing. Nothing was certain for any of them.

Caroline choked back a sob. "I want to go home."

Her heart breaking, Tilly stood and wrapped her arms around her shoulders. "Soon, I promise. Very soon."

Victoria crossed her arms. "You're ruining the tea party, crybaby."

Tilly straightened. "Be nice to your sister."

"How come I have to be nice to her?"

"Because you're stuck with her for the rest of your life, that's why."

The two were stunned into silence before erupting into peals of laughter. Uncertain of the joke, but wanting to be a part of the fun, Elizabeth giggled.

Tilly joined them. "You will meet many people in your life, but your sisters will always know you best, because they've known you the longest."

Following the brief spat, the rest of the tea party passed in smiles. For a moment Tilly forgot about everything that was happening. She forgot about the outlaws and New York City and the future.

She forgot about everything except Nolan. He was never far from her thoughts.

She stared at the half-eaten cake on her plate. Eleanor *did* know her best. She *had* quit on most things in her life. Tilly snorted softly. She was already quitting on the widows and orphans, and she hadn't even packed her trunks.

She toyed with her fork and recalled the kisses she'd shared with Nolan. Wouldn't Eleanor be surprised at how she changed?

Of all the things she'd quit on, she couldn't imagine ever quitting on him.

The mood among the captives deteriorated rapidly. Though the outlaws kept mostly to themselves, their presence was a constant reminder of the ticking clock on the hostages' fate. Each hour that passed took them further away from safety, and brought them closer to the ultimate danger. They endured days with constant rain and only the occasional break of sunlight through the relentless cloud cover, exacerbating the unrest.

The previous evening, the outlaws had stayed up well into the night, and their antics had kept everyone awake. They'd even fired off gunshots at one point. The girls had proved remarkably stoic in the face of the disruption. According to the stories Nolan had heard from the girls, they'd passed far rowdier evenings in Virginia City. The adults were not as understanding of the disruptions.

Bleary-eyed and annoyed, Nolan stumbled into the kitchen and discovered Tilly awake and making coffee. At least he hadn't suffered a violent nightmare the previous evening, and for that he was grateful.

Instead he'd dreamed of crowds of people. Hundreds of nameless, faceless people brushing against him. He'd spotted Tilly in the distance. She'd smiled and waved and he'd walked toward her. At every turn, someone had blocked his path, and she'd been swallowed by the crowd.

In desperation, he'd shoved his way through the mob, pushing and elbowing the press of humanity. He'd caught a glimpse of her and followed her through an open door, only to discover he was locked in a tiny room with only a single candle in the corner. The flame flickered and disappeared, plunging him into darkness.

He'd woken in a cold sweat, but at least he hadn't thrashed or taken a swing at the shadows.

He stood on the threshold, unwilling to disturb her. She'd donned the green calico dress she'd worn the day of her arrival. Humming softly, she tucked a lock of her chestnut hair behind one ear. A smile softened her expression, and she gazed into the distance with a contemplative look on her face.

He held his breath, keeping quiet, leaving her to her pleasant thoughts. There'd been few enough enjoyable interludes for any of them lately. She was looking to the future, no doubt.

Growing up, he'd always taken the few minutes before sunrise to plan the day ahead. He'd wake with the morning light, his hands threaded behind his head, his gaze fixed on the familiar crack in the ceiling. Looking back, he'd always been thinking and planning, experimenting with new farming methods and new seeds. He missed the familiar surge of anticipation. He even missed the arguments with his father.

His father had been content with the old ways of doing things, while Nolan had been focused on the future. In a twist of irony, he'd gradually become his father—always looking backward. He desperately wanted to turn back the clock and become the man he'd been before.

Following his release from the prison camp, he'd thought he could recapture the person he'd once been. He'd thought he could brush aside the ill effects from his internment as easily as brushing travel dust from a coat. Instead, the changes had settled into the very marrow of his bones. He'd grown around them. Like the old cottonwood tree on his farm that had threaded its roots around a misshapen boulder until the rock had all but disappeared from sight. He'd absorbed the changes the war had brought, and he couldn't cut himself free without hacking off a part of himself, as well.

He'd spent the past several years trying to free himself, yet he feared the transformation was too ingrained. Like the old cottonwood tree that was forever entwined with the boulder. There was no excising his past.

Tilly stifled a yawn behind her hand. "The girls are already stirring. I'll keep watch while you work on the boat."

Drawn to her, he moved closer. Over the past few days, he'd seen the beauty within her, and his first impression of her had altered. How could he have ever thought her looks were somewhere between plain and pretty? She was lovely. How had he missed her dazzling radiance at that first meeting?

Snared by the strength of his feelings, he remained stock-still. A prudent man would put some space between them, at least until the intensity of the moment passed.

Nolan took another step nearer. "The damage to the boat is worse than I remembered. I'll need more time than I originally thought to complete the repairs."

She turned her wistful gaze on him. "What time is the stagecoach today?"

"Noon." His stomach clenched. Another stagecoach pulling through town was another chance to reach help, and another chance for disaster. The injury to Captain Ronald had brought home the precarious nature of their situation. "You and the girls should leave. Now. While the men are sleeping. I've got two saddles. You can be on your way in less than a half hour."

"What about you?" She clutched the edge of the stove. "I won't leave you behind."

"I can't leave the captain. He's injured. He can't ride yet. We said we'd take the first opportunity that presented itself, and this is an opportunity. Wake the girls and leave. Get as far from here as you can. They'll be slow to follow."

"And then what?" She pushed away from the stove and pressed the heels of her hands against her forehead. "I don't know where I'm going. I'll be wandering through Indian country alone with three girls. It's too dangerous. They'd catch up with us before we reach safety."

"You're in as much danger staying here."

"I can't leave."

"Why not?"

"Because I don't want to face the danger alone." She dashed at her eyes. "Now you know the truth. I'm a coward at heart."

He had a sudden need to comfort her. To pull her toward him. To cup her head in his hands and pull her lips to his own.

"You're not a coward. The idea of letting you out of my sight terrifies me. I only want what's best."

"Do you truly think the girls and I are safer if we run now?"

"I don't know."

"Then work on the boat." Her movements jerky, she set two mugs on the table. "It's safer for us to stay and wait and escape together. We can travel faster that way, and we certainly won't get lost."

She laughed hollowly.

He took another step closer, crowding her nearer to the stove, halting her agitating pacing. "I only want to do what's best for you and the girls."

"I know." She covered her eyes and inhaled a shaky breath. "I'm sorry. I haven't slept well in days. I feel as though I'm going mad."

The walls were closing in around them all. They were living on borrowed time. He knew well enough what she was feeling, how constant fear was invading her thoughts.

Human beings were incredibly malleable, adjusting to even the most appalling living conditions. Yet everyone had their limits.

"Living in fear is exhausting," he said.

"How did you survive Rock Island?" She flattened both palms against his chest. "How did you live in the uncertainty without going mad?"

He started at the shock of the contact. "You don't. Not entirely."

Her fingers were long and tapered, with neatly trimmed nails. The faint blue veins on the backs of her hands reminded him of how fragile she was, how delicate. He was acutely aware of her, entranced by her gentle touch.

Her fingers trembled against the rapid beating of his heart.

"Why do you say that?" she asked in a breathless whisper. "You're not mad."

"You've seen how I live."

"If keeping tidy is a sign of madness, then half the world would be in a sanitarium."

"There are other things. I sometimes count things." She was looking at him with far too much admiration.

She deserved the truth of his nature. "Obsessively. I count them and count them again."

"I don't understand." Her fingers curled into the material of his shirt. "What was the last thing you counted?"

"The day you discovered the raccoon in the stove. I counted all the plates. I prefer even numbers."

She didn't appear disgusted, only curious.

"Why?"

"I suppose because even numbers signify order. I feel I have some control of the world around me if I can create that order."

"I envy you." She lifted one shoulder in a careless shrug. "I'm remarkably unmoved by disorder. I've never told anyone this, but there's a part of me that needs chaos. I worry that if I had control over events around me, then I'd be responsible for their outcome. My sister always said that I was irresponsible, and I'm starting to think she was right."

"You're not irresponsible." He'd seen how she doted on her nieces. "We're simply opposites, you and I."

"Perhaps we have something to teach each other."

"There's nothing from me you want to learn. I've gotten worse over the years. I can't stand the thought of losing control. I thought I would heal, but I'm not."

Her smile was sympathetic, and he searched for any sign of pity. He could tolerate her disgust more than her pity.

"It's no wonder you've gotten worse living in this wilderness with nothing but your own thoughts to keep you company," she said. "I can't imagine anything worse."

"You don't understand." Her censure of his living conditions brought an unexpected flare of anger. "I shouldn't have spoken so candidly."

Her posture tensed. "You're right. I don't understand."

He rubbed his forehead. Attempting to explain the inexplicable was a waste of time and breath. He appreciated her caring, but he knew the truth of his condition. Remaining isolated was his best chance of recovering.

His father's own words came back to haunt him: *They'll think you've gone mad.*

"I shouldn't have pried," she said.

"It's all right." He'd erased the adoration from her eyes. There was no need to share any more confidences. "You were only trying to help. Some problems simply can't be fixed."

Tears sparkled on the edges of her eyelashes. "I'm afraid."

"I know." Without pausing to consider his action, he reached out and caught the moisture on the tip of his thumb. "I won't let anything happen to you and the girls. I'd give my life for you."

"I know."

"Would you…?" She tugged her lower lip between her teeth. "Would you hold me? Just for a moment."

He opened his arms and she collapsed against his chest with sob. "I don't want to go to New York anymore. I want to go home and crawl under the covers and sleep for a week."

Holding her trembling against him was sweet torture. His feelings for her were unlike anything he'd ever experienced. He'd known infatuation, he'd known longing. Never before had he known this soul-deep yearning.

"You'll go home, Tilly, I promise." He would not break that vow. His own life meant nothing in comparison. "Whatever I have to do, I'll see that you go home."

He rubbed her back in soothing circles and her arms tightened around his middle.

"I'm tired and confused." She sagged against him.

"There's always been somebody telling me what to do and when to do it. There's always been somebody criticizing my actions. First it was Eleanor, and then my father. Nothing I ever did was good enough for either of them. I've lived my whole life wanting to be independent and self-sufficient. I thought once I was away from them, I'd be different. Better, somehow. But I'm the same person, making all the same mistakes. Except without the benefit of someone correcting me."

"I think you're doing fine, Tilly. Better than fine. You've been superb."

"Independence is far more grueling than I imagined."

She tipped back her head and met his gaze. He touched her forehead with his own and let his lips rest against her sun-kissed apple cheeks. Their noses bumped, and he felt her smile. Her breath whispered against his face. The longing within him deepened, and he traced his lips toward the corner of her mouth.

She turned her head and caught his lips against hers. Her hands slid up his back and she deepened the tender embrace. Melting warmth flowed through his veins, and he shook from the force of his raw emotions.

Noises stirred from where Captain Ronald was sleeping. Nolan loosened his hold. He desperately wanted to ignore the interruption and shut out everything that stood between the two of them. For just this moment, he could pretend he was whole again. He could pretend all the world was new. Instead, he nuzzled her lips and set her away from him.

She stared at him, her cheeks flushed, looking as charmingly dazed as he felt.

The captain limped into the room. "Is there coffee?"

Though Nolan had already put a space between them, they both jumped in guilty confusion.

"On the stove," Tilly replied. She turned away and fumbled with the burner setting. "Should be ready soon."

The captain hobbled toward the promise of morning coffee. "What's the plan for today?"

"The boat," Nolan replied, surprised to find his voice calm and modulated against the rapid tempo of his heartbeat. "Repairs."

"The boat? What good is a boat again?"

"They're keeping a close watch on the horses. The river is our best chance. The boat is small, little more than a dinghy, and in bad repair."

"Have you crossed the river lately?" The captain gave a negative shake of his head. "The current is dangerous. I've never seen the water this fast or deep. Is there no other way?"

Nolan flicked a gaze toward Tilly. "The girls can't travel without horses. You're injured. It's miles by land to Yankton. We can make the trip in a fraction of the time by river. Unless you think help is coming, this is our best option."

"I doubt help is coming." The captain sat back in his chair. "At least not in time."

Tilly fiddled with the bun at the nape of her neck. "Time is in short supply."

She turned her back, and the captain looked between the two with a keen scrutiny. "I can see you've thought this through."

Nolan braced one hand against the wall and worked his foot into his boot. "The outlaws have been in one place too long. They're growing desperate. When the gold doesn't arrive as expected, they'll be infuriated. We have to be well out of their path when that happens."

"You've made your point." The captain slumped in his chair and stretched out his injured leg. "What an abominable mess. I snared myself with my own trap. My pride has taken a blow, I can tell you that much."

"Your pride is the least of our worries. I need to make the repairs without attracting attention. They don't watch us very closely, but they do watch us. They'll notice if we change our routine."

"Why don't the both of you go before the outlaws wake?" the captain said. "I'll keep an eye on the girls. I'll send one of them to fetch you when the men stir."

Tilly nodded eagerly. "I'd like that. I want to feel useful."

"You've been more than useful," Nolan assured her. As much as he wanted space between them to sort out his deepening feelings for her, he also wanted her near. "We should go. Quickly. We can assess the repairs and gather supplies before the men are fully awake."

"Thank you." Her eyes shimmered with gratitude. "I'll fetch my boots."

She returned quickly, her cheeks flushed with anticipation. Though Snyder dozed at his watch post, they took the extra precaution of slipping around the back of town, just in case.

Once inside the dilapidated barn, Tilly gasped. "Are you certain that can be repaired?"

The boat had been propped against the wall. There were two large, jagged holes in the bottom boards. The paint was chipped and flaking, and the bow was warped. Under the best of circumstances, the project was daunting.

"It will float," Nolan replied grimly. "But it's going to take patience and time."

"The two things we don't have."

"If we plan to accomplish the impossible, then we'd best get started."

"You think we can achieve the impossible?" She flashed him a teasing smile. "I'm supposed to be the optimist."

"You've changed me."

The flippant words hung in the air. Her eyes held a mutual understanding, and warmth passed between them. The moment of sharing soon evaporated, and he turned his back to hide his confusion. He *was* changing.

Was he healing?

He reached for a wooden box and his hand came away dirty. He absently retrieved his handkerchief and rubbed at the smudge. The stain remained. He scrubbed until the spot grew red and painful. Unable to breathe, he hung his head.

Some wounds ran too deep to heal.

Chapter Fifteen

Tilly stifled a sneeze. "How can I help?"

"I need a place to work." He glanced over his shoulder, not quite meeting her gaze. "We can clear a space."

A droplet splashed against her head and she scowled at the hole in the ceiling. "Let's find a place away from the leak."

"Good idea."

"I am heartily sick and tired of all this rain." She stepped over the growing puddle from the hole in the ceiling, cringing at the mud on her hem. She hadn't felt clean in days. The damp air and the mud sucking at her shoes had grown from being annoying to unbearable. "Have you ever so much rain in your life?"

"Not here. Not like this."

They worked in silence for several minutes. Tilly slanted a glance at Nolan. There were times when she felt as though there was something between them, a growing understanding. But there were other times when she felt as though she didn't exist to him. As though she was standing next to Eleanor in a roomful of potential suitors, and she was invisible beside her beautiful sister.

Frustrated by the turn of her thoughts, she stacked several wooden boxes. The more she considered the boat, the more uneasy she grew. Events were building inexorably toward a precipice, and she was terrified of peering over the edge.

Her worry for the girls threatened to consume her. How had Eleanor survived all those years living in the rough conditions of Virginia City? The men inhabiting the coarse mining town had the same desperate look as the outlaws.

Lately the idea of traveling to New York left her feeling flat and uninspired. What was wrong with her? She'd turned into the manifestation of Eleanor's predictions. She was the sort of person who flitted from activity to activity, without ever being content with anything.

She *was* flighty and irresponsible. She didn't know what she wanted for herself, she only knew what she *didn't* want.

Overcome with uncertainty, Tilly sat back on her heels. "When were you the happiest?"

"Why do you ask?" Nolan replied absently, his attention focused on maneuvering a rotted bale of hay from his path. "Seems an odd topic under the circumstances."

"I want to think about something happy. I'm tired of worrying about whether or not I'm going to die in the next week."

"No one will die, Tilly. Not if I can help it."

"I know. But I want to take my mind off things."

"Fair enough. Let me think."

He rolled back the sleeves on his shirt, and her gaze was riveted to his muscled forearms. Her mouth went dry.

"I was happiest when both my parents were alive," he said. "At home. I enjoyed farming. Working with the earth. Growing something. There was always a challenge."

He grasped the bow of the boat. His shirt stretched across his back, highlighting his straining muscles.

Tilly dabbed at her brow.

"I drove my father to distraction," Nolan continued. "I was always trying to find a better way of doing things— a better plant, a better crop rotation, a better seed mixture. My father preferred the tried-and-true methods. He wasn't much for experimentation."

Tilly gaped. She'd expected a yes-or-no answer, or one of his terse replies.

Encouraged by his success, she continued. "Why don't you farm now?"

"What's the point? The land is gone." He moved to stand before her. "Stay clear. I'm going to right this thing."

She scooted backward.

He pushed off on the stern. The boat teetered before falling. She cringed, expecting the wood to splinter into a thousand pieces. To her relief, the frame held together.

"Couldn't you petition for the return of your land?" she asked. "As a former soldier, you deserve nothing less."

"A former Confederate soldier."

"But what about the Reconstruction?"

"The Reconstruction died with President Lincoln. The land is lost to my family forever. Had my father chosen to side with the Union, things might have turned out differently."

"Where is your family now?"

"My father is all that's left. He moved to Cimarron Springs, Kansas, after he lost everything. His sister and her husband settled there."

"And you didn't want to be near him?"

"I tried. It didn't work out."

"You can still homestead in Nebraska and Kansas," she said. "They can't deny you a homestead."

He grasped one of the boxes she'd moved and placed it beneath the bowed edge for support. "Maybe I will. Someday."

"What are you waiting for?" She knew immediately that she'd broached a forbidden topic. The muscles along his back tensed. "Never mind. Only I've seen your garden. There's no way you lost heart in farming."

"That garden will go to waste soon enough. The railroad surveyors have already been through town. Won't be long before the train tracks follow. Maybe Pyrite will rise from the ashes as a train depot."

"What will you do then?"

"I'll keep moving. The Wyoming Territory. Maybe California."

"You'll find another solitary occupation?" The idea made her unbearably sad. "Don't you ever get lonely?"

"Yes." He gave a rueful laugh. "I've grown accustomed to the solitude. It's better for me that way."

"I couldn't stand living that way."

"I know."

There was something in his gaze she didn't quite understand. An intensity and a sorrow that hadn't been there before. Despite his words, she sensed he wasn't as content with his solitude as he'd have her believe.

"I envy you," she said.

"Why?"

"You have the freedom to go wherever you want, to do whatever you choose. You have no family connections. Nothing to hold you back. You could easily pick up and leave tomorrow, and you'd never have to answer to anyone."

"Independence is grueling."

"That's not fair." She sniffed. "You've turned my words against me."

"Your turn," he said. "When were you happiest?"

Her cheeks flushed. He'd given her an honest answer, and he deserved one in return. An answer she couldn't give. She couldn't admit that she'd discovered a new strength within herself these past few days. She'd found a purpose, though a precarious one.

"I was happiest before Eleanor was married. Afterward, everything changed. Everyone changed. My father was different, Eleanor was different. I was too naive to understand that my place in her life would never be the same. As much as I chafed against her control, she was always the glue that held us together. Once she moved away, we drifted apart. I suppose in some ways I've been lost since then. As much as I complain about Eleanor, there's a part of me that's afraid of being on my own. Until this week, I hadn't realized how dependent I am. Rebelling against my family has been my only identity. I want something different, something better, I suppose. Except I don't know what that is."

"You'll find a way."

"We're a lot alike, you and me."

"How do you figure?"

"We're both trying to hide the worst parts of ourselves from the rest of the world." She immediately regretted voicing her words aloud. "I'm sorry. I don't know why I said that. I only meant that you and I both want something uniquely our own."

They were practically strangers. In another day, they'd be little more than acquaintances. It wasn't as though they'd exchange letters. What did they have in common? They'd been thrown together under harrowing circumstances.

Yet they were irrevocably linked in ways she was just beginning to understand.

"You shouldn't compare yourself to me." Nolan stood from where he'd been crouching beside the boat. "I've never met anyone more open and honest than you."

"I'm honest with everyone but myself. Eleanor is right to doubt me. I'm always saying that I'm going to set off on my own, but I never quite seem to make that happen."

"You're on your own now."

"And suffering miserably," she replied. "I wasn't supposed to be on my own. Eleanor was supposed to accompany me. She stayed behind at the last minute. As much as I say I want my independence, I'm afraid of failing. I'm afraid of being alone. I've never been comfortable in solitude. I've always needed people around. I'm afraid if I get to know myself, I won't like who I am."

"You might be surprised."

He turned away, but not before she caught a glimpse of his face. His bleak expression spoke more than a thousand words between them.

She preferred the bustle of activity and he preferred his solitude. They were different in temperaments but they were both the same in spirit.

They were both hiding from themselves.

As he waited for the next stagecoach, Nolan couldn't shake the feeling he was being watched. The hairs on the nape of his neck pricked and he hitched his shoulders. The brush between the buildings shook. Instantly alert, he studied the shadows. In a squall of feathers, a flock of blackbirds erupted into the sky.

He blew out the breath he'd been holding in a low whistle. This was the last stagecoach before the supposed gold shipment. Their time was running short, and the tension was robbing him of his common sense. Of course he was being watched. The outlaws had taken up their usual places. Charlie had positioned himself in his sharp-shooter perch, and Snyder was waiting in the relay station, ensuring Tilly played her role.

Dakota Red balanced on the top rung of the corral. "I'm going to miss you, stagecoach man."

"I don't return the sentiment."

The outlaw chuckled. "See? That's what I like about you. Your honesty. I can tell you're getting restless, which is why I'm keeping an extra close watch on you today. I don't want you getting desperate and trying something stupid. You've got them girls to think about, remember? We can't leave Charlie alone with your wife. Especially if you ain't around to defend her. You do right by me, and I'll do right by you."

A distant call came from the direction of the river.

"You better get out of sight," Nolan said. "That's the bugle call."

"We've got too many people up at the relay station. If there are passengers, tell them you're not serving lunch. I don't trust the captain to keep his mouth shut. That's the problem with those military men, they're always thinking they gotta be in charge."

"The passengers will question the change in routine."

"Tell 'em anything, but make it convincing. I don't have to remind you what's at stake."

Nolan slapped the reins against the horses and urged them into position. As the next stagecoach approached, the team struggled against his hold.

English Bob and his outrider, Gerard, were right on schedule.

Busy with the reins, he didn't immediately greet the driver.

English Bob leaped from his post and winked. "We've got some interesting passengers today, I'll tell you that much."

Nolan could only nod in return. The driver reached for the bridle of the lead horse. English Bob wasn't particularly tall, but was solidly built.

The driver cast a glance over his shoulder, then peered at Nolan from beneath the brim of his hat. "You're quiet today."

"We've had some trouble."

"What kind of trouble?"

"You'd better fetch the passengers," Nolan said. "I have an announcement that affects you all."

Without waiting for Gerard's assistance, two men emerged from the carriage. They were young, not yet in their midtwenties. They practically sprang from the confinement, their bottled energy evident. They had the sort of looks that brought to mind Captain Ronald's soldiers. A fresh-faced, clean-shaven exuberance with a hint of youthful smugness.

The first man stretched his arms over his head and arched his back before straightening. "That is a miserable mode of travel."

The second man caught sight of Nolan. "This is the supper stop, right? What are you serving?"

"No supper today," Nolan replied. "Change of plans."

"What do you mean?" the first man demanded. "We're hungry. We were told this is the supper stop."

The barrel of Charlie's gun glinted. Nolan slanted a glance at the driver. English Bob worked the buckles on the hitched team, his face impassive.

Nolan shifted. "One of the passengers came through town real sick. He's up at the house. Looks like scarlet fever."

The first man visibly recoiled. "Are you certain?"

"Not for certain. It's your hide if you want to risk it." Nolan shrugged. "The fellow looked real bad the last time I saw him. Don't know if he'll pull through."

The second man placed his hand on his friend's shoulder. "We can find something at the next stop."

His friend gave a look of disgust and jerked away.

"We'll just stretch our legs, if it's all right with you."

"Don't go far. The change of horses won't take long."

The two were liable to get themselves shot if they strayed too close to Charlie. At least one thing had gone smoothly. They hadn't put up more of an argument about supper.

A sharp rap sounded from inside the carriage.

"I'm waiting," a feminine voice called. Despite the closed door, her shrill voice carried the distance. "I will be informing your superiors at the Pioneer Stagecoach offices of this shoddy service."

Gerard's shoulders rose and fell with his deep sigh, and his face took an expression of long suffering. "Yes, ma'am."

The outrider stowed his shotgun beneath the driver's seat. His footsteps dragging, Gerard approached the door. He paused for a moment, as though gathering himself for a great ordeal. With deliberate care, he lowered the stairs. Before he could step out of the way, the door swung open, nearly clipping his nose.

Gerard reared backward, tripped over a dirt clod and landed on the soft earth.

An imposing woman with familiar blue eyes paused with her foot on the top stair. "Don't just sit there. I need a hand."

Nolan might have laughed at Gerard's predicament except the woman's eyes drew his attention once more.

Though her face was scrunched in an annoying frown, her looks were striking. She had the sort of flamboyant beauty that turned men's heads.

She wore a burgundy jacket over her white shirtwaist and matching burgundy skirt. A feathered hat topped her head. As Gerard struggled upright, she huffed and traversed the stairs unassisted.

Nolan felt the blood drain from his face.

Eleanor had arrived.

Chapter Sixteen

Nolan studied the new arrival. So this was Eleanor, Tilly's sister. Eleanor's hair was darker, and her complexion, unlike Tilly's, was untouched by the sun. But there was no mistaking those distinctive blue eyes, a trait both sisters shared.

Though he'd known her arrival was a possibility, Nolan was taken aback by her sudden appearance. The last thing he needed was another civilian in their midst. He already had enough complications and lies spinning around in his head. His gaze skittered toward the livery and back to the woman.

There might be a solution that benefited them all. He only hoped that fortune favored the foolish.

As long as the outlaws remained out of sight, Eleanor might escape this mess none the wiser.

"English Bob," Nolan called. "Can you see to the horses?"

The driver stood and dusted his pants. "Sure thing."

As Nolan handed over the reins, English Bob leaned closer.

"Anything to avoid dealing with that woman. Thankfully them other two men boarded when they did. She's a talker. Kept leaning out the window and complaining. I was sorely tempted to clip that feathered hat on a tree."

Eleanor paced before the stagecoach. "Is this the supper stop?"

"Yes," Nolan replied. "But there's been a problem. You'll have to wait here, ma'am."

In order for the plan to work, the sisters must remain separated until the right moment. As far as Eleanor was concerned, Tilly had traveled well ahead of her. Eleanor definitely wasn't expecting Tilly and her daughters in Pyrite. Which meant his plan had a slight hitch.

"I will do no such thing." She removed one of her gloves and slapped the leather against her palm. "I'm famished. We've been twice postponed this morning. I cannot afford any more delays. My children are waiting for me."

There was a catch in her voice at the mention of her children, and indecision temporarily rooted Nolan's feet to the ground. His heart went out to her. She was clearly tired and out of sorts. He shook off the hesitation. There was no time to explain. If he wanted to help both sisters, he had to speak with Dakota Red before he made any decisions.

"I need to check on something." Nolan touched the brim of his hat. "This will only take a moment, ma'am."

He ducked inside the livery and secured the door behind him.

Dakota Red pressed his gun against Nolan's side. "What's gotten in to you, stagecoach man?"

"The passenger that's just arrived. She's the girls' mother."

"What girls?"

"The, um, my nieces. Those girls. The girls that have been here the entire time. Who do you think?"

Dakota Red leaned around him and peered through the crack in the double doors. "So?"

"She's come to take the children home."

"I don't follow."

"My nieces." Nolan gritted his teeth. "She doesn't know what's happening. Let her take the children and leave. She won't know the difference, and you'll have three less people to watch."

"She's your sister-in-law?"

"Yes," he hissed.

He could barely keep up with the lies himself. He hoped the confusion of discovering her children in Pyrite overrode her other concerns, or they were all in trouble.

The outlaw studied Eleanor. "She's got a voice on her that could peel the paint off the walls." Dakota Red squinted. "She's prettier than her sister. I'll give her that much."

Nolan was surrounded by idiots. Blind idiots. "Let the children leave with their mother."

"I don't know. Something don't seem right. Why didn't you tell me she was coming? What are you hiding, stage-coach man?"

"She's early."

Nolan pressed his fingertips against his eyelids until he saw stars. He'd picked the most remote location he could find. Instead of finding solitude, he was playing host to an ever-increasing multitude of guests. The only thing that was missing was a regiment of Captain Ronald's men.

Dakota Red's gaze narrowed. "I don't trust you. Them girls will say something about us."

"They don't know anything, remember? They don't know why you're here. They don't know who you are."

The outlaw scratched his chin. "Where's she from? Their mother?"

"Virginia City."

"This place is getting awful crowded. I don't mind losing a few folks. But I'm taking a risk here, stagecoach man. I've got my face on Wanted posters wallpapering Virginia City."

"She hasn't seen you." Through the cracks in the door Nolan, watched the pacing shadow. "Please. On my honor as a Confederate soldier, I won't betray you. My concern is for the safety of the children."

The outlaw's mouth screwed up. "All right. You fetch them girls and send them on their way with their mother. You've got fifteen minutes. Don't try anything or I'll kill you myself."

Nolan whipped around as the door slid open.

"What is the meaning of this?" Eleanor demanded. "What is the delay?"

She caught sight of Dakota Red. "Who is this man?"

"A stable hand," Nolan replied easily.

"But he's so familiar." She stepped closer. "I'm certain I know you. I've seen your face."

"I don't think you have." The outlaw presented her with his profile. "I don't get out much."

"You are very familiar. Have you been to Virginia City? My late husband employed several men at his gold mine. Are you familiar with the Lehmann Mining Company?"

"Never heard of it. Never been to Virginia City."

"Oh." She opened and closed her mouth. "Oh, dear. You're a—"

Immediately following her shocked declaration, Eleanor crumpled in a faint.

Nolan lunged and caught her beneath the arms, then lowered her to the hay-strewn ground.

"Told you my face was all over Virginia City." Dakota Red nudged her with his foot. "Deal's off. She recognized me."

Nolan nearly shouted his frustration. He'd been so close to getting the girls safely out of town. If only Eleanor had waited.

The outlaw cocked his pistol. "I don't like killing women, but she knows too much."

Eleanor moaned and stirred, and Nolan splayed his hands. "She stays. I'll get rid of the stagecoach. Your plan will still work."

"This place is getting awfully crowded. I don't like being outnumbered."

"What have you got to fear? Your hostages are two women, three children and a lame cavalry officer."

"And you."

"And me."

"Don't sound so bad when you say it like that."

"We're hardly a threat," Nolan said. "There's still a way for your plan to work. We all want this mess over and done with. I'll steal the gold from the stagecoach. You can take all the horses, that will guarantee your head start. When they figure out the gold is missing, they'll think I stole it. You'll have a full day's ride ahead of the cavalry before they know you're missing. If you murder her now, and you don't get the gold, you'll hang for certain. I'd save the killing until after you've got the money."

"That was always the plan."

Nolan's blood chilled. Perhaps the outlaws would settle for killing him and the captain and letting the girls go free. "Your plan will still work."

Eleanor groaned and Nolan hoisted her into his arms

with a muttered apology. Even if he lived to tell the tale, no one was going to believe him. He had no sooner solved one problem than another one sprang up in its place.

Not to mention he currently had another difficulty. He needed the stagecoach and the two passengers gone before Eleanor came around, or she'd wake up screaming and guarantee them into an early grave.

Much to his relief, English Bob and Gerard had finished changing out the team of horses by the time he returned outside with Eleanor in his arms.

The outrider gaped. "What happened?"

"The lady has taken ill. She can't travel. She insists on staying here until she's well."

"All right." English Bob agreed with shocking speed. "You got enough rooms for all the sick people staying here?"

"Just."

The two male passengers circled around the corral, and Nolan adjusted Eleanor in his arms.

The first passenger did a double take. "What's wrong with her?"

"She's sick. She's staying."

The second man breathed a sigh of relief, then caught himself. "Sorry to hear that. We'll miss her, um, conversation. She enjoyed talking. A lot."

The driver and the outrider clambered atop the stagecoach. "C'mon, boys," English Bob called. "I'm leaving. With or without you."

With a last glance at Eleanor, the passengers swiftly returned to the stagecoach. No one wanted to risk Eleanor waking.

Nolan adjusted his burden. He'd taken this job for the peace and quiet. He was going to demand a raise the next time the owner of the Pioneer Stagecoach passed through town. They certainly didn't pay him enough for all his troubles.

The driver tipped his hat, and Nolan lifted his eyes heavenward, offering up a brief prayer of thanks.

This situation was growing more ridiculous by the moment. At this point, he wouldn't blink an eye if a traveling circus set up tents in town. He sincerely doubted anything would surprise him at this point. If they all survived unscathed, he'd have a good belly laugh remembering the look on English Bob's face.

He'd certainly never forget the look on Eleanor's face when she'd recognized Dakota Red from his Wanted poster.

Eleanor stirred in his arms. "What happened?"

"You fainted, ma'am."

"Set me down this instant."

"Certainly."

Nolan masked his grimace and set her on her feet.

The stagecoach driver shouted and the horses surged ahead in a rattle of harnesses. Nolan nearly collapsed. He'd dodged a disaster. For the first time in a week, something had gone has planned.

"Why is the stagecoach leaving?" Eleanor shrieked, her arms flailing. "I'm supposed to be on that stagecoach."

Her face flushed, and he noted the exact moment she recalled the reason for her earlier faint.

"Help!" she screamed. "I've been kidnapped!"

Tilly heard the commotion all the way from the relay station. Captain Ronald hobbled into the room.

"You have to be careful," she said, jerking her head over her shoulder. "You're supposed to be dying."

"Snyder is gone," the captain replied defensively. "He left as soon as the stagecoach took off."

Another scream sounded.

"What's wrong?" the captain demanded. "What's happened?"

"I don't know." Tilly wiped her hands on a towel. The captain was far too accustomed to giving orders. "Stay in here, and I'll see what's wrong."

"You're just a woman. You should stay here. Where it's safe."

"You've been shot."

"No matter."

She rolled her eyes. "You're risking our plan of escape. If the outlaws know how well you're getting around, they'll watch you."

"That woman is clearly in distress."

"I'll make you a bargain. If you can beat me to the door, you can see what's happening first."

The comment wasn't very charitable, but she didn't appreciate being referred to as "just" a woman.

As the captain limped behind her, Tilly stepped out the door. Nolan strode toward her, a woman marching beside him.

Tilly's stomach dropped. "Eleanor!"

"I demand an explanation! I have been kidnapped." Eleanor cupped her hands over her mouth. "Help me! I've been kidnapped. Someone help me!"

Tilly picked up her step and snatched her sister's arm. "Be quiet, Eleanor. I can explain everything."

"This man accosted me." Eleanor's expression shifted, and she tucked her hands against her chest. "There's an outlaw on these premises! I saw him."

"I know," Tilly soothed. "Come inside and I'll fetch the girls. I'll fix you a cup of tea."

"The girls? What are the girls doing in the middle of nowhere? What are you doing here, Tilly?" Eleanor pressed the back of her hand against her forehead. "Oh, dear, I fear I'm swooning again."

Tilly ushered her inside, where the captain waited. Eleanor glanced at the handsome captain and her cheeks flushed. She collapsed strategically, or so Tilly thought, and Captain Ronald caught her. He staggered against the strain on his injury.

"You'd best carry her, Nolan." Tilly heaved a sigh. "I'm so sorry. Eleanor has always had a flare for the dramatic. I'll fetch the girls."

"I'll see to her." Nolan gathered the prone woman. "I'll put her in the girls' room."

The captain reluctantly released his hold on Eleanor and Nolan rested her sister on the counterpane and backed away. As she went to fetch the girls, she noticed the captain smooth his hair and straighten his lapels.

Tilly returned with the girls, who'd been playing near the blackberry bushes. Since the incident with the jail cell, they'd limited the girls' play area during the time the stagecoaches passed through town.

Once inside, Victoria caught sight of her mother and dashed over. "She's fainted again, hasn't she? She's always fainting."

The three girls crowded around their mother.

"Your mother has had a shock." Tilly approached the doorway and stood beside Nolan "She wasn't expecting us to be here."

"Why *are* we still here?" Caroline asked. "Why didn't we get on the stagecoach with Mama?"

"I'll explain everything later," Tilly replied, unbearably weary.

Eleanor's arrival complicated an already impossible

situation. The chance of the seven of them escaping was slim. While Tilly was grateful the girls had been reunited with their mother, she feared for their safety.

"How come later never comes when you're an adult?" Carolina's quizzical expression matched her sisters. "Adults are always saying things like that, but then you never answer."

"I know what it means." Victoria harrumphed. "It means they don't want to answer. At all."

"Oh." Caroline gaped. "That explains a lot."

Nolan drew Tilly aside. "I'm sorry. I almost convinced Dakota Red to let Eleanor leave with the girls."

The frustration in his voice was obvious.

Tilly longed to comfort him as he'd comforted her, but she was painfully aware of their audience. "What happened?"

"She interrupted my plea. She recognized Dakota Red from a Wanted poster she'd seen in Virginia City. He couldn't let her leave after that."

Captain Ronald peered over Tilly's shoulder. "How is the young lady? Was she traveling with her husband?"

"My sister is widowed."

The captain slid his thumb down the muttonchops on his chin. "Widowed, you say."

Tilly stifled a sigh. At least she no longer had to contend with the captain's halfhearted flirtation. He'd be fully occupied with Eleanor from now on.

The captain gazed at Eleanor's beautiful face in repose, and his expression turned wistful. "Can I be of assistance?"

Tilly prodded him back toward the table. "She's fine. She's had a shock. Rest your leg. Eleanor will need you at your best if we find a way to escape."

"Yes. Of course." He stared past her into Eleanor's room. "I'll be at the ready. You may depend on that."

Tilly might as well have been part of the background for all the captain was paying attention to her. Even in a faint her sister attracted admirers. Though she sensed her sister's faint was more for effect than an actual affliction, she'd best check on her.

Eleanor's eyes fluttered open. "What is it? What's happened?"

Tilly groaned. Therein lay the difficulty. With the girls, they were dancing a line around the truth.

Tilly smoothed a hand over Victoria's hair. "Girls, I need a moment alone with your mother."

"But she's only just got here," Caroline said, pouting. "We haven't seen her in days and days."

"Seven days," Victoria chimed in.

"Mama." Elizabeth's lower lip protruded in a pout. "Want Mama."

"I promise I'll be quick." Tilly urged them from the room. "Run along."

Shoulders slumped, the girls dutifully exited the room. Tilly ignored her twinge of guilt. Though the girls were anxious to see their mother, they'd have to wait. Their lives were at stake, after all.

Tilly fluffed the pillows behind Eleanor's head and spoke in low voice. "You're being held hostage by three outlaws at a relay station in the abandoned town of Pyrite, Nebraska, along with me, your daughters, the stagecoach manager and a wounded cavalry officer."

"I never did understand your sense of humor, Matilda," Eleanor huffed. "I hold you to blame for this. I'm sure it's something you've done."

"Do not call me Matilda." Tilly clenched her jaw. "We

haven't told the girls that the men are outlaws. We didn't want to worry them. Don't say anything."

Recovering quickly, Eleanor pushed herself upright. "My girls are being held by outlaws? How could you have done this?"

"I've done nothing," Tilly insisted.

"These sorts of things never happen to me."

"Really? Because this sort of thing *just* happened to you. If you had listened to Nolan instead of butting in on his conversation, you'd be on your way to Omaha with the girls."

"Whatever are you babbling about? Who is this Nolan person?"

"Nolan, um, Mr. West, is in charge of this stagecoach stop. He was attempting to negotiate the release of the girls when you barged in and recognized the outlaw. Dakota Red couldn't let you leave after that."

"How was I supposed to know this horrible town had been overrun by outlaws? Blaming me is entirely unfair."

"Never mind," Tilly said wearily. There was no use arguing with Eleanor. She always had the last word. "Your girls have missed you. They want to see you."

She turned on her heel and stalked from the room. The girls rushed past her, calling greetings to their mother without giving Tilly a second glance. Tilly suppressed a sigh. Understanding the girls' enthusiasm only made the sting worse.

The two men exchanged a glance.

Tilly slammed a plate on the table. "Are you hungry?"

"Not particularly," Nolan said.

"Good. Let's eat."

Captain Ronald braced his hands on the table and lowered himself onto a chair. "Would someone mind explaining what's happened?"

Tilly clutched her head. "It's a long story."

"We appear to have an abundance of time."

Once she'd completed her explanations, the captain leaned back in his seat. "Your poor sister. She's had a tough time lately."

"Yes. Poor Eleanor." Tilly braced her chin on her hand. "This has been awful for her."

Eleanor appeared in the doorway.

She held a handkerchief before her mouth. "What is this I hear about guns?"

Tilly stood and took her sister's hand, leading her to the table. "Not in front of the girls." She plucked a basket from the counter. "Why don't you three gather some blackberries for your mother?"

"Mama!" Elizabeth clapped. "Boo-berries."

"Do we have to?" Victoria grumbled. "I want to stay."

"Run along." Tilly nudged her on the shoulder. "We'll make muffins tonight."

"You're not my mother," Victoria declared. "You can't tell me what to do."

"I'm your mother and I'm telling you to gather some blackberries." Eleanor straightened her spine. "Tilly, give them a smaller bowl. They'll never fill that."

"It's raining," Victoria whispered to her sister. "Mama hasn't even noticed that she's letting us play in the rain."

"Hush," Caroline ordered. "Or she'll change her mind."

Her cheeks burning, Tilly dutifully retrieved a smaller bowl. As though sensing her humiliation, Caroline gave her an encouraging smile. Tilly's stomach dipped. Eleanor had only just arrived and she'd already been demoted. Eleanor was treating her as though she was a child, and Caroline's commiseration only made it worse.

"I demand an explanation." Eleanor gracefully perched on the edge of a chair. "I have children. What sort of danger have you gotten us into, Tilly? What's this Caroline tells me about being locked in a jail cell? I entrusted you with a very simple task. You were to safely accompany the children home to Walter's parents in Omaha. I knew I never should have trusted you."

"Nothing was Tilly's fault," Nolan said. "She's the reason we're all still alive and planning an escape."

Eleanor flicked a glance in his direction, and Tilly sensed she'd eliminated the stagecoach man as an ally. Her sister turned her attention toward Captain Ronald, whose admiration was obvious.

"I don't believe we've been introduced." Eleanor held out a limp hand in the captain's direction. "I'm Mrs. Lehmann."

Tilly was fairly certain her sister's eyelashes fluttered.

"I'm Captain Ronald, ma'am." The captain awkwardly stood and bent at the waist. "I'll do everything in my power to keep your family safe, ma'am."

"The girls haven't eaten properly in days. Victoria says you've been feeding them nothing but berries and muffins." Eleanor stood. "Their clothing is a mess. Elizabeth is covered in stains."

"I haven't exactly had time for washing up."

"Even in the best of circumstances, you've never been responsible. They need routine. They need a schedule. You wouldn't understand, dear, not having children of your own."

"Captain Ronald." Nolan stood and shuffled his feet. "We should see to Eleanor's bags. They've been left in the rain. I'll bring them around back so you can assist me and still stay out of sight."

"Of course. Right away." The captain stood and limped after Nolan. He paused before Eleanor. "It's a pleasure to meet you, Mrs. Lehmann."

Tilly groaned. Though she was grateful for their polite exit, the humiliation stung. Her annoyance blossomed into full-blown anger.

She wasn't one of Eleanor's children, she was her sister. Her equal. And it was high time Eleanor started treating her as one.

Chapter Seventeen

Once the men were out of earshot, Tilly leaned forward. "I'm not your servant, I'm your sister. I set my own plans aside to help you, and all you've done is complain. If you didn't want my help, you shouldn't have asked me."

Eleanor assumed an expression of weary boredom. "I'd almost forgotten about your trip to New York City. We both know that was just another one of your foolish ideas. You'd have found an excuse not to go. Something else would have attracted your attention. You never could stay with one thing. You always find an excuse to quit."

"That's not true."

Tilly ducked her head. The widows and orphans seemed a lifetime ago. No one could blame her for being distracted by their current situation.

"It's true and you know it," Eleanor insisted. "I have a stack of partially embroidered towels that you never finished. Remember when you were going to write that novel? How many pages have you written? Five? Ten? Don't blame me because you delayed a trip you were never going to take in the first place."

"I'm sorry that I couldn't be as perfect as you, Eleanor."

"Don't take that tone with me. It isn't my fault you can't stick with one thing for very long. I'm hardly to blame. You have no idea what I've been through these past few months."

"What have you been through?" Tilly clenched her hands. "Why did you stay behind?"

Eleanor flushed. "I told you. I had things to do and the girls would have gotten in the way."

"The girls say that you despise the bank. An odd comment, don't you think?"

Eleanor shot to her feet and whirled away. "You can't pay any attention to what children say. Surely you know better."

"If you're having troubles, Eleanor, you should confide in me. Father and I can help."

"Help? From you? That's rich."

"Admitting you need help isn't a sin."

Eleanor spun back around and pointed her index finger. "Don't you dare pass judgment on me."

Tilly had obviously touched a nerve. Her history with Eleanor had taught her that this was the time for retreat. When Eleanor felt threatened, she attacked. And Eleanor had always been the better verbal warrior.

These past few weeks had stretched Tilly's nerves to the breaking point, and she wasn't afraid of Eleanor any longer. After facing down sure death at the hands of a band of outlaws, she was itching for a quarrel.

"Why shouldn't I pass judgment on you?" Tilly demanded. "You don't have any problems judging me. You've been criticizing me for the whole of my life. Nothing has ever been good enough for you."

"You brought it on yourself. I tried to give you direction, to give you guidance, but you never listen. Look where it's gotten you! You're still living under Father's roof."

"And you're living with your in-laws. How is that better?"

"I have children. It's different."

"Is that what this is about?" Tilly threw up her hands. "Am I some sort of low-water mark for you? As long as you're doing better than me, you're winning somehow?"

"That's not it at all, and you know it. Stop acting like a child."

"Stop treating me like a child. I'm not one of your girls. I'm your sister." Tilly heaved a fortifying breath. "I take that back. I'd prefer if you treat me like Caroline or Victoria or Elizabeth. You're far kinder to them than you are to me."

"I have never been unkind to you."

"Really? Since you have such an excellent memory for all of my transgressions, name one thing that I've done that's good enough for you. Name one thing I've done that meets your high standards. Give me one example and I will end this argument."

"This isn't an argument." Eleanor flicked her collar. "This is a ridiculous conversation. I haven't seen the girls for a week, and what are you doing? You're keeping me from them with your childish temper tantrum."

She stood and strode toward the door.

Tilly blocked her exit. "You're running away because you know I'm right."

"With all that's happening, I refuse to have this conversation with you. My only fault is expecting more from you than you expect from yourself. Low expectations have always been your downfall. You could have married that nice young man who worked for father."

"Marry one of father's law clerks? Like you?"

"You could have done worse."

"He wasn't interested in me. He was only calling on me in the hopes of seeing you."

"How do you know?" Eleanor fiddled with her collar. "Did you ever give him any encouragement?"

"Maybe I didn't try as hard as I could have. But you, Eleanor, have always demanded far too much of people. And that has been *your* downfall."

Tilly turned, stormed from the room and continued outside. She expected Eleanor to be close on her heels, shouting and calling for her to stop. Eleanor had never let another person get the last word in an argument.

She'd nearly reached the end of Main Street before she realized she was standing alone. A sharp breeze rippled the overgrowth of bushes between the abandoned buildings. Tilly shivered and cupped her elbows.

Eleanor's words rang in her ears. She'd never finished the stupid towels because Eleanor had criticized her stitches, and she'd lost interest. She hadn't quit her work with the war effort—the work had ended when peace was declared. Then again, why travel all the way to New York when there were plenty of widows and orphans who needed assistance in Omaha?

She'd made her plans to leave shortly after learning that Eleanor was returning to Omaha. She hadn't put together those two events until just this moment. She'd had three years of modest success. She'd worked with Father in his law office, and she'd served on her committees.

She didn't want to go back to living in Eleanor's shadow. Was she quitting on her sister, or quitting on herself?

Her head throbbed and she pressed her fingers against her temples. Snippets of conversation from the girls came rushing back. Despite Eleanor's protests, Tilly recalled her arguments with Eleanor over the years. Eleanor grew most critical of Tilly when her own life was faltering. Shifting the focus onto Tilly deflected the notice from her own failings.

Tilly dropped her hands to her sides. She was done being Eleanor's scapegoat. Recommitted to finishing their argument, she spun on her heels and froze.

Charlie strolled from the shadows beneath the eve of the abandoned hotel.

His lip curled up in a sneer. "Where do you think you're going?"

Fear quickly replaced her self-righteous anger.

Tilly took a cautious step back. "Nowhere."

She searched for any sign of Captain Ronald or Nolan. How long would it be before they noticed she was missing? She'd broken the most important rule in dealing with the outlaws: never be caught alone with Charlie.

"I didn't think you were going anywhere." He grinned. "Or maybe you were coming to find me."

Charlie cradled the scattergun in his hands. His newly acquired sidearm was stowed in a gun belt strapped around his waist. Tilly frantically searched for an escape. They were too far from the livery and the relay station. There was a chance no one would hear her shouts even if she called for help.

Charlie advanced on her. "You're not as pretty as your sister, but old Charlie likes you," he drawled. "That has to mean something. Come on over here and talk to me."

She pivoted on her heel, ignoring his softly spoken order. There was no help coming, and she had no way of defending herself.

As she strode toward the relative safety of the relay station, she felt his steps behind her. Her heart pounded in her chest. She glanced over her shoulder. She'd lengthened the distance between them, but he showed no signs of abandoning his pursuit.

Her blood chilled. He wasn't chasing her, he was stalking her.

Tilly broke into a run. Something caught her sleeve and she shrieked. Strong arms closed around her. She fought like a wildcat, scratching and kicking.

"It's me, Tilly." Nolan's voice broke through her panic. "You're all right, I'm here."

"I thought you were Charlie." Her wild gaze focused on his face. "He was right behind me. He was following me."

"Charlie isn't there." Nolan cupped the side of her flushed face. "He must have seen me approaching and lost interest."

Nolan had seen Tilly exit the relay station and wanted to give her a chance to collect herself. He and the captain had moved as far away as they dared under the circumstances, but they'd both heard the voices raised in anger.

Tilly ducked her head. "Thank you. For looking out for me."

Nolan placed his hand over hers. "Why don't you take a walk with me?"

"What about Eleanor and the girls?"

"Captain Ronald will look out for them."

Tilly raised a mocking eyebrow. "I don't doubt it."

Even Nolan had noticed the mutual attraction. The captain had done nothing to hide his obvious admiration for Eleanor. "I think the captain is smitten with your sister."

"Everyone is smitten with Eleanor."

"I'm not."

While Eleanor was pretty, she was too aware of her

own appeal. He'd seen her type before. She'd immediately latched on to the captain's admiration because she needed the attention.

Tilly slanted a disbelieving glance in his direction. "She's very pretty."

"There is more than one kind of beauty." Nolan gestured ahead. "Follow me."

"Where are we going?"

"It's a surprise."

She gave a pointed look at the undertaker's house. "What about the outlaws?"

"I doubt they care about us. They're well aware that we can't travel far. They also know we'd never leave the others behind."

"I suppose you're right."

He led her past the edge of town. Grasshoppers sprang from their path and cicadas called. He parted the tall prairie grasses and she followed behind him. When the way became too rough, he grasped her fingers and pulled her the rest of the way. At the top of a small, rocky hill, he pointed.

He pointed to the snake of blue in the distance. "Do you see that?"

Her expression was sulky. "The river?"

The argument with her sister had clearly affected her. He'd never seen her this cross before.

"Yes. But look to the left of the river. See that hill with the white top?"

She shielded her eyes with one hand. "Yes."

"Meriwether Lewis and William Clark stood on that hill. They discovered a colony of prairie dogs in that very spot, and sent one back to President Jefferson for study."

"Are you certain that's the hill?" She crossed her arms

over her chest. "There could be a thousand hills that look the same."

"That's the hill. I'm certain. I've read all of their diaries, and studied their maps. That hill is nicknamed Old Baldy." He gestured toward the toes of her boots peeking out from beneath her muddy hem. "They might have stood in the very spot where you're standing."

The air was sultry and a mellow breeze stirred her chestnut hair. He couldn't imagine a day without her gentle teasing or her joyous laughter. He hadn't expected to discover friendship in this remote location under such demanding circumstances. Yet he'd found just that, and something more. He was afraid he'd discovered something deeper in their time together, something he wasn't ready to face.

Her expression remained bemused. "Why did you bring me here?"

Why had he brought her here? He'd wanted to separate her from Eleanor. He'd wanted to separate her from the constant threat hanging over them. Mostly, though, he wanted a moment alone with her. She offered so much of herself, and he had given her so little in return.

"Do you wonder what they thought about?" he asked, recalling their conversation in the abandoned hotel the day after her arrival.

"Who?"

"Lewis and Clark. They were traveling into the unknown. They didn't know if they'd live or die. Doesn't that make you wonder what they dreamed about?"

"Don't tease me," she said dully. "I'm not up to the challenge."

Her pessimism chilled him to the bone. He needed her wit and her optimism. He'd become addicted her joyous spirit. "I'm not teasing you, Tilly. The ugliness in the world is only exceeded by the beauty. I forgot that, but you reminded me."

She'd reminded him of the joy, and he'd brought her the opposite in return. They'd developed a friendship, but only one of them had benefited.

Her eyes misted over. "Thank you, for bringing me here. I shouldn't have doubted you. Except speaking with Eleanor always leaving me feeling annoyed and out of sorts."

He wanted to hold her and comfort her and find a way to make everything right. He wanted to change the world, he wanted to change himself. He wanted a million things that were out of his reach.

And yet there she stood. Close enough to touch. Within his reach. His fingers curled at his sides. Perhaps the greatest gift he could give to her was letting her go.

"I don't have any siblings," he said. "I confess I'm at a loss."

A delicate mist had settled over the valley below them, blurring the view. The vivid green of the rain-soaked basin dissolved into the lush blue of the sky.

Tilly moved nearer to the edge of the embankment. "She's older than me by five years, but you'd think it was decades."

"I don't have much to offer by way of insight."

He hesitated long enough that she turned quizzical blue eyes on him. "But you do have some insight?"

He tugged on his ear. "Most of us are inherently lazy. We take the easy path. I suspect the easy path for Eleanor depends on her looks. When folks are used to handling their problems in one way, they don't always know what to do otherwise."

"I don't know. She's always done everything right, everything well. I don't think she can admit failure."

"Not everyone has the insight to recognize their faults."

"Is that a blessing or a curse, do you suppose? I'd much rather have Eleanor's confidence."

"I'd rather lack confidence than live in oblivion."

"Not me!" Tilly laughed. "We're sisters. We were raised in the same house, and yet sometimes I feel as though we're strangers. How could two people share the same parents and the same experiences, and yet be miles apart in understanding?"

"The greatest distance in the world is between the hearts and minds of two people who love each other. The length of a room might as well be a thousand miles."

"That sounds like Eleanor and me." Tilly snorted. "We are each outsiders in the other's thoughts."

"Perhaps you should try starting fresh. You've known each other as children, and you've known each other as sisters, but you've never known each other as equals. Treat Eleanor as a stranger, as someone you've never met. Treat her without any fixed notions."

Tilly plucked a goldenrod flower from the tall grass. "I don't know if I want to know her better. I love Eleanor, she's my sister. But when Eleanor is around, I'm invisible. I don't want to be invisible anymore."

Her words invoked a forgotten pang of sorrow. A long-buried memory came to the surface of his thoughts. "I did have a brother once. He died shortly after he was born."

Tilly started. "I'm sorry."

"To be honest, I haven't thought about him in years. I was barely more than four or five years old myself when he was born. I don't remember him, but I remember how I felt after his death. How you spoke of Eleanor brought back something I'd forgotten. For months after he died, my mother became little more than a shadow. She'd wander from room to room for no reason. She was always losing things. I'd speak to her, and sometimes she wouldn't even answer me. I felt as though she was looking through me instead of at me. I felt as though I was invisible."

"That must have been difficult."

"It was a long time ago."

"I shouldn't have said anything." Tilly fidgeted with the sleeve of her gown. "I shouldn't have reminded you of such a sad time."

He regretted his confession for only an instant before recalling why he'd confided his thoughts. "Don't be sorry. I feel better talking about him. I feel better putting solid words to vague feelings I've had for years. For a time his death overshadowed my life, but I was too young to understand."

"To a much lesser degree, of course, that's how I feel about Eleanor. As though she was such a bright light, I was always cast in the shadow."

A plump bumblebee hopped on the breeze before settling on Tilly's flower. She laughed and held the stem away from her. "We're still invisible. This fat fellow hasn't even noticed us."

"You're not invisible to me, Tilly," he said. "I'm sorry for the circumstances, but I've enjoyed getting to know you these past few days."

The air around them was thick and humid. The clatter of insects filled the afternoon, and the rushing river sounded in the distance. He ached to reach out and touch her, but held himself in check.

He had already changed her, in just a few days, and not for the better. Instead of mitigating his own compulsive actions, she'd joined in his foolishness. She was stacking the plates in even numbers and carefully positioning the pans in their chalked outlines. How long before she grew frustrated by his habits? How long before she started treating him as his father had? How long before she grew tired of making excuses for his actions and covering his eccentricities when company came to call? She accepted him now, but how long until her understanding turned to frustration and disgust?

A gust of wind caught the flower in her hand, bending the stalk. The bee clung to the surface before bounding away once more.

She lifted her face to him, her lips parted slightly. His throat tightened. She was offering an invitation, one that he couldn't accept.

He clasped his hands behind his back. "At least it's not raining, for once."

She ducked her head and stepped away. "This has all gotten too ridiculous. There are too many people in Pyrite. Dakota Red knows that he's losing control, and he's going to do something rash."

Nolan appreciated the change of topic. She'd taken the awkwardness from the situation and put them on solid footing once more. He caught the wounded look in her lush, blue eyes before she quickly masked her expression. Regret stabbed him, but he held firm. Putting some distance between them was for the best.

"I know." His jaw tightened. "We'll give them a wide berth."

"That might prove difficult with Eleanor. She's never been known to give anyone a wide berth."

Nolan caught sight of something in the distance and moved his head for a better look.

Tilly followed his gaze. "What is it?"

"I thought I saw something." A prickling ran along his nerves, an intuitive warning of danger. "But it was nothing."

There was no need to worry her.

He searched the horizon once more, unable to spot the glimmer of movement he'd seen in the distance. A boat, perhaps. Or an animal crossing the river.

Tilly smiled at him. One thing had come of their time together. He hadn't lost everything. He had her friendship. Feeling wonderfully warmed by her smile, he felt his mood lighten.

"We should get back before they send out a search party," Tilly said.

He took her hand to assist her down the hill, pausing momentarily to glance over his shoulder, then shook his head. Whatever he'd seen must have been a trick of the light.

Chapter Eighteen

The following day, as Nolan fed the horses in the corral, a lone rider galloped down Main Street. The sight ignited a brief flare of hope before he recognized Lieutenant Perry. Nolan dropped the bucket, splashing water over the side, and scooted into the shadows. There'd be no help there.

The lieutenant had obviously ridden hard. He was breathing heavily and his horse's sides were flecked with foam. He leaped from the horse's back and took the stairs leading to the undertaker's house two at a time.

The lieutenant hadn't seen him yet, and Nolan used the distraction to his advantage. He slipped around the side of the house and positioned himself near the porch. The lieutenant was fired up about something, and Nolan wanted to know why. The information might prove useful.

"Quit your racket." Dakota Red stumbled over the threshold. "What's happened? You ain't supposed to be here."

"You've been discovered." The lieutenant slapped his hat against his thigh. "The cavalry is only an hour behind me."

The outlaw strode to the edge of the porch and looked

right and left, as though the cavalry might be galloping down the street at that very moment. Nolan reared back. When the footsteps receded, he crept closer to the corner once more.

"What do you mean?" Dakota Red demanded, snatching the lieutenant's collar. "Did you snitch?"

He slammed the lieutenant into the side of the house.

"No, you fool." Lieutenant Perry struggled free, his breath coming in harsh gasps. "Two passengers came through town yesterday. Did you see them?"

"Sure. But they didn't see us. They didn't stay longer than the time it took to change out the horses."

"They saw something, all right. Apparently one of the drivers thought the stagecoach man was behaving strangely. Then the captain went on patrol and didn't report back like he usually does. Turns out the captain suspected your stagecoach man of aiding outlaws. Two of the captain's men decided to hitch a ride on one of the stagecoaches and scout the town, see if they noticed anything strange going on at the relay station."

"Well, they didn't see us." Dakota Red's voice had taken on a defensive note. "They didn't even get close to the relay station."

"No. But they saw the captain's horse. Your idiot brother left the horse in the corral for anyone to see. What happened to the captain, anyway?"

"Shot him."

"Good."

Clearly the lieutenant thought his captain was dead, and Dakota Red hadn't corrected the assumption. But why? "How was Charlie to know some fool cavalrymen would have the brains to sneak through town? You told me they were all a bunch of idiots."

"Apparently, I was wrong."

"*Apparently*, you were. What do we do now?"

"If you want to live, I suggest that you run," the lieutenant replied. "Fast and far. They didn't see you, they only saw the horse. Right now, they still think the stagecoach man is involved. Leave him as bait while you make for the border. By the time they figure out he's innocent, you'll be long gone."

The boards creaked as Dakota Red paced the porch. Nolan flattened his back against the chipped paint of the house.

"If you're fortunate, the rain will slow them down," Lieutenant Perry said. "Cross the river and head north."

"I thought you said they was gonna be watching the river."

"The captain called off the watch two days ago. They think they have the element of surprise on their hands. Once you get across the river, cut the ropes. They won't be able to follow you."

"You're being awful helpful," Dakota Red said. "How do I know that you're not setting us up?"

"I don't want you getting caught. They don't know that I've been helping you. Let's keep it that way. If something happens and you do get caught, blame everything on Nolan West. He's such an odd fellow, he's the perfect man to take the fall for us. Tell the cavalry he killed their captain. He was a real favorite with the men. They'll hang him before he can prove his innocence."

"You'd let him hang to save your hide?"

"Sure. And you'd do the same."

Nolan's chest seized. He'd considered the lieutenant a friend at one time. How could the man set him up to hang?

What a coward. The captain had more honor in his little finger than this spineless idiot.

Dakota Red grunted. "We'll do what we have to do."

"Just make sure my name stays out of it."

The cavalry officer left the porch, grabbed his reins, and mounted his horse. "I can't stay. They think I've ridden ahead to scout the place."

"What do we do with the rest of the hostages?" Dakota Red scraped his hand through his greasy hair. "They may not know about you, but they know about us."

"Lock them up. Let the cavalry deal with them. Just make certain the stagecoach man is blamed for the captain's death. No one will believe anything that odd fellow says. The cavalry won't care about a botched kidnapping when they have a murderer on their hands."

Nolan's ears buzzed. The lieutenant was as good as caught, but he was too arrogant to see his own mistake.

Lieutenant Perry kicked his horse into a canter.

Charlie joined Dakota Red on the porch. "What was that all about?"

"We've got trouble."

"Then why is the lieutenant running? Shouldn't we nab him?"

"Let the lieutenant run. If he turns on us, we'll turn on him."

Shouting orders, Dakota Red quickly returned inside.

Nolan stepped from the shadows. The only thing that had kept them safe these past days had been the promise of gold. Without the promise of instant riches, there was no way Dakota Red and his men were going to simply abandon the town without taking something of value.

His throat tightened. There was only one thing of value left: the hostages.

Tilly had no more stepped out the door than Charlie grasped her around the upper arm. "C'mon."

Her stomach clenched but there was no time to acknowledge her shock. He shoved her into the relay station once more and crowded in behind her. Dakota Red must have entered from the back. He had hold of Eleanor, and he forced her into a chair.

The girls whimpered and crowded around their mother.

"Stop!" Tilly shouted. "You're frightening them."

"That's the idea, lady," Charlie drawled.

Snyder dragged Captain Ronald from the bedroom. The captain limped behind him, his face ashen.

"He ain't dead." Snyder chortled. "He's not even close to dead. They was exaggerating his wounds."

Dakota Red sneered. "Not surprised. Whatever you was planning, it's too late. The cavalry is coming."

Tilly narrowed her gaze. "Where is Nolan? What's happened to Mr. West?"

"You'd best worry about yourself, little missy. You got your own problems."

Charlie had that same speculative gleam in his eyes.

"What about the gold?" she asked.

"There's not going to be any gold."

Nausea pitched in her stomach. *They knew.* They'd somehow discovered the ambush. The glint in Charlie's eyes sent a ripple down her spine. Since they weren't getting the gold, they had nothing to lose. She made a desperate lunge but something in her eyes must have given her away.

Charlie snatched her arm with such force she feared her shoulder was separated. A second later he released her. He jerked sideways and fell. It took a moment for Tilly to comprehend what had happened.

Charlie grappled with Nolan on the floor.

Her heart seized in her chest. Nolan was safe. At least for now. Charlie was out for blood.

Dakota Red snatched his brother's collar and hauled him upright. "We don't have time for this, you fool."

Nolan pitched to his feet and caught her around the waist. Shock and fear muddled her thoughts. She sagged into his embrace and rubbed her sore shoulder.

"C'mon." Dakota Red nudged the captain with the barrel of his gun. "We're locking y'all up for safe keeping." He threw back his head and laughed at his own joke. "Ain't that rich? It's y'all going to jail."

They gathered all the hostages and led them to the jail cell. As the outlaws marched them down Main Street, Tilly's feet sank into the earth. Standing water had puddled in the low spots along the road. A sudden sense of foreboding shook her.

Nolan followed her gaze and she nudged him. "What does this mean?"

"The river is flooding."

Charlie caught up with them. "What are you talking about, stagecoach man?"

"Feel the ground," Nolan said. "Look at the standing puddles. The river is starting to flood."

"It ain't." Charlie spat into the puddle. "It's rainwater, is all. What are you playing at?"

"This isn't from the rain. The water table is rising. If the Niobrara breaks the embankment, the whole town will be swept away."

Dakota Red pushed Eleanor ahead of him. "Don't make me no never mind. The boys and I are leaving just as soon as we lock you all up tight." He glanced over his shoulder with a grin. "I sure do hope you're wrong, stagecoach man. Otherwise y'all are going to drown."

Tilly gasped. "What are we going to do?"

"We'll think of something."

The outlaws crowded all seven of them into the jail cell. Tilly carefully watched Nolan. He glanced at the piece of floorboard he'd cut out when he'd freed Caroline. The water beneath the boards had risen. They might have a reprieve. The outlaws didn't have a key, which meant there was no way of locking them inside.

Snyder appeared and handed something to Dakota Red.

The outlaw waved the key before them. "Look at what we found in the house. Thanks for fixing the door, stage-coach man. You've been a real help. This wouldn't have worked before."

He turned the key with a resounding click and stowed it in his pocket.

Eleanor sobbed. "What's going to happen to us?"

"Maybe the cavalry will get to you in time." Dakota Red shrugged. "Or maybe they won't. Ain't my problem anymore."

With a last tip off his hat he hurried out the door.

Eleanor collapsed on the cot and hugged the girls to her side. The captain sat beside her and wrapped his arm around her trembling shoulder.

Tilly narrowed her gaze on the pair. Eleanor didn't protest the contact.

The captain stretched out his injured leg. "Don't listen to him, ma'am. My men will reach us in time."

"They're not far behind," Nolan said hoarsely. "The lieutenant came through town a few minutes ago with the warning. He was riding hard. They'll be here."

Tilly shivered and tried not to look at the water seeping through a low spot in the floor. Omaha had flooded in the past. The rushing water was swift and unmerciful.

Elizabeth whimpered and the captain hoisted her onto

his knee. "Don't you worry, little lady. My men are the fastest and the bravest. You'll be riding out of town soon."

Since her attention was focused on Nolan, Tilly noted how his demeanor shifted the moment the door closed behind them. His breath came in quick shallow gasps and his eyes turned glassy and unfocused.

They'd left a chair propped in the corner the day they'd rescued Caroline, and she dragged the legs through the puddle. Nolan didn't appear to see her as she guided him toward the seat.

She crouched beside him and brushed the hair from his forehead. "Are you all right?"

"Nothing is wrong," Nolan said, his voice strained. "The captain's men will be here."

Victoria and Caroline each rested their heads on their mother's opposite shoulders. Eleanor stroked their hands and murmured soothing words. Tilly's heart softened toward her sister. Eleanor could be harsh and unyielding, but she adored her girls.

Nolan's words rang in her ears. Eleanor only knew how to be perfect. Her marriage to Walter had not turned out the way she planned, and Walter's death had come as a shock. Eleanor had lashed out the only way she knew how. She'd lashed out at Tilly. Nolan was correct: their relationship needed to change, and Tilly was the only one who could force that change.

Once they were free, Tilly vowed to renew her efforts to get to know her sister. Eleanor had changed over the years. They both had. And it was time they were reintroduced to each other.

"It's being locked up, isn't it?" the captain said, startling Tilly from her reverie. "Don't worry. We'll be out soon."

It took a beat for Tilly to realize the captain was speaking to Nolan.

Nolan braced one hand against the wall and stood. "It's the confinement."

"Do you get the nightmares?" the captain asked.

Tilly glanced between the two. They were speaking to each other as though no one else was in the room. Eleanor and the girls were lost in their own world, oblivious to the conversation.

"Yes," Nolan said. "I get the nightmares."

"I used to get them, too." The captain glanced at Eleanor's profile, his gaze filled with unmasked longing. "For a year after the war, I didn't sleep a full night. I'd wake up screaming. Thought they were going to cart me off to the sanitarium."

"Did you have any other, um, problems?"

"I drank all the time when I first got back. My wife died while I was gone. A fever. I left for the war with the whole world ahead of me, and I returned to nothing."

Eleanor's hands clenched in her lap. Though her attention was focused on the girls, she was most definitely listening to the conversation.

"I know the feeling," Nolan said wearily. "Too well."

"You don't like me much, do you, West?" The captain's wide grin was at odds with his words.

"The feeling is obviously returned." Nolan's breath rasped. "You thought I was riding with Dakota Red."

"I apologize. We were both prejudiced in our actions."

"I don't follow."

"I can tell a man who served in the war just by the look in his eyes. I'll walk across the street to avoid that look. I came out here to forget about the war."

"As did I. Being locked up like this, I want to tear myself apart."

"Why do you suppose there's so much regimentation and order in a soldier's life? When the world has gone mad around you, a man needs to feel as though he has control over something. Except it's all a lie, isn't it? All that forced order is a lie."

"You're a good man," Nolan said, his voice gruff. "I'm sorry I didn't see that before."

Tears burned in Tilly's eyes. She was an unwelcome observer in these events. The two men had suffered, and they were bolstering each other as best they could under the circumstances. Neither would admit weakness, and nor should they. Such circumstances were bound to leave their mark on a man.

From the moment they'd arrived, Nolan had been warning her away from him. Not overtly, but subtly, with his actions more than his words. Her chest tightened. She'd teased him about the thing he most dreaded. She'd cajoled him for his idiosyncrasies, feeding his unease. What an insensitive idiot she'd been.

"I owe you an apology, as well," the captain said. "My instincts were wrong, and I've cost us. I should have left the military when I'd planned."

"You're leaving?" Eleanor asked, her eyes wide. "You're leaving the cavalry?"

"There's no honor in our fight with the Indians. I can't be a part of it anymore."

"What will you do?" Eleanor tucked a strand of hair behind her ear. "We might as well pass the time with conversation."

Tilly smothered a grin behind her hand. She'd never have believed it, but Eleanor was as taken with the captain as he was with her. They made a fine pair. With all that was happening around them, what harm could come from a little flirtation?

"My family owns a seed company and plant nursery in Wichita," he said. "My older brother took over the business, and there wasn't room enough for the both of us in the beginning. The business has grown over the years, and he needs help. There's rich farmland in the area. Everyone is moving west. Why shouldn't I profit?"

Eleanor gazed at the captain with a look Tilly had never seen her bestow on Walter. Certainly Eleanor had loved Walter, but he'd been their father's choice. Had Eleanor been more in love with the idea of marriage than the man she'd married? Tilly sighed. None of that mattered, she supposed. Walter was gone and Eleanor had a wistful gaze that Tilly had never seen before.

Nolan slid his arm around her waist and she rested her head on his shoulder. He took her hand and placed it over the steady beating of his heart and placed his fingers over hers. Outside a heavy rain fell, and water seeped through the cracks in the roof.

"What about you, West?" Captain Ronald tipped back his head. "What did you do before the war?"

"Farming. We lost the land to carpetbaggers after the war."

"I could use a good man."

Eleanor glanced at them and blinked. Tilly stiffened, preparing for a lecture. Eleanor only flashed her a rueful smile and turned her attention to the captain once more. Tilly's shoulders sagged. Things were changing between them already.

"I'm honored by the offer," Nolan said. "But I'll probably travel farther west after this. Maybe the Wyoming Territory."

"You'll run out of places to run one of these days." The captain chuckled. "What will you do then?"

Nolan tensed. "Maybe by then, I won't need to run anymore."

She desperately wanted to apologize to him. To assure him that her teasing had meant nothing. She didn't think there was anything wrong with them. Nothing more than anyone else. The space was too close and her feelings were too raw. She couldn't expose herself before all these people. Tilly shivered and Nolan tugged her closer, rubbing her upper arm.

The door opened and Dakota Red, Charlie and Snyder appeared. "Change of plans. They're closer than the lieutenant led us to believe. We need some insurance in case they catch up to us while we're crossing the river."

He worked the lock and nudged open the barred door. Both men kept their guns trained on the hostages. Tilly cringed and Nolan tucked her behind him.

"We need a hostage." Dakota Red grabbed Caroline's arm. "This one will do."

Nolan reached for the man and a pistol shot sounded. Tilly screamed. Nolan staggered backward and collapsed. Blood oozed from a wound on his arm. The captain struggled to rise but Charlie cocked his gun.

"I'll kill you all," the outlaw declared. "Don't make me no never mind."

Caroline struggled to free herself from Dakota Red. "Mama, help."

"No!" Tilly shouted.

Eleanor clutched her daughter around the waist. "Don't you dare take her."

"Don't fuss with me, woman, or I'll shoot you."

"Then shoot me, but you're not taking my daughter."

The captain threw his body before Eleanor. "You'll have to shoot us both."

Tilly gaped in horror at the growing commotion. "Take

me," she shouted. "Take me. I promise I won't cause you any problems."

"You're better off alone." Nolan clutched his bloody shoulder. "If you take a hostage, the cavalry won't give up on tracking you. If you leave us safe, you might have a chance."

"Maybe we ought to listen to him," Snyder said, shifting on his feet. "Nothing has gone right on this job from the beginning. Maybe we ought to cut our losses and get out of here."

Dakota Red's face took on a fiery hue. "I didn't bust you out of jail because I was interested in hearing your opinion. We're surrounded by the cavalry. What do you think is going to happen? Do you think they're going to let us ride out of here? We need the hostages, at least until we get across the border."

Tilly scooted toward the door. "Then take me."

Charlie yanked her from the cell and slammed the door. Nolan staggered to his feet and fought with the outlaw through the bars. Charlie slammed the butt of his gun against Nolan's fingers.

"Don't fight them," Tilly pleaded.

The girls sobbed and she offered a watery smile. "Don't worry, girls. Everything is going to be all right, isn't it, Eleanor?"

"Oh, Tilly."

Eleanor collapsed against the captain, who still held a whimpering Elizabeth. He'd care for her and the girls. They'd be all right. They'd survive this, because they had each other.

Charlie shoved her toward Snyder, who grasped her upper arms, her back against his chest. Her gaze locked with Nolan's. She had no doubt of her fate. Nolan had a wild, murderous look in his eyes.

He'd see that she received justice. Snyder tugged her toward the door and she fought against his hold. She only had a second to impart everything she had to say.

Nolan caught her fingers, his jaw set, his hazel eyes fierce. "I will come for you."

If she told Nolan how she felt, she'd only make things worse. He was standing between three desperate outlaws and escape. Dakota Red and his men wouldn't go down easily.

Nolan would come for her, but there was good chance she'd be dead before he caught up with them.

"Be kind to yourself," she said, reaching out a hand. "No matter what happens, forgive yourself."

Snyder jerked her from the room and dragged her into the rain.

Chapter Nineteen

Nolan fought against the doors like a madman.

"She'll be rescued," the captain said, prying him away. "Let the cavalry do their job. They'll save her."

"I can't. I have to try." Nolan spun around and searched the cell. The bars were solid. They'd tried everything else the day Caroline had gotten stuck. He nudged the piece of flooring he'd cut out. "This wood is rotted through in some places."

He searched the ceiling and traced the watermarks down the walls. Once he discovered the worst of the damage, he dropped to his knees.

Eleanor sniffled. "What are you doing?"

"These buildings were built in a hurry. The foundations are raised off the ground with a space beneath the floors. Tilly discovered the space the hard way."

"Are you certain?"

"There's a wooden bib covering the foundation. If I can break through the floorboards, I can crawl out from beneath the building."

"That might work." The captain tested the floorboard with his foot. "We need a pry bar."

The two men glanced at the rickety cot at the same

time. They quickly disassembled the legs and set about levering the floorboards loose.

Despite the rotted wood, the floorboards were remarkably stubborn.

The captain mopped his brow. "The men who built this jail obviously didn't want anyone escaping."

After the first board came free, two more followed in rapid succession. The captain peered down into the space.

"There's standing water."

Nolan rolled to his side, his arm stretched above his head. He'd have to wade through a tight, muddy dark space to free himself.

Marvelous.

The nightmare of Tilly's situation was far worse.

He quickly pried another board free. There was no way the standing water had been there before, or the buildings would have collapsed by now.

"I wasn't lying before," he said. "The river is on the verge of flooding. When the cavalry arrives, have them take you to higher ground as quickly as possible."

He stretched his torso through the opening, and his hands sank to his wrists in the soft mud. Nolan grimaced and crawled forward. The space was tighter than he'd thought. In order keep his face above the water, he had to crawl on his elbows.

The captain stuck his head through the opening. "You'll need this."

Nolan accepted the pry bar with a curt nod. "Whatever happens, take care of Eleanor and the girls."

"I will. Always."

Nolan shook his head with a half grin. The captain was love-struck. He'd never believed in love at first sight, but the pair made a good match.

His knees and arms sank with his stuttering progress.

The walls closed in around him and the breath locked in his lungs. His vision blurred and he felt a scream rising in the back of his throat.

Tilly's face swam into his vision. His chest seized. She'd sacrificed herself for Caroline without a second thought. He was a coward for hesitating. Swallowing back his panic, he searched for the glimpse of daylight he'd seen ahead. His head grew cottony. Using all his mental strength, he fought against the physical reaction. After taking several deep, heaving breaths, he moved forward.

The bib covering for the raised platform had been exposed to harsher weather than the floorboards. Using the pry bar, the first board splintered. He removed the next two and squeezed through the narrow opening. His shirt caught on a splinter and tore. His bare skin scraped against the jagged surface, drawing blood.

He stood and hooked his bloodied fingers over the high, narrow window ledge.

"I'm free," he shouted. "Follow my escape route and get the girls to higher ground."

His first instinct was to blindly rush after the outlaws. Instead, he staggered toward the livery. After retrieving the gun Lieutenant Perry had left him, he chose the fastest mount and hurriedly saddled the horse with shaking fingers.

The outlaws couldn't go backward, which meant they'd move forward. They'd cross at the ferry and cut the lines to slow their pursuers.

The ride to the river took an eternity. Rain sluiced across his face, obscuring his view. By the time he reached the ferry crossing, the men had loaded their gear and their horses onto the platform. He could only assume they hadn't left a lookout because of the hasty escape and hazardous conditions.

All three were concentrated on controlling the ferry against the swollen river. Even with the outlaws distracted, he couldn't risk being seen. Once again he corralled his instincts. If he stormed the outlaws without a plan, he risked Tilly's life.

His heart racing, he secured his horse out of sight behind a copse of trees and belly-crawled toward the rise of a small embankment.

Tilly sat alone on the shore, her hands bound before her. Her chin was set at a defiant angle. His blood chilled and he concentrated on his objective. He'd take out their leader first, and then he'd aim for Charlie. Dakota Red's brother was a wild card, the most likely of the bunch to shoot first and think later. Nolan was counting on Charlie's first shot going wild.

Except a wild shot risked Tilly's life. Nolan closed his eyes and willed her to run once the bullets started flying. She was smart and he'd never seen her panic. She'd keep her head and scramble out of the way. He was counting on it. He was counting on Tilly.

The water had crept over the banks and partially submerged the ferry dock.

The violent current tugged the lead ropes taut, and the men struggled against the swiftly flowing current. Nolan checked the pistol. He had six shots against the three men with an innocent hostage in their midst.

If they crossed the river, he'd never catch up with them, and she'd be as good as dead.

Despite the odds, he had to act.

His elbows sank in the mud. He flexed his bloodied and mud-splattered fingers over the gun barrel before carefully setting his sights on Dakota Red. After pinpointing his focus, he took a steadying breath and fired the shot.

Dakota Red slumped forward.

The horses bucked, throwing the ferry off balance. Tilly took one look at the prone man and frantically crawled higher up the embankment, away from the river.

"Good girl," Nolan muttered to himself.

As Snyder struggled with the horses, Charlie fired off a shot. The bullet ricocheted near Nolan's head, splattering his face with mud. He swiped at his cheek and aimed once more. Charlie was focused on Tilly's escape. With a snarl the outlaw lunged toward her from his perch on the ferry.

Nolan easily picked him off.

Snyder drew his weapon and began firing blindly. Another bullet ricocheted off the ground near Nolan's head.

The spooked horses bucked and lunged. One of them bumped into Snyder, knocking him sideways. The outlaw tripped backward over the rigging and tumbled into the river.

Nolan emerged from his hiding place and sprinted down the hill. He quickly covered the distance, his feet splashing in the rising water. Dakota Red had tumbled into the river along with Snyder, but Charlie was still a threat.

Nolan discovered the outlaw on his back, his eyes lifeless. With a grimace he tossed his coat over the man's face.

Tilly had crawled several yards away. He dropped down beside her and she threw her tied wrists over his head.

His heart in his throat, he crushed her against him. "Are you hurt?"

"No." She sobbed against his neck. "How did you escape?"

Relief flowed through his veins. "I used the Matilda Hargreaves escape."

"What's that?"

"I went through the floorboards and broke out."

"But you hate small spaces."

"Turns out, I only needed a fraction of your bravery, and I did just fine."

She pulled back and stared at him, a half grin on her face. "You're filthy."

"I know."

He absently swiped at his face.

She pressed her forehead against his. "You've made it worse."

Moisture seeped through his pant legs and Tilly shivered. The river was rising. They weren't out of danger yet. He ducked from her hold and fought with the knots at her wrists. She was muddy and bedraggled and absolutely beautiful. He cradled her face and kissed her lips after untying her.

She pulled back and stared at something over his shoulder.

"He's still alive."

Nolan followed her gaze and discovered Snyder clinging to the ferry. His eyes were wild and desperate. Of all the outlaws, Snyder was the only one who had shown them any mercy.

"Stay here," he ordered Tilly.

Nolan jumped from the bank onto the ferry and leaned over the side. Snyder had hooked his arm over the tow rope.

"I can't swim," he shouted. "Help."

"Give me your hand."

Nolan caught the man's arm and hauled him onto the ferry platform.

"You owe me," Nolan said. "Remember that."

Snyder gasped and coughed. "I won't forget."

"You're not going try and kill me now, are you?"

"No. I'll take the ferry across the river, and I won't stop until Canada."

"You'll never make it."

"I'm gonna try. You won't see me again."

Strangely enough, Nolan believed him. The man had nearly fifty pounds on him, but he hadn't attacked. The outlaw grasped the ferry rope and heaved. Nolan left him and returned to Tilly's side.

"You're letting him go?" she asked.

"I have more important things to worry about. We have to fetch the others and get to higher ground before the river floods."

He helped her upright and held her upper arms until she'd steadied herself.

She took a halting step and gasped. "I've hurt my ankle."

He kneeled at her feet and studied her dainty ankle. "I don't think it's broken. Only bruised."

He stood and hoisted her against his chest. She wrapped her arms around his neck. "You can't carry me. I'm too heavy."

Nolan glanced down. The water had risen to his ankles.

"No argument. The river is flooding."

He set her astride the horse and mounted behind her, then kicked his mount into a canter. By the time they reached Pyrite, the cavalrymen had arrived. A dozen men on horseback had mustered outside the jailhouse.

The captain stood in the center, his weight leaning heavily on a stick as he shouted orders to his men. Seeing Nolan and Tilly, he stepped away from the cluster of horses and soldiers.

"What happened?"

"Dakota Red and Charlie are dead," Nolan said.

"What about the big fellow?"

"Last I saw, he was taking the ferry across the river. Don't know how far he'll make it. The river is over the banks and the tow lines are stretched thin."

"If he manages to make it across the river alive, we'll catch up with him later. Our concern now is getting these women and children to Yankton before the river floods."

The cavalry officers mounted and the girls were divided among the men. Captain Ronald kept close to Eleanor.

Nolan tightened his hold on Tilly's waist.

She glanced at him, and her hair whipped across his face. "What happens now?"

Her words held a deeper meaning and greater question— a question he wasn't ready to answer. "I'll see you safely to Yankton."

"And then what?"

"We have a long way to travel today," he said evasively. "We have to move fast to stay out of the river's path."

He felt her stiffen and he didn't dare look at her. He was afraid that if he did, he wouldn't be able to follow through on the promise he'd made to himself.

Because of her injury, Tilly rode with Nolan. As Nolan had predicted, the water rose swiftly. The fort was on the other side of the river, but Snyder had cut the ropes on the stagecoach ferry crossing. They stayed on the south side of the river and made their way toward the ferry crossing in Yankton.

They moved quickly, wanting to ensure they made the crossing near Yankton. The captain predicted that the large basin where the Missouri River met the Niobrara would mitigate the worst of the flooding. They switched horses at least once during the day in deference to the added weight.

Since they'd gotten a late start, the cavalrymen made camp that evening on a hill overlooking the bend in the river just before the Missouri. Captain Ronald waved them over.

"Come look at this."

The river was twice the width as when Tilly had passed by the first time. She'd expected the rising water to be noisy and agitated, but the wide expanse was remarkably calm. Save for the enormous trees washed from the banks that floated along the surface, she might not have realized the extensive damage.

The captain pointed at a crook in the river where debris had piled up. The growing mound was as large as a building.

It took Tilly a moment to make out the shapes. "Is that a roof?"

"Sure is."

Nolan squinted. "I think that's part of the relay station."

"Looks like it." Captain Ronald chuckled. "You're out of a job, West."

She grasped his arm. "I'm so sorry. You've lost everything."

"Not everything."

The captain tilted his head. "My offer still stands. I could use a man I can trust."

Tilly held her breath and waited for his answer.

"I'm looking at a job in the Wyoming Territory."

She quickly masked her disappointment and turned away. She'd thought something had changed between them. An understanding. But Nolan had grown distant. He was polite and solicitous, looking out for her needs, but she sensed he was pulling away from her.

Both physically and mentally exhausted, she returned to the camp the cavalrymen had hastily erected for the evening.

She was staring into nothing when Eleanor took a seat on a blanket beside her. "I wanted to speak with you. I wanted to apologize."

Shaken from her troubled thoughts, Tilly blinked. "For what?"

"You were right. I was far too critical of you. When mother was dying, she asked me to look out for you. I took my job too seriously. I was too young to know any better."

"You were too young to be given such a grave responsibility."

"Yes. But I should have known better as I grew older. I set a high standard for myself, and I expected too much of the people around me. Even the girls. You showed me that."

"They're fine girls, and they adore you."

"I should have trusted you more with them. When Victoria was born, I'd never felt anything like what I felt for her. I wanted to protect her and shelter her. I hardly even let Walter near her. I wouldn't be separated from her. I thought I was being a good mother."

"You *are* a good mother."

"But I drove Walter away. I thought our lives would be better once he returned from the war, but he never felt a part of our lives. We grew apart while he was gone.

I'd become accustomed to doing everything for the girls myself. He didn't have a place anymore."

"What an odd thing to say. Of course Walter felt as though he was part of your family."

Eleanor's smile was tinged with sorrow. "The girls and I had our own way of doing things, and we excluded him. I think that's part of the reason he wanted out of Omaha. He thought we could start over. The change didn't help. After we moved to Virginia City, we rarely saw him. I felt as though I was married to a stranger."

Tilly covered her sister's hand. "I'm sorry. I wish you would have said something. I didn't know how difficult these past few years have been for you. I'm sorry about Walter."

"I was angry when he died." Her lips tightened. "Angry that he'd thought so little of the girls and me that he'd leave us destitute."

Tilly's heart softened. "I'm sure he thought the mine would eventually pay out."

"That stupid hole in the ground. The only thing it ever paid out was heartbreak."

Captain Ronald approached them, tins of coffee in each hand. "I thought you might like something warm against the cold night."

Eleanor blushed and accepted the offering. The captain touched his forehead and moved away.

Tilly stifled a smile. "He's very handsome."

"Yes."

"I think he's smitten with you."

Eleanor's expression crumpled. "We're destitute, Tilly. What man would want to be saddled with a woman and three children, when all we own is the clothes on our backs?"

"I don't believe he minds."

"He's moving to Wichita."

"Wichita isn't such a bad place." Tilly glanced at the cavalryman. "What if he asks you to marry him?"

"I've barely been widowed a year. I have the girls to think about."

"That's not what this is about, though, is it?" Tilly asked.

"I made so many mistakes with Walter." Eleanor stifled a sob. "What if I make all the same mistakes again?"

"No one is perfect, Eleanor. Not even you. If you allow someone to love your imperfections, you might be surprised."

Eleanor blinked rapidly. "When did you grow up?"

"When you weren't looking."

Her sister hugged her close. "Thank you. For what you did for Caroline."

"You're welcome." Tilly rubbed her sore ankle. "Before I say anything else, I need to know something. How do you feel about the captain?"

"I haven't known him very long, certainly, but I think we're suited."

"Could you love him?"

"I think I'm already falling in love with him, Tilly. He's been so good to the girls. After you were taken…" Her voice hitched and she gathered herself. "After you were taken, he was the only thing that kept us going."

"This is all so sudden." Tilly assumed the role of older sister for once. "He's a good man, but perhaps you should spend some time thinking about your future."

"I've been alone this past year. I don't want to be alone anymore."

Her sister appeared truly fond of the cavalryman, and he obviously returned the sentiment. He was a good man who would treat Eleanor and the children with love and respect. What else did they really need? Still, it wouldn't hurt to give Eleanor a little nudge.

"That doesn't mean you have to rush into something you might regret later," Tilly said.

Eleanor sighed. "All my life I've done everything exactly how I ought to. I was the perfect daughter, and I did everything that was expected of me. I married the man Father chose for me. I tried to be the best wife and mother I could. And what has that gotten me? I'm miserable, Tilly. This time I'm going to do what feels right for me."

Tilly grinned. "Then I think you should marry him."

"He hasn't asked."

"He will."

Eleanor caught her gaze. "What about you? I've noticed you spending a lot of time with Mr. West."

"I think I love him."

To her credit, Eleanor only clasped her hand. "How does he feel about you?"

"I think he likes me. I think he could even love me, but he's unsure of himself."

Eleanor met her gaze, her expression intent. "I'll tell you something, and I'm not saying this to be unkind. I'm sharing something I learned over the years. Men don't change. When I married Walter, I knew he chafed at his work in Father's law office. I thought he'd change once we were married. I thought he'd change once the girls were born. I thought he'd change once we moved to Virginia City. I was wrong every time. He didn't change, and neither did I. If he isn't willing to be with you now, he never will."

Tilly's heart squeezed painfully. "I'm afraid you're right."

"Then find someone who doesn't have to change to love you."

A commotion sounded at the edge of the camp, and they both turned. A man leading his horse strode through the line of soldiers, parting the ranks.

Her heart thumped against her rips and she half stood. "Lieutenant Perry."

Even as she registered the thought, Captain Ronald strode into view.

The lieutenant took one look at the captain and reached for his sidearm. The captain was quicker.

His men quickly apprehended the lieutenant.

"I thought you were dead!" the lieutenant shouted. "I've done nothing."

"It's too late, Perry." The captain gave a sad shake of his head. "You never can trust an outlaw to kill the right man."

The crowd parted, revealing Nolan, and the lieutenant sagged. There was no escaping his lies.

Eleanor rushed toward the captain. "You could have been killed. What were you thinking?"

The captain caught her against his chest and buried his fingers in her hair. "I would never risk death now that I've found something to live for."

The two embraced and Tilly leaned back on her hands. Eleanor was definitely going to be married. And soon.

She glanced in Nolan's direction. Where did that leave her?

Chapter Twenty

The village of Yankton had the feel of a boomtown. Steamships traveling along the Missouri had swelled the population of the town. There were numerous thriving business, and Nolan even spotted a photography studio along one of the bustling streets.

The cavalry had taken up residence in the stockade built in the Dakota War of 1862. The enormous stockade had been built to house the settlers from surrounding areas. Since the attacks had never manifested, the stockade remained in good repair. Captain Ronald pointed out the territorial capitol building on their trip to the fort. The building was an uninspiring white two-story structure located at Fourth and Capitol Streets.

The evening after Nolan and the rest of the group arrived in Yankton, the fort hosted an impromptu celebration. He was reluctant to attend, but the captain was insistent. Nolan withdrew some money from the bank, surprised at how much the balance had grown. That afternoon he went into town and purchased a new suit. The kindly proprietor rushed the alterations.

By now, most of the town had heard about the outlaws, and they were eager to hear Nolan's story. The townspeople treated him as though he was a hero, and he quickly ducked away from their regard. He hadn't done anything that anyone else wouldn't have done.

That evening he took extra care with his appearance. He planned on leaving for the Wyoming Territory the following day. He'd already wired his superiors at Pioneer Stagecoach and let them know about the town. He'd miss Bill and English Bob and the others, but the time had come for him to move on.

The mess hall teemed with the people, and he paused on the threshold. The Dakota Territory was growing with the steamship business, bringing scores of settlers. Since here were few enough reasons to celebrate most days, it appeared as though everyone within miles had turned out for the party.

Wearing his full dress uniform and holding a glass of punch, the captain approached him. "I brought your money."

Nolan plucked a thread from his lapel. "What money?"

"For the capture of the outlaws."

Captain Ronald named a sum that had Nolan frowning.

"I think you've made a mistake."

"That's the sum. A fellow could make a good living in the city on that amount of money."

"I've never been one for the city," Nolan said. "A man like me needs open spaces."

"Suit yourself."

"What about Snyder?" Nolan asked. "Has he been caught?"

"He's been captured. He barely it made it across the river. The flooding on that side was worse. It was either drown or be caught. He decided to finish out his jail term."

"I hope the judge goes easy on him. He was the only one who showed us any mercy."

"I'll make certain the judge is aware of your feelings. You're quite a hero around these parts. Your word means a lot."

Nolan's face heated. "You would have done the same for Eleanor."

"Without pause."

The captain spotted Eleanor and his face softened. "If you ever pass through Wichita, stop by for a visit. We're friends now, I think."

"We are."

"Then wish me well." The captain raised his glass. "I have a very important announcement to make."

Tilly's sister was glowing. The girls had been scrubbed clean and wore matching pink dresses with white sashes. Elizabeth had a smudge on her hem already. They crowded around him and he dutifully exclaimed over the ribbons in their braided hair and their satin bows.

Their mother soon gathered them near.

He caught sight of Tilly before she spotted him, and he took the chance to admire her. She'd swept her head into a crisscross of braids atop her head that revealed the enticing curve of the nape of her neck. She wore a dress in a vivid shade of blue that brought out the lustre in her eyes. His heart swelled. She caught his gaze as the captain raised his glass.

"If I could have your attention, please," the captain called, one arm wrapped around Eleanor's waist. "I'd like to make an announcement. This beautiful lady has agreed to be my wife."

The room erupted into whoops and hollers. Eleanor blushed and kissed his cheek. The girls crowded around them. He felt an odd pang in his chest. The girls had already transferred their attention to the captain. He caught himself. They hadn't transferred their attention, they'd shared their affection.

Nolan wove through the crowd until he found Tilly. "Isn't that rather sudden?"

"Yes." She reached for a glass of lemonade. "The captain was smitten."

"What about Eleanor?"

Despite his words, he was more interested in hearing how Tilly felt about the marriage.

"I think she likes him. I believe she'll even grow to love him. Living with Walter's parents was never an ideal solution, but she didn't have another choice. Now she does."

"What will you do?"

"I'm going with her to Wichita. Just until the girls are settled."

His eyebrows shot up. "But what about New York? What will happen to all the widows and orphans?"

"They'll find assistance without me, I'm sure. Having spent time with my nieces these past few weeks, I don't want to be away from them. I'm tired of making decisions based on what I don't want. I want to make decisions based on what I do want."

"I'm happy for you, Tilly."

"What will you do?"

"I'll move farther west. It's what I always planned."

"You said your father lives in Cimarron Springs."

"Yes."

"If you ever pass through Wichita on your way to Cimarron Springs, I'd enjoy seeing you."

"And I you." He paused. "They've given me the reward for the outlaws. I'd like you to have it."

Her eyes grew red. "You don't have to pay me off. I won't ask anything of you."

"No." Regret immediately engulfed him. "That's not what I meant at all."

"I'm fine, Nolan. You don't have to worry about me or take care of me. I don't know what my future holds. Not exactly. And you know what? I don't care. I'm going to spend the rest of my life starting things that I never finish and I'm not going to care what people think."

Someone bumped against him and murmured an apology. The skin beneath his collar itched and his palms grew damp. There were too many people in too small of a space. He needed some fresh air, but he didn't want to leave Tilly just yet. Not when their time together was growing to a close.

He wouldn't live out his life with her. He'd probably never see her after today, but he'd been fortunate to call her a friend for this span of time. He'd been fortunate to love her.

He tugged on his collar. "I can't change, Tilly. You know that."

"I never asked you to change." A sad smile lifted the corners of her mouth. "My sister can be an unmitigated pain, and the captain adores her. The problem isn't counting plates or arranging your tools. The problem is that you can't accept who you are."

"Tilly…" The word hovered on the tip of his tongue. "It's not that easy."

"You'll be all right, Nolan West. As long as you're kind to yourself, you'll be just fine."

His throat closed, preventing from saying anything more than a gruff, "Goodbye."

She pressed a kiss against his cheek. "Goodbye."

He watched her walk away, and the crowd swallowed her.

His chest seized.

He'd done the right thing.

Then why did everything feel so wrong?

Tilly rested her hand on her chin and stared out the window. She didn't regret moving to Cimarron Springs, even though she sometimes felt foolish living in the same town as Nolan's father without ever introducing herself. She didn't know what she'd say, or how she'd explain herself.

After Eleanor and the girls had settled in Wichita, she'd been a third wheel. Captain Ronald's family was more than comfortable, they were wealthy. The captain hadn't shared that particular tidbit of information with Eleanor, and she'd been furious at first, but her temper had quickly faded.

While Captain Ronald clearly adored Eleanor, Tilly had noticed that her sister more than returned the affection. She'd caught Eleanor staring at the captain when he wasn't looking. She'd seen the blush of color dusting her sister's cheeks when the captain looked in her direction.

Eleanor had made her own choice, and it was clear she didn't regret her actions. Their father had taken their move with his usual aplomb. He'd always preferred his solitude, and he didn't seem to mind the absence of his two daughters.

When she'd grown restless in Wichita, she'd asked the captain to help her find work. A friend of a friend had gotten her work at the post office in Cimarron Springs and a room in the boardinghouse.

All in all she was content. Lonely. But content.

A knock sounded and the boardinghouse proprietress peered into the room. "You have a visitor."

Tilly heart jolted. She stood and smoothed her dress. "Who?"

"An older gentleman."

Her brief spark of hope faded. "I'll be right down."

She checked her appearance in the looking glass and descended the stairs.

Tilly met the bearded gentleman in the parlor. She couldn't recall ever meeting him before, and her confusion increased. He stood and doffed his hat.

"My name is Jericho West. I believe you know my son."

Tilly's step faltered before she took the gentleman's proffered hand. "I met your son, yes. How is he?"

"Well, I suppose. He wrote to me recently. He doesn't do that very often. He mentioned your name. He asked, well, he asked me to check on you."

"That's very kind of you. And kind of your son." Tilly gestured. "Won't you have seat?"

The man took an awkward seat on the edge of a chair while she sent for coffee and refreshments.

He cleared his throat. "Imagine my surprise when I traveled to Wichita, only to discover you were living right under my nose."

"Oh, dear." Of course Nolan would have assumed she was living in Wichita. That's where she'd planned to stay the last time they'd spoken. "I hope you weren't inconvenienced."

"Not at all, no." Jericho rested his hat on his knee and fumbled with the brim. "He's always been whip smart. Neither his mother nor I had much schooling, and we couldn't give Nolan much schooling, either. There was too much work to be done on the farm. When the war broke out, he warned me. He told me that we were sitting on the wrong side of history. I didn't understand. No one ever thinks they're on the losing side of history, do they?"

"I suppose not." Tilly stared at her clenched hands. Nolan had made his choice. He'd chosen his solitude. "I'm not certain why you're telling me all of this."

"He fought because he's honorable. After the war, I moved to Kansas to be near my sister. Nolan came home to live with me, and I could see that he'd changed. I didn't understand. I was hard on him. I wanted him to be the same boy he was before the war because I was selfish. I didn't want to face my own guilt."

Mr. West's eyes grew red around the rims.

Tilly blinked rapidly. "You don't have to say any more."

"I do. I do have to finish. I didn't want to see him suffering because I knew I was responsible. He fought because of me—he fought for a cause he didn't entirely believe in. Seeing him every day was eating me up with guilt. Instead of helping him, I drove him away. I made him think there was something wrong with him, when really there was something wrong with me." Mr. West retrieved a handkerchief from his pocket and swiped at his nose. "When he mentioned you in his letter, I came straight away. It's the first thing he's asked of me since he was released from Rock Island. You see?"

"Yes. I think so."

Mr. West clearly loved and missed his son, and she sympathized with his dilemma.

"Why are you here?" Jericho asked. "Why are you in Cimarron Springs and not Wichita?"

"Because I didn't have any place else to go, and this is the closest I could be to Nolan while my heart mended."

Jericho brushed at his eyes. "I hoped so. I hoped you'd say that."

"It doesn't do us a lot of good, does it? He's never coming home."

"Maybe. Maybe not." Jericho reached for his hand. "But if he does come, at least he'll have someone to welcome him."

Tilly took the older man's hand. She'd be fine if Nolan never returned. She'd discovered her own strength, and she didn't mind the solitude anymore. She'd looked inside herself and seen something worth nurturing. She was no longer afraid of being alone. She was no longer compelled to live up to someone else's idea of who she should be and what she should do.

Despite her newfound strength, she mourned the loss of her friendship with Nolan. Jericho was offering her a chance to know someone who understood what she was feeling. They were both healing from the loss of someone they loved. At least they could heal together.

"If he ever decides to come home." She squeezed Jericho's fingers. "We'll be here for him."

Weary from traveling, Nolan thought his eyes must be deceiving him. He rubbed them with the heels of his hands and looked again.

Tilly glanced over her shoulder and her eyes widened. "You startled me. I wasn't expecting you."

His pulse thrummed. He felt as though he'd stumbled into a dream. A dream he'd been having since the day he left Yankton. A dream where Tilly wandered through the spaces of his heart.

Since nothing made sense, he said the first thing that came to mind, "Who were you expecting?"

He glanced around, but he was in the right place. This was his father's home. The house was exactly the same as he'd left it. The kerosene lamp was the same, the rag rug was the same, even the crooked framed sampler his mother had stitched was the same.

Yet Tilly stood before him, her bluebell eyes twinkling. "Your father, of course."

"Tilly, what are you doing here?"

The change of events was too abrupt. His mind couldn't keep up with the frantic beating of his heart.

"It's a long story," she said. "Perhaps your father should tell you."

She set a package on the counter and turned.

Still mute and stunned by the encounter, he let her slip past him.

She'd nearly reached the door when he discovered his voice.

"Where are you going?" he asked.

He felt as though she'd disappear forever if he let her out of his sight, even for a moment.

"Home."

"Home?" he asked. "This is your home?"

"Cimarron Springs is my home now. I've been working at the post office for the past several weeks. There was a package from Wells Fargo for your father today, and I decided to deliver it myself. I was hoping to speak with him, but as you can see, he isn't home yet."

She stepped outside and inhaled deeply. "I love the smell of burning leaves, don't you?"

"Yes." Dusk was falling and he searched for a pony cart or some other means of conveyance. "It's several miles to town. Did you walk?"

"I did. There's a shortcut over the stream."

He scrambled to form a lucid thought. "Let me walk with you."

"I'm fine on my own. I walk the distance almost every day."

"I insist."

"All right then, if you insist."

"I do."

She slipped her arm through the crook of his elbow, and he felt the shock of her touch all the way to his toes. Until that moment, he hadn't realized how much he missed her, how much he truly loved her.

She smiled at him as they walked. "Beautiful weather we're having."

A thousand questions danced on the tip of his tongue. "How long have you been living in Cimarron Springs?" he asked.

"Three months. I traveled with Captain Ronald and Eleanor to Wichita, but you can imagine the difficulties. They're newlyweds, after all. I helped them settle in and spent some time with the girls. I'd already moved here when your father came to call."

Part of the reason for her appearance at his father's house fell into place. "I asked him to check in on you. I hope you don't mind."

"Not at all. We struck up a friendship. What about you? How have you been?"

His throat tightened. Why hadn't his father written him about their growing friendship? Why had they excluded him?

Nolan swallowed past the lump in his throat. "I'm well."

"Your father says that you've been traveling."

"I have."

"Anyplace interesting?"

"No place I wanted to stay." He paused. She was behaving casually, as though they hadn't been through torment together. Not knowing what else to do, he mimicked her casual talk. "Then Eleanor and Captain Ronald have found happiness?"

"Yes. It's work, mind you. They're both used to getting their way." She held her bonnet with her free hand and tipped her head to the sky. "I'm coming by your father's tomorrow to help with his garden. I hope I'll see you."

"Tilly. What's happening here?"

This wasn't right. None of this was right. She wasn't supposed to be here. He'd planned on living with his father for a while. He'd planned on trying to explain why he'd left before, and why he'd come back. He hadn't planned on meeting Tilly in his father's kitchen, and all his carefully erected plans crumbled.

Her smile was serene. "Nothing is happening here. Absolutely nothing."

His stomach twisted. Certainly her presence meant something. Certainly there was hope for them if she'd moved to the one place he might someday return to.

"Why were you at my father's house?" he asked, his voice hoarse. "Why are you in Cimarron Springs?"

"I told you. I was at your father's house delivering a package. Your father and I are friends."

Had her feelings for him been deeper than he thought? Or was he reading the situation all wrong.

"Unusual friends," he prodded.

"Not so unusual if you really think about it. We both love the same person. Having something in common is often how friendships begin."

His footsteps halted. She'd spoken the most precious words he'd ever heard. But he couldn't let her stay here. He couldn't let her waste her life on something that was never to be. More than once he'd thought of making the trip to Wichita, and more than once he'd stopped himself. He'd finally returned home to seek his father's advice.

"You can't love me, Tilly," he said. "I'm not right, and I don't think I ever will be. I've tried everything. This is who I am."

Her gaze was peaceful and unmoved. "I know."

"And that doesn't bother you?"

"Yes. Of course it bothers me. It bothers me because it bothers you."

"I can't subject you to the sort of life I live. You deserve better. I don't want you to become like me."

"I think we could both move closer to the center of things."

"People will talk," he said. "They'll talk about me. Which means, in turn, they'll talk about you."

The edges of her mouth drooped. "Do you think so little of me that you don't suppose I can tolerate a little gossip?"

This wasn't going at all as he'd expected. She was countering his words at every turn. "I didn't mean to insult you."

"You haven't insulted me, you've hurt my feelings."

A lump formed in his throat. "I didn't mean to do that, either."

She faced him and clasped his hands, her gaze earnest. "I know that you mourn the man you were before the war, but I don't, because I didn't know that man. I can't mourn for someone I never met. I know this man. I fell in love with the man standing before me."

He didn't dare breathe. He didn't dare hope. "Life with me would not be easy."

"Life is sloppy and messy and nothing ever turns out the way we suppose. I don't need someone who is perfect. I'm not perfect, either. If I married someone perfect, I'd simply feel as though I was under Eleanor's rule once more, and I'm through living like that. I don't know what you were like before the war, but, according to your father, you weren't without flaws."

"I don't want you to hate me." He closed his eyes. "I don't want your love to turn to disgust."

"Love is not finding the perfect person with the perfect smile and the perfect disposition. Love is finding the beauty in someone's flaws and imperfections. Love is finding someone who is willing to accept you as you are and grow together with you. I won't be the same person in a day, or a week, or a month. I'm not done becoming the person I want to be."

She didn't understand. "You'd be better off with someone normal," he said.

"I have spent the better part of my life running away from things. For the first time in my life, I have chosen to run toward something I want. I have chosen to risk my heart and my happiness trying. I came to Cimarron Springs because I refused to give up on you. You may shun me. You may refuse me. You may walk out of my life and never return. I will not, however, allow you to dictate what's best for me. Not now. Not ever."

The tone of her voice gave him pause. "Then you're willing to take a risk on me."

"Only if you're willing to take a risk on me."

"I don't deserve you," he said, his hope rising. "But I would spend the rest of my life trying to be worthy of you."

"That's all I'll ever ask of you. I've given up on a lot of things, but I will never give up on you. I will never give up on our love." Her teasing smile returned. "Of course, you'll have to try very hard."

His heart seemed to lighten. "You'll have to try a little, as well."

"I suppose."

He caught her against him and kissed her long and hard before pulling away. "I love you, Matilda Hargreaves. Will you marry me?"

"Yes. But you have to promise me something."

His stomach knotted. "I'll do my best."

"You are not allowed to say that you don't deserve me. I'm through with that nonsense. I love the man you are, and I won't have you questioning my judgment."

The knots in his stomach unraveled. "You have excellent judgment," he said. "Because I'm actually quite a catch as a husband."

A slow grin spread across her face. "Tell me more."

"My domestic skills are unparalleled."

"That sounds promising."

"I come from an excellent family."

"True," she said, tapping her lower lip. "I'm quite fond of your father."

"I once saved a damsel in distress from a band of outlaws."

"You're brave, too." Her eyes twinkled. "I'm marrying a real hero."

In that instant he let go of the burden he'd been carrying since his imprisonment. He'd survived. He'd changed. He wasn't completely healed, and he might never be, but he had enough love in his heart to fill the gaps. He no longer had to prove he was deserving of this life, he simply had to live and love and move forward.

Clinging to the past was selfish. People were meant to mourn, but they were also meant to move on.

"You have to promise me something, as well," he said.

She fiddled with a button on her cuff. "What is that?"

"Stop comparing the worst parts of yourself to the best parts of others."

Her expression turned somber. "You are the first person who ever looked at me and didn't compare me to something better."

"No. I wasn't."

"I already love you." She ducked her head. "You needn't flatter me."

He tucked his knuckles beneath her chin and urged her to meet his gaze. "Miss Hargreaves, you could use a little more confidence in yourself."

"How fortunate that we seem to bring out the best in each other."

"How fortunate indeed."

She caught his hand and tugged him in the opposite direction. "We have to tell your father. I think I see a light in the window. He must have returned home."

Nolan looped his arms around her waist. "He can wait. This cannot."

He kissed her tenderly and pulled away. She gazed at him with so much love it took his breath away.

She loved the flawed man he was, and that was the most perfect gift he'd ever received.

Epilogue

The train whistle blew, scattering the chickens pecking along the track. With pistons chugging, the engine rumbled into the station. Steam vapors hissed over Tilly's feet.

Beside her, Nolan fidgeted. She clutched his sleeve. "Relax."

"What if he doesn't like us?"

"He'll like us."

"What if he doesn't?"

"He'll like us. Who wouldn't like us?" Tilly said. She hadn't seen Nolan this nervous since their wedding day. "You once said you'd give me anything my heart desires."

"This wasn't what I expected."

Her heart lurched. "Are you very sorry?"

"I'm very happy. I'm simply nervous." He straightened his tie. "Do I look all right?"

"You look fine." She smoothed his collar. "He's going to like you. Don't worry. Do I look all right?"

"You look beautiful. Radiant. Show a little confidence."

"You're one to talk."

They shared a knowing grin. They brought out the

best in each other. The worst, too, sometimes, but they always managed to find their way through the difficulties.

She anxiously smoothed a hand down the growing swell of her stomach. Her father's cousin, who served on the board of the New York Widows and Orphans Society, had written several months ago about a very special case.

Even though Tilly had foregone her trip to New York and her work with the widows and orphans, she'd still wanted to help. She and Nolan had discussed several possible ways they could assist those left homeless, and they'd chosen adoption.

A gray-haired woman wearing a severe black dress and a starched apron emerged through the steam and the crowd of departing passengers. A young boy with his shoulder wrapped in a sling stood meekly beside her.

Nolan and Tilly exchanged a glance and he squeezed her hand. After deciding to adopt a child, they had both come to the same conclusion: only the most unique child would do. They were two people who understood what it was like to be different, which meant they were looking for someone very special to join their family.

The gray-haired woman gave a brisk nod. "I'm Mrs. Blankenship. I believe you were expecting us."

Tilly's gaze skittered to the boy. "We were."

When her father's cousin had written about the child, they'd both known their prayers had finally been answered. With the support of Nolan's father and their extended family, they'd made their decision.

He was too thin for an eight-year-old, with a mop of dark hair and a solemn expression far beyond his age.

Everyone was anxious to meet the new addition to Cimarron Springs, but they'd decided to wait for introductions to the rest of the town lest they overwhelm him. Eleanor and the girls were visiting the following week.

"He's been a good little fellow," the woman said. "Not so much as a peep out of him the whole way. I'll leave you to get acquainted."

Nolan bent at the waist and shook the boy's free hand. "My name is Nolan, and this is Tilly. Your name is Kevin, right?"

"Yep. I'm Kevin."

"It's a pleasure to meet you, Kevin."

The boy set his jaw at a defiant angle. "Did the orphanage tell you that I don't have an arm?"

"They did."

"Did they tell you why I don't have an arm?"

"We didn't ask."

"I fell under a carriage and the wheel crushed my arm. The doc said it was too broken to ever heal right. My ma said she had too many mouths to feed to keep a child who couldn't work." Kevin's gaze was skeptical. "The lady from the orphanage told you all that, right?"

"She told us you wanted a home," Tilly said. "That's all we needed to know."

"I can't always do the chores real quick, but I can work longer if you need." The boy's lips quivered and Tilly's heart melted. "If you're going to send me back, I understand. They didn't tell the last family about my arm, and they were real mad."

Tilly longed to reach out and hug the boy, but Nolan gave an almost imperceptible shake of his head. Watching the two, she held her breath.

"We adopted you because we want you to be a part of our family," Nolan said. "Not for chores."

The boy sniffled. "At the orphanage, they said I wouldn't get a family because I'm not normal. Because of my arm, and all."

Nolan rested his hand on the boy's shoulder. "Who's

to say what's normal? Around here, we think folks who are a little different are a lot special."

The boy's face softened. "No fooling?"

"No fooling," Nolan said. "I'll tell you something else."

"What's that?"

"I'm not perfect, either."

"Then you're not disappointed with me?"

"Nope," Nolan replied, his voice husky with emotion. "We're very happy with you. You answered our prayers."

"Then you're keeping me? Forever?"

"Forever."

The boy's chin lifted a notch. His gaze flicked toward the train and back again. "Then let's go quick, before you change your mind."

Tears pooled in Tilly's eyes and she groped for Nolan's hand. "Let's go home."

Kevin didn't believe in them, but he would, in time. Love had a way of bringing out the best in people.

Nothing was ever perfect, and she wouldn't have it any other way.

* * * * *

Don't miss these other PRAIRIE COURTSHIP *stories from Sherri Shackelford:*

THE ENGAGEMENT BARGAIN
THE RANCHER'S CHRISTMAS PROPOSAL
A FAMILY FOR THE HOLIDAYS

Find more great reads at www.LoveInspired.com

Dear Reader,

For this installment of the Prairie Courtship series, I decided to explore other areas of the Great Plains during an earlier time. In the years following the Civil War, trains and steamships opened the American frontier. I'm fascinated by the people who decided to settle such a harsh and unforgiving land.

Nolan was a challenging character for me. I'm the exact opposite of him. I have an alarmingly easy time living in chaos. I organize my desk between each book, which means my desk is clean for precisely two days a year. Most of us, however, can relate to anxiety. We all find ways to feel as though we have some control over events swirling around us. Nolan and Tilly had both learned to manage their anxiety in solitude, but circumstances forced them to work together.

I love connecting with readers and would enjoy hearing your thoughts on this story! If you're interested in learning more about this book, or others I've written in the Prairie Courtships series, visit my website at SherriShackelford.com, or reach me at sherrishackelford @gmail.com, Facebook.com/SherriShackelfordAuthor, Twitter @smshackelford, or regular old snail mail: PO Box 116, Elkhorn, NE 68022.

Thanks for reading!
Sherri Shackelford

Get 2 Free Books,
Plus 2 Free Gifts—
just for trying the Reader Service!

Love Inspired HISTORICAL

*When local rancher Bo Stillwater finds abandoned triplet
babies at the county fair, the first person he turns to is
doctor's daughter Louisa Clark. But as they open their
hearts to the children, they might discover unexpectedly
tender feelings for one another taking root.*

Read on for a sneak preview of
THE RANCHER'S SURPRISE TRIPLETS,
the touching beginning of the series
LONE STAR COWBOY LEAGUE:
MULTIPLE BLESSINGS.

"Doc? I need to see the doctor."

Father had been called away. Whatever the need, she would
have to take care of it. She opened the door and stared at Bo in
surprise until crying drew her attention to the cart beside him.

"Babies? What are you doing with babies?" All three crying
and looking purely miserable.

"I think they're sick. They need to see the doctor."

"Bring them in. Father is away but I'll look at them."

"They need a doctor." He leaned to one side to glance into
the house as if to make sure she wasn't hiding her father. "When
will he be back?"

"I'll look at them," she repeated. "I've been my father's
assistant for years. I'm perfectly capable of checking a baby.
Bring them in." She threw back the door so he could push the
cart inside. She bent over to look more closely at the babies.
"We don't see triplets often." She read their names on their
shirts. "Hello, Jasper, Eli and Theo."

They were fevered and fussy. Theo reached his arms toward
her. She lifted him and cradled him to her shoulder. "There,

there, little man. We'll fix you up in no time."

Jasper, seeing his brother getting comfort, reached out his arms, too.

Louisa grabbed a kitchen chair and sat, putting Theo on one knee and lifting Jasper to the other. The babies were an armload. At first glance they appeared to be in good health. But they were fevered. She needed to speak to the mother about their age and how long they'd been sick.

Eli's wails increased at being left alone.

"Can you pick him up?" she asked Bo, hiding a smile at his hesitation. Had he never held a baby? At first he seemed uncertain what to do, but Eli knew and leaned his head against Bo's chest. Bo relaxed and held the baby comfortably enough. Louisa grinned openly as the baby's cries softened. "He's glad for someone to hold him. Where are the parents?"

"Well, that's the thing. I don't know."

"You don't know where the parents are?"

He shook his head. "I don't even know *who* they are."

"Then why do you have the babies?"

For an answer, he handed her a note and she read it. "They're abandoned?" She pulled each baby close as shock shuddered through her. He explained how he'd found them in the pie tent.

"I must find their mother before she disappears." Bo looked at Louisa, his eyes wide with appeal, the silvery color darkened with concern for these little ones. "I need to go but how are you going to manage?"

She wondered the same thing. But she would not let him think she couldn't do it. "I'll be okay. Put Eli down. I'll take care of them."

Don't miss
THE RANCHER'S SURPRISE TRIPLETS by Linda Ford,
available April 2017 wherever
Love Inspired® Historical books and ebooks are sold.

www.LoveInspired.com